THE WORLD
BEFORE

Everything is connected.

Roland Amariah Gonzales

The World Before

The World Before

Roland Amariah Gonzales

DEDICATION

I dedicate this, my second work, to those insistent whispers dancing upon the peripheries of my mind. Those echoes that somehow, in some way, *everything* is connected.

TABLE OF CONTENTS

PREFACE

This was an exercise in self-indulgence...driven by nothing less than pure *avoidance* in continuing my personal story, part two of my autobiographical account. I made it about ¾ through the rough draft of that painful tome before past demons, given life anew, tormented me near to oblivion. Stepping back, I gathered those raw and visceral emotions, condensed them into a small cardboard box with "this way up" imprinted on the side, then casually threw it into a dark and lonely room where it could fester.

Months passed. I found myself moving from Georgia (the country) to China, my wife deciding to attend a university in Chongqing. For *fun,* if you can imagine! When inspiration inevitably kicked my door in, I took stock of my surroundings, stared off toward the sunset for a few days, then calmly entered that forgotten and dusty room. After locating and retrieving my box, now blackened and gnarled, I emptied its contents into the inkwell from which I dipped mine quill to pen that before you.

...and when I began, oh *how* it did pour! I have discovered an undeniable truth, the likes of which must surely be secret from mere mortals – it is far easier to write about *anything* other than one's self. Sadly for your truly, "the work" must continue. Until it is finished, expect more sci-fi, fantasy, and whatever else my procrastinating mind can create as a defense mechanism.

You will now embark on a journey, dear reader. One of *terrible* loss. One of *tragedy* and triumph. At times, oh...how you will *weep!* Others...you *may* laugh! Anger...*altruistic* anger...yes, that may find you as well. Rest assured that, throughout it *all,* I *will* be there with you...in spirit. Or...perhaps it is better to say that *you* will be joining with *me,* albeit briefly, for in this work lies an aspect of my being. A microscopic *nano-bit* of my psyche. My *existence.* Wholly unremarkable, certainly!

Every *artist*...from the "lowly" craftsman to the "highest" self-assured musician, painter, geneticist or, yes, even writer...every *creator* gives of themselves in their creation.

It's a compulsion, you see...to do otherwise, to create *without* imparting yourself is to make a thing lacking spirit. To birth a creature with no soul. A pitiful thing cursing its existence as well as that which begot it. It would be a tremendous disservice to one's self and to those exposed to the creation, wouldn't it?

Strive to love your creation and in it, give of yourself! Do this, live in this way, and you will *never* know regret. Or...to quote an old book, "to thine own self, be true."

| | ≡ -| |‐ ‐

"To live is to suffer, to survive is to find some meaning in the suffering." Friedrich Nietzsche

An unforgiving star reached outward, caressing a pitiful barren orb. The orb, lashed by the cruel whip of an unforgiving mistress, shuddered as fire cascaded through its thin atmosphere. Vast deserts full of forgotten things as unforgiving as the star shined briefly as sand molten and made glass remained. A small figure clad in a tattered, grey, hooded-cloak gazed in the downpour's direction. It observed with awe the distant conflagration sent from beyond, pausing only for a moment to consider its significance. Pressing need brought it back to reality. The creature turned upward and struggled against a tide of coarse sand as waves of unbearable heat washed over it.

The lone figure winced in pain as crimson flowed from its side, blemishing the dune's orange face. Its movements were uncertain...difficult, before finally cresting the dune. Reaching the cool shade of a large boulder, the lone figure collapsed. It lay there and caught its breath, a pitiful form draped in rags, torn and shredded after a precipitous fall. Only good fortune had preserved its breather.

The entity drew in a ragged, hoarse breath before rolling onto its side to violently cough up blood. Replacing its breather, it stared downward at the massive dune it had just conquered, then upward toward the plateau it had left behind, its home. Another torrential downpour of fire tore through the atmosphere, further away. Bright, searing, golden streaks left indelible glowing marks on the ground. The

1

figure's thoughts stretched as they drifted to the safety of its home...a distant thing in practicality as well as memory.

...how the...the Burning Wastes...seek to...to claim me.

The lone suddenly became *acutely* aware of its cloak's warmth and haphazardly tore it away, revealing the countenance of a young boy with grey skin, grey eyes, and shoulder-length white hair. Grimacing at both heat and injury, the boy tossed his scalding cloak to the side. He then lay there, enveloped in shadow's embrace with eyes closed, drawing in cooler air as eagerly as he would water, had he any.

He opened his eyes then rolled onto his front, moaning pathetically at distant sharp pain as he crawled along the sand. The boy struggled to lift a weathered and beaten far-sight glass as he shakily thumbed at a torn and empty water skin. He licked along dry and cracking lips, his tongue swollen...his breathing shallow as his vision momentarily blurred. His arm collapsed before he fainted.

He awoke and hazily perceived The Rift, a stretch of land violently torn asunder before the Elders' time. Curious, he brought the far-sight glass to bear and saw for the first time, an impossibly-long, thin metallic-grey line extend from somewhere deep within The Rift. Sitting atop was a red eye, slowly blinking. The boy studied the eye then looked outward and beyond as his vision blurred again. He was dangerously near oblivion, his thoughts broken and scattered like so much inconsequential sand.

Desert...stretching on and on...to the horizon...forever...forever and ever. At least the...the path down...is easier...easier than 'up.'

The boy steeled himself, replacing his hooded-cloak before struggling to his feet and shuffling forward. A misstep brought him to the edge of The Rift in record time, cursing, crying out, and grunting in pain the entire way. He came to a stop beside another large boulder, pausing a moment to ponder the gargantuan thing. His vision tunneled as he grew more delirious, his pain much more distant.

How did...here? Same from...above? No...from where? ...everywhere?

The World Before

The boy struggled to his feet then leaned against the boulder, unease creeping through him as he perceived faces along its face. Some were contorting in rage and screaming in terror. Some were even laughing. Shaking away the unpleasant images, he brought the far-sight glass to his eye and panned over The Rift's bottom, gasping in surprise at what he discovered as something near focus returned.

A dilapidated building, much of it crumbled away to nothing, lay at the bottom of the chasm. It was from this ruin that the metallic-grey line extended. Intrigue overrode injury as the boy's senses focused upon the oddity. Taking great comfort in temporary distraction, he gently squeezed the far-sight glass, its worn but familiar sun-metal casing reassuring in his hand. It was a piece of the plateau. Of home. The boy had...borrowed it from the sacred pedestal at the base of the Moonstone.

Stolen, that I may...find he who has...he is here. In...this...this place. Will I make it back, I wonder?

Burning agony tore a path through his body, his consciousness empowered, emanating from his open wound. The boy hissed in pain then brought his grey hand to his faded blue tunic, now purple. He brushed his hand to his wound as he whimpered before bringing it before his eyes, and beheld blood.

...probably not.

The boy tried to weep in sorrowful self-pity, but found he could not. He returned his attention to the ruin, noting faded shapes and lines, nearly imperceptible, jutting from above the ruin's entrance.

$$| \, | = - | \, | - -$$

...what does it mean? This place...it is very strange.

Observing a path downward, the boy plotted a course over the more-manageable rocks. Taking a few quick breaths, he again steeled himself and began the arduous trek, whimpering as he lurched from rock to rock, gathering just enough energy to make a new, desperate bound. Dusk arrived by the time the boy did the same, dizzy and clinging to life by a thread. He first leaned then collapsed against the shambled remains of an outer wall. His body was beyond its breaking point, yet his spirit persisted, driven. Wrapped in its dried and withered husk.

This world...is dead. Dead or dying. Maybe...maybe it's time to...just lay here...in the cool shade. Blessed shade. Maybe I should...just lay here and...and go to sleep. Forever...sleep.

A faint clicking noise followed by a low hum slowly roused his senses. He warily cocked his head to the side, eyes closed, listening.

The noise comes from...within the ruin? It sounds like...like Falling Stars, but...I'm not on the plateau...and...we've no dead to send... perhaps...what if I am on the plateau. I'm dead and being sent. Maybe this is...this is all just...fantasy.

The boy lay there, frowning as curiosity won over his hard-earned rest. He found it impossible to stand and instead crawled, shuffling forward at an agonizingly slow pace, grateful for the continued shade. Grateful that he could hardly feel anything, anymore. He came to a stop as he discovered a barrier to the humming sound, a large, metallic-grey rectangle marred with several indentations and...

...streaks of blood?...his?

The metallic-grey rectangle rested on the face of a tiny square room, surrounded by the what had once been a mighty edifice, now lost to time. The boy reached up and placed his palm against the rectangle, gently running his fingers along the bloody streaks, poking at the indentations.

The rectangle...it is...similar in function to an iris, I think...but it does not respond?

The boy repositioned his body, pressing his back against the rectangle as he considered what to do next. His thoughts were interrupted as his weight, however slight, caused the metallic-grey rectangle to collapse inward, resounding with a dull *thump* against the ground. The boy remained on his back and blinked slowly, eyes burning from lack of moisture, before closing them. Exhaustion claimed him before thoughts stirred.

4

The World Before

*Wait... *thump*? Wet ground equals *thump*. Wet ground means water. Get up. Get up!*

The boy strained his neck to look upward, perceiving the dark chasm of a sharply downward-sloping tunnel. He stared in confusion as a singular thought entered his brain.

...how...?

The boy had expected a small room...perhaps enough space for a sleep pod. Not a lengthy tunnel.

Perhaps...perhaps delirium has finally taken its toll. ...have I lost my mind?

Faces from the boulder at The Rift's mouth flashed across the boy's mind.

...yes. I do believe so.

Moisture wafted from the tunnel, tickling his dry and burning eyes. With great effort, he rolled over then crawled past the metallic-grey rectangle, discovering damp soil underhand. His eyes widened, crazed as he repressed a mad urge to tear away his breather and devour the soil. With strength anew he struggled to his feet and, leaning heavily against the smooth and damp wall, lurched forward. The humming grew louder now, pulsating. The boy practically drank in the air, his dried lungs slowly gaining full breaths. He licked at the inside of his lips as his pulse quickened, a feverish need for water providing him purpose.

A soft red glow emanated from below. The boy's slow, clambering gait gained momentum as he journeyed downward. Damp soil gave way to metallic stairs, rusted to powder in some places. The boy brushed his right hand along dark metallic columns unphased by moisture. He marveled at impossibly smooth walls, in wonder of it all.

The stone here is cut so precisely...and so much metal! It's nothing like our sun-metal, it's dark. It's...I don't know.

He reached the bottom and, turning a corner, beheld a glaring red eye. The boy froze in place as the eye slowly closed. Beneath it was another rectangle the color of the metallic columns, similar to that

5

above. Sharp pain once again jolted through his body, collapsing him against a large cube extending from the floor. Whimpering, the boy remained on the floor.

The angry red eye flared open, brighter than before. The boy dared not look away as his hands probed the ground behind, out of sight. He could *feel* water nearby. It was thick in the air and sticky on his fingers as he shakily rubbed them together. Reaching upward, he grabbed onto the cube, lifting himself to his feet. He tentatively stepped forward then spoke to the eye in a hoarse voice he hardly recognized, "I-I *cough* *cough* I...need. Do you...where?" Receiving no response, he cautiously drew near enough to reach out and touch the eye, or at least tried to. It was covered in a material similar to the lens of his far-sight glass.

What is this place?

Satisfied that the eye posed no threat, the boy took a step backward to study this new metallic rectangle. The aches of his failing body were drifting away, hand-in-hand with his consciousness. He barely perceived a flat square next to the rectangle, affixed to the wall. The boy cocked his head in curiosity before blacking out.

He violently crashed against the cube, an explosion of fire in his side ripping awareness to the forefront. Leaning heavily against the cube, he took a deep breath before tearing away his breather, violently hacking up blood. With trembling hands, he replaced it then steadied himself, his chest rapidly rising and falling in shallow breaths. He sobbed as he tried to stand upright, both hands pressing down upon the cube. The boy yelped in surprise, little more than a dried croak, as he pulled his hands away from an almost alien sensation.

...water...?

The boy brought his fingers to his nose, smelling the liquid before removing his breather. He touched his fingertips to the tip of his swollen tongue, wincing in relief at the stinging sensation.

Water!

The World Before

The boy replaced his breather and looked down at the cube, running his hands over the thing. It was difficult to make out details, the only light in the room emanating from the blinking red eye.

...and even if I...I could see clearly...I have no idea...there must be...some way...

The boy realized with a start that light from above, from *outside*, was fading rapidly.

Nightfall. Oh no.

The boy frantically ran his hands over the cube, hysterical and on the brink of tears. His eyes attempted tears yet none came out, only more burning pain.

Please...oh please give me some, just a little...please! Pushing down...seemed to work before. Maybe...maybe if I push down harder?

The boy blindly grasped at the cube until he felt a raised surface on its side, then pushed against it. Water spurted from the cube's small metallic mouth. The boy tore at his breather in a frenzy before pouncing on the metal mouth with his own. He gurgled, choking for a moment as searing agony washed away, replaced by liquid relief. He stopped and considered his waterskin, pausing briefly to fill the thing before remembering its state. With some difficulty, he managed to push against the cube's side with his body while filling cupped hands. He gingerly brought them to his lips and relished the swishing of his tongue about.

The boy replaced his breather before a distant loud and wet *thump* sounded from above, from *outside,* commanding his attention. There was a moment's pause before it was followed by another sickening wet thump, *much* closer this time. The crash of a wall decimated by something much larger sounded. The boy slowly peered around the corner then looked up toward the distant rectangular opening.

Only stars.

A baby's ear-splitting wail, a dying animal's high-pitched screams...hideous laughter and ecstatic moaning...terrified screaming and enraged shouting...*insane* gibbering. All sounded from above, all at once, a hundred times over. The boy stopped breathing as he froze in shock, eyes wide in abject terror.

Stars above, no. Please, no.

The stars answered, disappearing from sight as an indiscernible mass slammed against the entrance and roared in a cacophony of rage, sorrow, and moaning laughter. The boy cried out and fell backward, his hands covering his ears. The sharp pain returned as his vision blackened for a moment. Vision restored, he saw a large fleshy and barbed appendage with unblinking, hateful eyes snake down the stairs.

He scrambled backward along the floor, screaming, "no! NO! Begone! Leave me be!" The monstrosity continued stretching outward as it continued its maddening assault on his hearing, paralyzing him in fear as his hands clasped against his ears. His shoulders slumped as he whimpered and resigned himself to the inevitable.

An enormous, serrated appendage made of bone, muscle and sinew suddenly erupted from within the mass in a spray of black ichor as the boy stared in disbelief. It slammed down onto the outstretched limb, sawing back and forth in a blurring motion as the creature continued its paradoxical moans of ecstasy and shrieks of agony.

The outstretched limb fell to the floor and spasmodically writhed before another lanced out to seize the fleshy oozing prize. It quickly dragged it into ravenous maws, devouring it in moments. The boy looked on in horrified fascination as the serrated limb plunged back into the creature. A moment of confused relief gave way to shock as an orifice tore open on the creature's front, spraying more vile ichor. For a singular moment, the boy thought he heard the creature moan "RAAAAAGHEELLLLLL," before firing three pseudopods into his chest.

The boy grunted in pain, looking downward just in time to see three wriggling tails disappear into his chest. He screamed in horror and disgust. The creature above began to stretch out another barbed appendage toward him, much faster this time. Adrenaline surged as he

8

scrambled backward around the corner, out of sight of the raging creature. Wild-eyed, he glanced upward and noticed first the metal rectangle, then the blinking red eye. Using the water-cube for support, he struggled to his feet and slammed his open palms against the black metal rectangle as he shouted for help.

The small metal square beside the black metal rectangle became illuminated by a faint green light as it spoke words he couldn't understand. He slapped at its face repeatedly with open palms. The boy felt a tiny pin-prick of pain from the face, drawing back his hand to see it had pierced him. After a moment, the faint green light changed to blue as the red eye did the same, causing the metal rectangle to swing inward as he fell into a dark room.

The boy scrambled to his feet then turned to face the metal rectangle, slamming it shut. He waited with bated breath before he heard the loud thumping of flesh against metal, screams of joy and pain just beyond. After a brief eternity, the thumping ceased, though the cries remained. The boy sighed in relief then turned inward to survey the room, his mind struggling to comprehend that before him.

Sleepy red eyes stretched on and on, seemingly into infinity, unblinking and illuminating – though just barely. *Ancient*, desiccated corpses rested underneath, silently observing the interloper. The boy shook his head in disbelief, eyes wide. It was too much. His mind broke as he backed against the wall, mumbling unintelligibly before sliding to the floor.

...I...

A sudden squirming sensation from *beneath* his skin demanded attention. He slowly looked down in horror then peeled his bloodied, faded blue tunic aside to expose the source. Small tendrils wriggled outward from his gaping wound before clasping together and pressing tight. The boy yelped in terror, unspeakably violated, then rolled onto his side. He clutched his hand over his wound, eyes darting about madly as he fought a wave of nausea.

Roland Amariah Gonzales

His sight fell upon a distant red eye, moments before his vision blurred, before wrapping his cloak tightly about his body as he convulsed on the floor. Exhaustion and terror supplanted his consciousness, the plaintive and desperate wails of the creature outside growing distant before fading entirely.

The World Before

ASPIRANT OF THE PLATEAU

Traces of bioluminescence flitted about fungal lines. Pulsating then growing in intensity, they formed a steady stream which flowed into a growth affixed to the ceiling. Blue light slowly filled the sleep pod, illuminating in resplendence a small figure underneath. The figure lazily rubbed sleep away, flicking the grit aside onto his lichen bed. There was a slight *pop* as two tendrils exited his ears before receding into the lichen. Countless others whispered across his bare form, *popping* as they released him before following suit.

The figure rose to his knees and, with eyes closed, slowly drew in a deep breath through his nose before releasing it through his mouth. He stretched his arms and neck before brushing his hands against one another in a downward motion. Opening his eyes, he saw the last tendrils waggle before disappearing.

He half-smiled then murmured softly, "still hungry? All must earn their keep...we can't *all* afford to lay about." The lichen bed did not respond...though the figure surmised the bed was content in its role, all the same. The figure's half-smile melted to melancholy, its owner lost in thought.

Would that I could say the same for myself. Being assigned to the Watchers is a role envied by most – certainly my two younger siblings...yet...I want more. There has to be more. I want to go beyond the plateau. There's a world both frightening and full of wonder, so close. ... "sacrilege!" the Elders would likely cry out, were I to suggest.

The figure sighed then despondently looked upward, breathing in time with fungal lines above as his sleep pod's wavering blue glow ebbed and flowed. The figure raised his arm slightly overhead and absentmindedly touched the fungi-light, again losing himself in thought.

Roland Amariah Gonzales

Watching from the plateau's edge for…what? I may as well be *embedded in the rock, feeding on dead skin.*

The figure glanced downward and apologized for dismissing his bed's purpose so callously. Sighing, he gingerly pulled his red tunic and sash from the lichen bed then dressed himself. He murmured "thanks for the clean," before briefly pausing to wonder if others talked to their beds. The fungi-light above pulsed three times.

Time to go.

Remaining on his knees, the figure pulled aside the pale-red skin flap which separated his room from a narrow and roughly carved tunnel, then crawled out. The narrow tunnel was filled with males, each traversing barefoot along soft lichen-floored tunnels. They moved with purpose and spoke little, if at all, waiting for the figure to take his lead position. Fungi-lights ran the length of the tunnel, bathing it in red. Fungal lines spiderwebbed between the lights and into each sleep pod, pulsating with energy. With life.

The figure felt a nudge from behind a moment later. Startled from his musings, he glanced over his shoulder and, seeing his younger brother, smiled then said, "Rael! Hello, *little one.*"

Rael huffed indignantly and, feigning hurt, replied, "*not* little, Faeleor. Only Younger!" They both chuckled as all made their way to the Sustenance Chamber. After a short trek, Faeleor, Rael, and the other males arrived at a fungal iris barring their path. Faeleor placed his palm against the iris which separated male sleep pods from the Sustenance Chamber. The iris rippled for a moment before opening. Faeleor stepped through, seeing the females step through precisely in time with the males.

All shuffled along wordlessly to their places, a throng of identical shapes and forms. 75 of them bore the same skin, pale and grey as a fungi stalk. Only the Watchers were darker than most and the Elders? …well, who knew what they looked like under their large dark robes and masks. Faeleor glanced at and offered a genuine smile to his Young sister, Iwik. She responded in kind.

12

The World Before

The Sustenance Chamber was a large, crudely-cut circular cavern. The floors were relatively smooth stone. The underbelly of a *massive* crystalline formation, blue in color, occupied its center. The room possessed no fungi-lights as the crystalline formation itself, the Moonstone, provided a soft white glow, illuminating the room.

100 lichen beds were positioned below the crystal, spreading outward in concentric circles increasing by five, the innermost-circle possessing ten. Each lichen bed was wide enough to accommodate one sitting individual. The Elders, draped in dark black robes with their faces masked and hidden, were firmly rooted to their innermost circle, facing away from the crystal toward those assembled.

Faeleor took up his position on the Watcher's circle, all clad in red, and faced the Elders. Behind him stood his brother Rael with the Menders, clad in blue. Behind Rael stood the Cultivators, clad in green, followed by the Young, clad in white, where Iwik stood beaming. When all were in place, the Elders intoned with a singular voice both wet and dry, hoarse yet eloquent, "we are they who remain. We are the guides. We are the preservers. We are the shepherds. You are our flock whom we *love*. We are your Elders."

Those assembled intoned, "we thank you, Elders."

Faeleor and the other Watchers intoned, "we are they who stand *on* the plateau. We are the seekers. We are the anointers. We are the sentinels. You are our flock whom we love. We are your Watchers."

The assembled intoned, "we thank you, Watchers."

The next circle spoke, Rael among them, "we are they who create. We are the crafters. We are the caretakers. We are the producers. You are our flock whom we love. We are your Menders."

The assembled intoned, "we thank you, Menders."

The Cultivators spoke next, "we are they who nourish. We are the farmers. We are the deliverers. We are they who inter the dead. You are our flock whom we love. We are your Cultivators."

The assembled intoned, "we thank you, Cultivators."

The Young, with little Iwik, spoke last, "we are they who learn. We are the hopeful. We are the eager. We are your future. You are our flock whom we love. We are your Young."

The assembled intoned, "we thank you, Young."

The Elders raised their arms upward as one, toward the Moonstone, and intoned, "as our Moonstone deems it, so mote it be. Rest."

All assembled lowered to their knees atop lichen beds as the Elders remained standing. Thin tendrils rose from the lichen beds and, snaking up the tunics of those assembled, firmly but gently penetrated their navels. Sustenance flowed. All were fed. All were content. Faeleor glanced upward as a thought struck him, one he was surprised to have *never* considered before.

I've never seen the Elders feed. Why do they not feed?

Thereafter, all were pensive for a time until the Moonstone pulsed three times. The tendrils withdrew as all assembled rose to their feet. The Elders intoned, "sustenance has been rendered. Now, all must toil."

The assembled intoned, "that we may be one with all. And that all may achieve ascension."

Faeleor and the Watchers exited first, to the north, then journeyed upward through the caprock to begin their duty. Once gone, Rael and the Menders exited through the south toward the Production Chambers to begin theirs, followed by the Cultivators. Lastly departed the Young. 10 apiece to the Cultivators, the Menders, and the Watchers, to *learn*. When all had left the chamber, the crystal grew dark. The Elders' remained, upright. Unmoving.

The World Before

Faeleor's sighed inwardly as he trudged along with his fellow Watchers, at odds with his thoughts.

It's not that I don't like being on top of the plateau...above ground...it's just...once you see how much is out there...I wonder if other Watchers think in such a manner.

Faeleor recognized light, not of the Moonstone, emanating from ahead as he and the others set their breathers in place. He smiled despite his restlessness – he *loved* being above ground. Faeleor emerged, greeted by a beautiful, shining, pale-white orb set against a sky as dark as any cavern bereft of fungi. Dotting the sky were innumerable lights, twinkling as if they blinked at him.

Faeleor's smile widened as he recalled his first night atop the plateau, as a Young learning, believing he had emerged only to find himself in an even larger cavern.

I was so disappointed!

It was only after being whisked back underground at the first fiery streaks of twilight that he had realized this was not the case. Faeleor's nostalgia waned as his gaze ran from the gargantuan Moonstone, embedded in the plateau's surface, to the sky-orb. He sighed as he shook his head and looked downward.

Time spent in the plateau...as good as spores on the plateau's surface. Without purpose, without aim. Sometimes hurried, mostly not. ...but hey, I can tolerate four hours after sunrise now, with only mild irritation. I'm the reigning Sun Champion. ...that's something...isn't it?

Faeleor nodded in amused satisfaction.

He and the other Watchers plucked small mushrooms thick with grease from a lichen bed near the entrance, then made their way toward the Moonstone. Their task was to perform the Ritual of Cleansing: cover the crystal with nutrient-rich oil, a daunting task which took much of the night. Three stone paths spiraled upward, circling the Moonstone. These sturdy fingers gripped the Moonstone, keeping it safe and secure, its many surfaces accessible. The Watchers went about their work, shadowed by Young. After some time, the work was done.

The Ritual of Cleansing complete, the Watchers retrieved one far-sight glass apiece from a pedestal at the base of the crystal, then ventured out across the plateau to patrol, to watch. Faeleor looked outward and surveyed the Burning Wastes, now cooled by the sun's absence. They stretched in all directions as far as the eye could see. To stray from the plateau and its loving womb was to embrace death, for in the Burning Wastes lay not only *blistering* heat sure to cook one, boiling their blood until it burst forth...no, at night, something *far* more terrible emerged.

The Watchers had no word for the creatures. They knew only that they moved about at night when the grounds below were cooler. One could slightly make out their forms only with the aid of a far-sight glass, so high up was their vantage. What was able to be perceived defied logic and reason, threatening the very sanity of the beholder. Before the sun rose the next day, the creatures fled out of sight and over the horizon.

Faeleor chose to flirt with madness as he peered through his far-sight glass, tracking one of the monstrosities. It ambled below, seemingly aimless...twitching ...writhing. Convulsing forward at times toward the unknown. It was large, even from a distance, as it lumbered about in nonsensical movements and unknowable purpose.

Faeleor stared, mouth agape and brow furrowed in disgusted fascination, his head beginning to ache from the sight.

I swear, sometimes something between a faint whine or cry can be heard on the wind. It sounds like...I don't know. ...that time Rael, clumsy as he is, tripped over a Young's fallen sash. Yes, that's it. Rael fell and hurt his knee...he made a sound like that...but this...this is so much worse...I think it's ...it's getting louder? I –

Faeleor jerked his sight away from the thing, breathing heavily. It had looked right at him. *Into* him. The pain in Faeleor's head began to fade.

The World Before

How. How could it possibly see me? Can it even see? Does it have eyes? This feeling is...I am terrified. But why...why am I so worried? They've never been on the plateau, let alone looked up here. ...maybe that's it. They've never looked up here.

Faeleor took a deep breath and looked up to the sky-orb. He found peace in this, peace enough to look out once more across the plateau, careful to avoid gazing upon the horrors below. It was then that he saw something he'd never seen before.

A red...fungi-light? No...an eye? It...is blinking but...from so far away. It cannot be a fungi-light. What is that? Why does it keep blinking? To be seen from so far away...it must be huge!

He lowered the far-sight glass and realized he could still see the light. Sunrise would occur soon. He glanced at his feet and saw a small rock. Holding it in hand, he etched a mark pointing toward the odd red eye. He briefly looked out across the now-cool Burning Wastes, both fearful and longing. He decided he didn't want to compete with the other Watchers for Sun Champion this cycle.

He trudged back to his sleep pod, disrobed, then lay on his lichen bed and closed his eyes. He relaxed as the lichen bed's tendrils slithered over his body to begin the clean, wincing as sleep tendrils entered his ears. The sensation was...unpleasant. But that was his role as a Watcher. To be the eyes of the Moonstone. To Watch. Faeleor's sleep cycle began as the Elders' words, ever a reminder that one must be faithful both to the Moonstone and they, the Moonstone's voice, resounded in his mind.

Roland Amariah Gonzales

The next day proceeded much the same as before. Faeleor awoke, donned his red tunic, said hello to his siblings, took in sustenance, then performed the Rite of Cleansing. He hurried back to his position and, after locating his etched marking, pulled out his far-sight glass to gaze at the distant red eye. It gazed back into him. Inviting. Seductive. ...*terrifying?* An ear-splitting roar broke his reverie and he fell backward. Faeleor crawled to the plateau's edge, then peered over.

The creatures, numbering in the *thousands*, slammed long barbed appendages into the plateau's sheer face, rapidly ascending. Faeleor cried out and ran to alert his fellow Watchers. All ran in terror to the caprock's entrance, then sprinted to the Sustenance Chamber. Faeleor cried out in dismay to the Elders, "they are *coming*! I *should not* have looked upon them! The horrors are upon us!" The Elders spoke as one, directing the Watchers to gather everyone unto the Commemoration Chamber.

Cruel, vile flesh and bone slammed against the Moonstone, noble and pure. All assembled, minus the Elders, cried out in surprise and looked upward as the Moonstone's soft white light was first punctuated then completely overwhelmed by darkness. The relentless staccato of pounding continued before reaching a crescendo as all trembled in the void. A moment of silence encapsulated all as they awaited the final blow, their hearts heavy with dread. A piercing shriek rang out as a large fracture began then quickly split down the entirety of the Moonstone. The Elders wailed in unison as the Moonstone suddenly exploded into chunks and fragments. One of the creatures plummeted downward from above, slamming against the Sustenance Chamber's floor in an explosion of viscera and gore, such was the size of the Moonstone.

It lay there for a moment as all stood paralyzed in fear, their world undone. What remained of the monstrosity slowly reached out and devoured its outlying matter, immediately regaining form large enough to convulse forward. In a whirlwind of bladed-bone slaughter, it rapaciously devoured those nearest. Countless others rained downward in an impossible downpour of fleshy, wrathful howling and giggles.

18

The World Before

Faeleor wept as he fled toward the Production Chambers, the sounds of carnage behind replaced by mournful laughter, hysterical and insane. He gathered everyone into the Commemoration Chamber as the plateau *shook* from the invaders.

Rael held Iwik close as both stood terrified, all silent as the furious pounding and shrieks of the monsters drew nearer. One of the monstrosities breached the Commemoration Chamber and tore apart all before it. All but the three siblings were gone in an instant, their voices a brief chorus of horror. Faeleor turned to his terrified siblings, cracked open by fear...emptied of hope. His eyes shimmered with hopeless tears, his world gone. He would not let those things take his family.

Faeleor produced a blade in hand then plunged it into Rael's heart before pushing him back into dark, quiet waters. He turned to a terrified Iwik. She begged him to spare her, to leave her be. She wept and said she loved her big brother. Faeleor wept too as he thrust the blade into her chest again and again, the blade-wielding arm suddenly a fleshy, barbed appendage that sliced Iwik into pieces before Faeleor greedily shoved them into his many mouths. He looked into dark waters and saw Rael's body floating in the distance. Then he saw himself, a horrifying thing.

Faeleor bellowed in terror, in anguish, in delight. A deafening, thunderous groan shook the ground as the plateau was torn asunder. A gargantuan, glowing red eye glared down at Faeleor, full of hate and malice. The creatures in the Commemoration Chamber surrounded Faeleor and drew closer before pouncing as one.

Faeleor awoke with a start in his sleep pod, his heart pounding as his chest heaved, the dream consuming his waking self. His blue fungi-light pulsed slowly as his mind raced.

...I killed them...and then...oh, little Iwik...everyone...gone. All gone.

He felt, for the first time, disgusted by the lichen bed as it writhed over his bare form. In one fluid motion, Faeleor sat upright and violently tore himself free, snapping a few tendrils before the rest quickly receded. He frantically donned his red tunic and sash, desperate to be away from the sleep pod, the cavern, even the plateau! A feeling of suffocation nearly *overcame* him, his breathing shallow and vision narrow as he pulled aside the skin flap and emerged into the tunnel, finding himself utterly alone.

...wait. This...isn't right. Where is everyone?

Faeleor stepped toward the Sustenance Chamber, trepidation his only companion. He reached out to touch the iris, hesitating briefly. Understanding *beyond* understanding enveloped Faeleor as he saw himself standing on a precipice overlooking the shores of oblivion. For a fraction of an instant, he was painfully aware of his minor but vital role in something much larger than himself. And then, it was gone.

A surge of energy coursed up Faeleor's spine, his hair tingling. Fear gripped his heart. Part of him longed to flee back to his sleep pod, to forget standing here, to forget everything and just go back to his everyday life...but he was compelled. A solitary tear formed before descending down his cheek before he touched the iris. *Blinding* light assailed his eyes as he hissed through his teeth and jerked away.

The Moonstone, gone!? ...no. Mid-day? I've never seen the Moonstone so bright! My eyes will adjust...after a few minutes. Gah, how it stings!

He approached the Elders, intending to ask much of them. He noticed that their forms, while upright and standing, were limp and lifeless. He tentatively reached out and touched an Elder's robe. There was no response. He tugged at it and softly spoke, "Elder?" There was no response. He tried shouting.

Nothing.

Emboldened further, he reached up and brushed his fingers against an Elder's mask, intending to remove it. He even gave it a tug but found it as firmly set in place as the Elders themselves. He sighed then lowered his head, lost in confusion.

...what is going on?

Faeleor made his way to the female's iris, intent on awaking Iwik. He placed his palm against it and felt it ripple for a moment before becoming rigid. He tried once more and, perceiving no reaction, returned to the male iris, intent on awaking Rael. He placed his palm against it and it, too, remained unphased. He struck it in panicked frustration.

Nothing.

Faeleor's shoulders slumped as he looked downward. Then, he heard the Elders speak from behind, calling as one, "Faeleor. You have awoken. Come. Come near to us, child."

Faeleor's body lurched toward the Elders, despite himself. He blinked then found himself atop a lichen bed a moment later. Its tendrils snaked upward and grasped his wrists and knees, gently pulling him downward in supplication. He turned his head to look upward into an emotionless and uncaring mask before they spoke as one, "Faeleor, you have been the reigning 'Sun Champion' for many cycles. It is, therefore, time we told you of another role within our people, one that has gone unfulfilled for far too long. The Aspirant. You have...felt the pull, yes? To leave this place? Your people? ...your home?"

Faeleor was stunned as he cast his gaze downward in shame.

To even think of leaving the plateau is sacrilege. To openly speak of it, let alone hear it from the Elders themselves! I...I don't...

Faeleor looked up toward the Elders as the tendrils softened their grip and, after a few moments, spoke in earnest, "...yes, my Elders. In your infinite wisdom you know what lies in my heart, even if I alone do not."

The Elders nodded as one and spoke alike, "yes, you *will* be our Aspirant."

Faeleor felt then an odd nagging that he couldn't quite place...but his trust in the Elders was complete. He asked, "my Elders, where will I go? ...what would you have me do?"

The Elders paused for a moment then spoke, "the red eye. Yes...you have seen it. Fear it not, for this is your destination, far beneath the gaze of the eye. Therein, you will find a relic. Something crucial to our people's survival, indeed, to *ascension itself!* You will take your far-sight glass, a waterskin, and these garments-divine. You must endure the burning heat of the sun, for that is when the monsters sleep. Now...prepare yourself."

As the Elders spoke, a bundle of clothing lowered from the ceiling by lichen tendrils. Faeleor was released from the bed's tendrils and stood to reach upward and receive the Elders' gift. He turned it over in his hands for a moment, examining it. It was different from anything he had ever known. He donned, with some effort, boots made from mushroom leather – to protect his vulnerable flesh from burning rock. He received gloves made from the same for the same purpose. Then, long flowing robes as well as a hooded cloak.

He fitted a mask with attached breather which clung to his face by means of tiny lichen tendrils. He received a waterskin made from mushroom leather thicker than that which he thought possible.

...where did this come from? The Menders do not make such things...

Once he was fully dressed, the Elders spoke again, "go now, and retrieve your far-sight glass. Then, return."

Faeleor bowed and replied "yes, my Elders," then walked with slight difficulty toward the surface tunnel, his new boots taking some getting used to.

The World Before

I no longer feel rough stone underfoot...nor the softness of lichen paths. I have become numb to all.

As he reached the last bend of the upward tunnel he found himself besieged by a light more blinding than he had ever experienced. The mid-day sun shone overhead, the heat on the caprock nearly unbearable. After a few moment his eyes adjusted, or rather the eyelets of his mask possessed a film which reacted inversely to light. The brighter the light, the more they filtered and absorbed, allowing him to see. Faeleor shook his head in wonder.

Incredible. Simply...incredible.

Faeleor retrieved his far-sight glass and took a moment to look across the Burning Wastes. The air shimmered hazily as he stood in wonder at infinite sand and nothing else. Turning away from the incredible sight, he made his way back to the Elders. Faeleor stepped onto his lichen bed and asked the Elders, "my Elders, why not send more than one Aspirant? Why not send *several* Watchers to the red eye? If what lies within is so important...why send me alone?"

The Elders considered only for a moment before speaking, "we send those whom we deem worthy, Aspirant. Yours is not to reason why. Reach the red eye and what you seek, indeed, what seeks *you*, shall be revealed. Now go! To the Commemoration Chamber where you will find means to depart from here. There, will you begin your journey."

Faeleor bowed then turned toward the Sustenance Chamber's south exit, reserved for Cultivators, Menders and Young. He touched the iris which rippled a moment before opening, then stepped through. A series of green fungi-lights illuminated his lichen-floored path as he journeyed downward. He reached the end and came upon a four-way intersection, three blocked by an iris. To the left lay the Cultivators' Fields, to the right, the Menders' Craftspace. The Commemoration Chamber lay directly ahead. Faeleor paused for a moment as he realized he had not been this way for some time.

Roland Amariah Gonzales

I've never liked this place...I was glad to be done with it when I became a Watcher. It's not the dead that bother me...there's...something else.

The iris rippled briefly before opening, and he stepped through. Faeleor surveyed that before him, rough rock illuminated by inverted fungi-light casting a dim, purple glow. A number of exceptionally-bright fungi-lights shone upon a distant wall, the illuminated spot itself encircled by lichen beds.

They shut off a moment after Faeleor's entrance.

Odd. Those lights always illuminate...though I know not why.

The people of the plateau laid their dead to rest under the inverted fungi-lights, though their repose was brief. Large black and gray-mottled reclamation fungi grew here. They emitted a sweet smell, constantly dripping a substance which hissed and fizzled flesh and bone, dissolving it into the lichen bed below. The lichen bed itself seemed unfazed by this liquid as its tendrils quickly broke apart then reclaimed dissolved tissue.

Beyond the reclamation beds lay the water reservoir. This water was drawn from the external thin atmosphere by the Moonstone itself, a near-impossible task which produced no more than a handful per day. This meager amount was then channeled through the mycelial network and deposited in the reservoir. Faeleor walked up to the edge and marveled at the infinite yawning chasm, stretching as far as he could see.

I always forget just how much water is down here. Why does the Moonstone collect so much?

He kneeled and filled his waterskin then turned and went back to the reclamation fungi, observing two rapidly decomposing bodies as they were ravenously pieced apart by tendrils. He observed dispassionately the bodies' forms, their decay.

This one...three arms. The other, only half a head. Young defects. ...it happens.

The World Before

A low rumbling sounded from the far corner, past the reclamation fungi, somewhere near where the bright fungi *had* shone. This was a noise Faeleor had not heard before...save for his nightmare. He cautiously approached the wall, pausing to observe his peoples' Timetable as the rumbling died down.

The Timetable was a smooth wall in the cavern containing the record of all that had been. Carefully etched was their history, not in letters or words but pictographs. Faeleor found much of it incomprehensible though the portion establishing the five castes, from Elder to Young, was apparent. He wondered at the impossible depictions of what came before and their meaning before his attention was commanded elsewhere.

Faeleor seized in horror at what befell his eyes.

The encircled rock surface, formerly illuminated, began to crumble away. It then became animated as, underneath, fleshy appendages writhed and burst through the rock. Faeleor had only a moment to think.

The monsters, here!? They are the wall!?

A chorus of plaintive wailing, terrified shrieking, hideous laughter and more assailed him. Faeleor threw his hands up to his ears and fell to his knees, eyes shut in despair, sure the creature would be upon him in an instant. The horror's song shifted from mindless rage to indignant agony. Pain. Faeleor squinted to see the lichen beds, formed around the wall for this very purpose, shoot out countless tendrils with sharpened ends, piercing the monstrosity's fleshy middle.

The tendrils sawed back and forth as they drove deeper into the creature. A terrible *squelch* and cracking of bones and sinew was faintly heard beyond the mask of hysterical laughter and ecstatic moans as the creature was bisected. Light flooded the Commemoration Chamber, causing Faeleor to squint for a moment before his mask adjusted and a thought struck him.

This is...that's...outside.

Roland Amariah Gonzales

The monstrosity continued its raucous performance as it tried to reach through the lichen-bed's tendrils, only to have its fleshy appendages torn back by a violent web numbering in the thousands. Faeleor's chest rose and fell in rapid succession as he looked toward the outside. He willed life into leadened limbs, taking a few hesitant steps toward the opening. He faltered for a moment as his boot caught against a rough patch, then snapped his attention upward and broke into a full sprint.

A thousand voices speaking incomprehensible languages. Pleading, laughing, shouting, screaming. Walls of flesh...blood. Bones *snapping* apart as limbs reached outward, trying to grab him, only to be pulled back in an instant by vicious lichen tendrils. *Faces.*

So many faces.

Absolute terror. Absolute loathing. Envy. Longing. *Hunger.* Most of the faces were malformed and hideous but more horrifying still...some were almost recognizable as "normal." This is what surrounded Faeleor as he ran shouting through the gauntlet of madness. This is what would forever stay in his mind as he bolted through blood and gore, past the monstrosity with its anguish and rage. He fled past the bloody arch into a long tunnel facing the Burning Wastes, then, fell to his knees and brought his hands to his face, sobbing that such a thing could exist.

The World Before

Faeleor laid on the cavern floor in the fetal position as he faced the Burning Wastes. Time passed as he recovered. Too much time. Hearing the creature's cries grow muffled and smothered, he warily looked over his shoulder to see that its flesh was solidifying into rock. Faeleor shook his head in disbelief and confusion.

I...I don't understand.

Faeleor observed long shadows of the plateau cast across the Burning Wastes. Steeling himself, he rose to his feet and moved at a brisk pace until he exited the tunnel. Once more he was in awe of being apart from the plateau, a newly birthed child suddenly made aware of a larger world. Faeleor took out his far-sight glass and scanned the horizon. An impossibly-large dune, once made small by the sheer size of the plateau, now lay before him. Beyond and just above that, he perceived the red eye blinking at him. Calling to him.

He began a light jog and paused to drink water when needed. The heat, while assuredly less suffocating than it had been earlier, was still quite torrid. After a while his pace slowed before he stopped and surveyed his surroundings.

...there's nothing! There's nothing here. No lichen, no...anything! Just hard dirt. Small rocks. And sand. This world is dead. Dead or dying.

He began a light jog once more until he reached the base of the dune, then began his arduous climb. In good shape and well-hydrated, he reached the top of the dune in decent time, gasping in awe as he beheld The Rift, full of oddly-shaped boulders gargantuan in size. After a moment of wonder, he withdrew his breather and took a swig of water, then brought his far-sight glass to his mask. He could see the red eye *much* more clearly now, and found that it was affixed to a tall metallic-grey cylindrical rod which jutted from a small ruin. He lowered the glass and shook his head at the impossible discovery, numb from earlier terror.

The red eye isn't so far off, now.

The structure was square-shaped and had smooth, upright walls. Much smoother than the flattest surfaces in the plateau. They were a color similar to fungi-stalk but also browned from the surrounding terrain. There were strange symbols jutting above the structure's entrance.

$$| \, | = -| \, | - -$$

Faeleor could not discern meaning.

...odd place.

He quickly but safely made his descent into The Rift and arrived at the ruin. He walked around the structure, not overly large, then returned to its face where the symbols resided. The last rays of sunlight fled from The Rift as twilight neared. Faeleor exhaled in relief. He preferred the dark with its silver sky-orb. He longed for it now and sighed wistfully. Slight movement caught his attention in the distance, past where he had descended from. He retrieved his far-sight glass and peered through it.

I thought I saw...wait. There!

Faeleor looked on in fascinated horror as boulders began to move, almost imperceptibly. Fragments of rock at first fell away before fleshy growths probed outward and tore off other bits of rock. He heard faint muffled noises in the distance and gasped in horror as he made the connection. Faeleor lowered his far-sight glass and quickly surveyed his surroundings.

There are boulders in the near-distance though they seem solid. ...they're still, but for how long?

Faeleor entered the ruin through an open rectangular archway and sought whatever he thought the Elders had sent him for.

What am I looking for? This place is barren. No lichen beds, no fungi lights. It's all so...dead.

Faeleor's stomach gurgled as he felt hunger. He realized he had no food.

I need to reach the Sustenance Chamber. Wait. ...how will I get back to the plateau?

The World Before

He looked through the archway up toward the top of the rift, and saw the near-distant boulders begin to move.

No. Oh, no no no!

Faeleor frantically tore deeper into the ruin through more archways but found nothing. The awful cries of monstrosities sounded from all directions as they howled for blood. Faeleor huddled against a hard, grey rectangle affixed to an archway. He buried his face in his knees and tried not to breathe.

Silence.

He cautiously stood up and turned to face the rectangle He perceived its function to be similar to the plateau's skin flap barriers, only much harder. Curious, he placed his palm against it. It did not ripple or open.

Is this what the Elders would have me find?

A thunderous crash shook the structure, collapsing most of it as Faeleor cried out in terror. A huge flesh-arm covered in eyes, hair, and screaming mouths exploded through the wall. It slammed Faeleor into the hard rectangle with such force that it violently swung inward. The arm launched Faeleor backward as he tumbled down a sloping tunnel. He landed with a thudded *crunch* and after a moment opened his eyes, facing another red eye which blinked at him. In *immense* pain, he struggled to draw in air and realized he couldn't, his breather smashed to pieces. He coughed up blood then shakily turned his head upward to see the monstrosity surging against the archway, terrible and unrelenting as it bellowed and giggled hysterically.

I'm going to die here. I'm sorry Rael. Little Iwik. Elders. I –

The monstrosity's flesh-arm flung against the nearby wall with a *splat* as fingers erupted from it at odd angles, pulling itself forward and downward toward Faeleor as he looked on in horror. It stretched itself thin with sickening *pops*, *snaps*, and the sound of bursting blood sacs. It drew closer to Faeleor until it seized his boot and began pulling him upward. Faeleor grasped onto the grey rectangle before the creature furiously yanked him backward, slamming the rectangle shut.

29

Roland Amariah Gonzales

The red eye blinked stoically as rasping cries from above ended violently, followed by the rending of flesh pulled into hundreds of mouths. Menacing silence broke as a single chorus of pathetic mewls and raucous laughter filled the air, then nothing.

THE WONDERFUL WORLD OF
AZ-0731

The man jolted upright from his sleep cycle, awoken by the jarring screech of a wake-alarm paired with blinding red light. He mechanically donned a grey jumpsuit as the noise and harsh glare continued. Numbly setting his body in motion, he hit the *EXIT* button. The pod's surface thinned, allowing the man to permeate and step onto a platform, waiting to take his position on the conveyance lane. The pod's clamoring awakening system silenced as it solidified.

The man stepped off the platform and grasped the conveyance ladder, looking upward as he descended. His blank gaze fixated on a golden, sparkling sleep pod, *PC AZ-0731* emblazoned on its surface. *Beautiful.*

Overhead, a bright red sky as harsh as the sleep pod's light bore down upon all, flickering momentarily. All plunged down, down into the unfathomable, dark depths of the city.

The man's pace increased to a blur as he observed innumerable sleep pods, golden and beautiful all, stacked atop one another. They stretched out farther than he could perceive, attached conveyance ladders casting an endless stream downward. He smiled as a pleasant citrusy scent washed over him as he shot through several cleansing fields, ridding his body of any bacterial contaminants. Nearing his assigned workspace, the man suddenly detached from the conveyance lane and plummeted toward oblivion.

His falling form, a single mote of grey amidst a flurry in an inky-black void, tore through several gravi-catch nets which first slowed then completely halted his movement, allowing him to step onto a thin, gilded, gleaming walkway. Hundreds of others merrily strode before him, a procession of the blessed. They departed the main path, disappearing down forgotten corridors to perform forgotten functions. The man joyfully marched forward, drooling a bit as static filled his thoughts, numbing his senses.

A young adult female equipped with a half-face breather stood in his path, wildly waving her arms about and shouting, desperate to gain his attention. The man cocked his head in confusion.

Odd.

The man smiled and waved, knocking the woman over as he continued his stride, unaware of her futile attempt to grasp his leg as tears streamed down her face. The woman released her grasp, crying out in pain after being drug along the walkway's rough and rusted metallic grating, her legs now torn and bleeding. She collapsed inward, clutching at her wounds and sobbing as the man joyfully disappeared in the distance.

The man quickly forgot the woman, grinning as he admired surrounding walls of alabaster and gold. Holo-placards projected motivational messages, words of encouragement, and praise directed solely at him.

I truly am the luckiest.

The man's gait brought him before a large iris made of gemstones and inlaid with gold. A blue holographic figure, roughly the same size as the man, appeared in a cloud of smoke, projected from a nearby holo-point. It resembled a dark haired female with fair skin who wore a purple bandana and sported several ear piercings. She spoke with a comically-thick accent, "Madame Zostra zays provide your palm zat I may read your future!"

The man's unwavering smile widened as he proffered his hands, palms up, taking a moment to admire his handsome reflection against an opposite reflective panel. Madame Zostra placed her palms atop his as two thin telescoping cords with monomolecular ends snaked out from the sides of a Sec-Palm reader. They gently wrapped around the man's wrists before violently penetrating between well-scarred knuckles. Blood was withdrawn then immediately analyzed. The man laughed as he shook his head in mirth and merriment, eyes vacant.

Madame Zostra spoke again, "AZ-0731, you are clear to proceed to your vorkplace. Be *very* wary of wolves!"

The man's face turned solemn. He nodded then said with great concern, "one can *never* be wary *enough* of wolves." The beautiful shining iris opened in response and the man stepped through, entering a large room somehow *more* beautiful than the previous corridor. Pillars of jade lined the room's corners, platinum filigree running between them. Intricate woven tapestries were mounted on every wall save that which bore the iris. Above, the ceiling bore a serene sunny day of resplendent silvery clouds. A glittering metallic catwalk lined the interior border of the room, the center possessing two massive gleaming silver doors. The man moved opposite the iris to his work platform, then pressed a large red button. The double doors slowly opened, settling with a jarring *CLUNK*.

The man observed the pit and its contents, grin deepening. With beaming pride, the man turned his back on the pit then pushed a large green button. Large grinders began churning as nozzles positioned above sprayed outward. A cool breeze constantly wafted from the pastoral ceiling.

The liquid sizzled and hissed as it, along with the grinders, dissolved the contents of the pit into a chunky paste. This sludge fell into holding vats. Molecular mechanites then broke inorganics down to their base compounds to remove toxicity. The resulting paste was chemically-treated in a separate vat by various nutrient additives and preservatives before depositing into a mold. This mold was then sprayed with another solution, hardening it and allowing it to be grasped. The final product was conveyed elsewhere for packaging and distribution.

Once the pit was empty, nozzles and grinders came to a halt until a full batch was again ready. Rainbow-colored clouds poured intermittently into the pit, filling it dozens of times over the course of the man's shift. Once the glorious cloud-rain ceased, the man pushed the large green button to begin the process anew.

The man paused only once for his five minute nutrient intake, retrieving a thinly-wrapped meal-stick from his grey jumpsuit. As the man chewed the flavorless bar he couldn't help but grin, shaking his head at having such great fortune. Meal break complete, the man resumed his work for an indiscernible amount of time. The piercing screech of an alarm filled the room along with harsh red light, momentarily blinding him.

Work's done. Time to go home!

The rainbow clouds slowed to a trickle before coming to an end. The man gazed lovingly at the clouds in the pit, waving to them before pushing the large red button and sealing the floor panels. He crossed over the floor then stood before the iris. Madame Zostra's holographic image projected from a nearby holo-point, smiling, "Great job AZ-0731! You performed *most* admirably. Vere you very wary of wolves?"

He replied earnestly, "Yes Madame Zostra, thank you so much!"

Madame Zostra clapped her hands together then said, "fantastic. On your way then and zee you at home!"

The iris opened and the man stepped through. He trudged along the gilded metallic walkway behind countless others wearing healthy and vacant smiles to match his own. As he neared the conveyance lane, the woman from earlier re-appeared from and approached him.

The odd female.

She spoke, "It's me. Do you...do you recognize me?" Tears welled up in the woman's eyes as she gingerly reached out and brushed her fingers against something on the side of the man's head. The man jerked away from the woman's touch, unsure of who she was or her motives.

She could be a wolf! ...why is she sad? I'm the luckiest man in the world!

He offered the sad woman a mock frown followed by a supportive smile then said, "aww, don't be sad little one, all are happy in the

Production Center, and I am by *far* the happiest!" He strode through her again then reached out and grasped onto the conveyance lane. It slowly ascended before rapidly building momentum, carrying the man upward in a blur. The female shouted in despair as he disappeared from sight. The man arrived at pod PC AZ-0731 after some time, passing through several cleansing fields along the way.

He reached out and touched his palm against a Sec-Palm Reader which pulsed three times before the pod thinned. The man entered it and, after removing his grey jumpsuit, laid down. Madame Zostra appeared and said, "welcome home AZ-0731, I'm zo glad you made it back. Have you zeen the news today? Zome people were *not* very wary of wolves!"

The interior of the pod was filled with rapid images and sounds, too many to count, all violent and horrific. As the images and sounds played, thin telescoping metal cords snaked outward just beside the man's head then entered his ears, interfacing with his brain-case. The man, oblivious to the probes, swallowed and said sadly, "all those people lost to wolves... *what* a shame." He dwelled on how lucky he was before sleep initiated.

Roland Amariah Gonzales

The man jolted upright from his sleep cycle, awoken by the jarring screech of a wake-alarm paired with blinding red light. He mechanically donned a grey jumpsuit as the noise and harsh glare continued. Numbly setting his body in motion, he hit the *EXIT* button, the pod's surface thinning. The man exited, stepping from the pod's platform to take position on a conveyance lane. The pod's clamoring awakening system silenced as it solidified.

The man looked upward as he descended, his blank gaze fixating on a golden, sparkling sleep pod, *PC AZ-0731* emblazoned on its surface.

Beautiful.

Overhead, a bright red sky as harsh as the sleep pod's light bore down upon all, flickering momentarily. All plunged down, down into the unfathomable, dark depths of the city.

The man's pace increased to a blur as he observed innumerable sleep pods, golden and beautiful all, stacked atop one another. They stretched out farther than he could perceive, attached conveyance ladders casting an endless stream downward. A pleasant citrusy scent took hold of his senses as he shot through several cleansing fields, ridding his body of bacterial contaminants. Nearing his assigned workspace, the man suddenly detached from the conveyance lane and plummeted toward gravi-catch nets below.

He stepped off onto a walkway and proceeded to his workstation. He was suddenly accosted by a strange woman whom he could not recall, equipped with a half-face breather. He regarded her sad, angry face in confusion before she plunged something into his neck. She stepped back and clasped her hands over face, weeping and murmuring something too low for the man to hear. He began to console her saying, "don't be sa-sad little...one, a-all...all...," then fell to the ground. He weakly slurred then shouted, "...woo...olf...WOLF!"

Sec-Cameras emerged from unseen places and scanned the woman. Red lights began flashing throughout the corridor as the woman's likeness was projected from thousands of holo-points. Terrified, she fled down a walkway and disappeared.

Darkness took the man.

Roland Amariah Gonzales

Kael awoke in terrible pain. His head ached and his body throbbed. He struggled to draw in thick, choking, noxious air. A sharp stinging pain flared from his neck.

*That's...odd. I...I can't...*remember *the last time I felt pain.*

He shakily rose to his feet, legs wobbling and unsteady. Every movement felt like swimming in lead as he struggled toward the Sec-Palm Reader, observing his reflection against a reflective metal panel. He stared in horror at a face he didn't recognize, eyes sunken in, cheeks gaunt, and head completely shaved. A small metallic cube was implanted on the left side of his skull. He turned his head in disgusted awe to see a cheery yellow face with *IO Placidity Implant: AZ-0731* imprinted below. A small red light on the device pulsed slowly.

Hands shaking, he first touched the device before giving it a light tug. An explosion of stars took his vision as he fell to his knees, an ear-splitting wail sounding from within his head. Kael's mouth gaped as he silently screamed, desperately hugging his knees to his body. The wail lasted a brief eternity as Kael lay there, breathing heavily. Grasping the Sec-Palm Reader for support, he rose to his feet, back to the iris.

He observed his surroundings, seeing nothing but old decayed metal and stonework, rusted and rotten. Filth stained the walls, the walkway, even in the air, choking him with a noxious stench he couldn't place. All around were holo-placards warning those not sentenced to the Production Center to vacate immediately or be at risk of bio-contamination.

His existence one of misery and horror, he turned toward the Sec-Palm Reader and noticed in the reflective panel, a large medi-ringe jutting from his neck. He fearfully reached for it and grit his teeth as he slowly pulled out a needle as long as his middle finger. A small trickle of blood flowed as Kael whimpered in pain.

He looked at the medi-ringe and turned it over carefully, pocketing it just before a blue holographic figure appeared. It was a dark haired female with fair skin who wore a purple bandana and had several ear piercings. She spoke with a comically thick accent, "Madame Zostra says provide your palms that I may read your future!"

Kael jumped back in surprise, shouting. He tentatively placed his palms on the reader, crying out in pain as blood cords tore into him, verifying his genetic sequence and lack of contamination, his key to this place. He yanked his hands backward after being released, nursing them, then observing hundreds of scars.

How long have I been here?

Madame Zostra wagged her finger at him before giving him a thumbs up, "it seems that you have seen wolves, yes? Good on you for spotting them! Do not vorry, Hunters vill find them and vhen they do, *vhat* do we do?"

Kael stared in stunned silence then began weakly, "I-I don't know what I'm doing here, I-."

Madame Zostra nodded in satisfaction then smiled cruelly before she said, "that's right, AZ-0731! Vee *burn* them! Now proceed to your happy verk!"

Kael nodded slowly, at a loss for words, though took solace in her reminding him of one thing: his happy work. The light on the P.I blinked yellow for a few moments before resuming a static green.

That's right, I have a job to do. A wonderful job!

The metal iris opened and the man entered a large room filled with beautiful decoration and vibrant color. He moved to the workstation opposite the iris and pressed a large red button, the doors opening then settling with a jarring *CLUNK*. The man observed the pit and its contents, tears of joy pouring forth. With beaming pride, the man turned his back on the pit then pushed a large green button. Large grinders began churning as nozzles positioned above sprayed outward. A cool breeze constantly wafted from the ceiling's pastoral depiction.

The liquid sizzled and hissed as it, along with the grinders, dissolved the contents of the pit into a chunky paste. This continued until it was time for nutrient-intake. The man shoved his hand into his pocket to retrieve a thinly-wrapped meal-bar, then felt something prick his hand.

Curious, he withdrew his hand to see a long needle embedded between his knuckles, attached to a cylindrical tube.

Odd.

The man yanked out the needle, followed by a squirt of blood, then threw it on the ground. He then reached into his pocket and pulled out his nutrient bar. As he happily munched on the blood-soaked nutrient bar he thought on the new flavor and how lucky he was to work at such a great job. He walked to the pit and threw trash in it as rainbow clouds rained from the sky, then, stepping toward the console, tripped on the medi-syringe.

The man flailed his arms upward as he fell forward, slamming his head against the ground.

The World Before

Kael awoke in agony. His head felt like it was splitting in two. As he reached out and touched his skull, his fingers glanced over a heavily-dented cubic structure, a shattered glass object atop. He gingerly probed the object before an odor he couldn't put words to commanded his attention. Rotting, burning flesh. Waste. Filth. Something sweet? Garbage. Kael struggled, first not to vomit, then to his feet and, hearing noise, looked toward it. What he saw shattered his mind.

Innumerable bodies, mostly corpses. He heard moans and cries of anguish from the pit of the damned, central to and below a ceiling which stretched upward into infinite blackness. Some in the pit were strangely serene. In repose. Some weakly begged for help. Some were missing limbs...some were just torsos. Kael *remembered*. Blood and gore stained the walls. The floors. Him.

...I work the Redemption Pit. Mine is to grind bodies, living or no.

Kael saw a nutrient bar's thin wrapper amidst the bodies then fell to his knees, vomiting. After he shakily rose to his feet, he noticed something familiar. He looked at the charnel pit, this pit of death and despair, and saw something...pretty? In the middle of the pit lay a flower. A charred corpse with an unmarred face...twisted in agony as the body was redeemed by fire.

...wolf...daughter? My daughter. ...I did this.

Kael fell to his knees, mustering a sorrowful wail that almost made it past countless air movers above as they kept *filth* from below contained. He slammed his fists against metal grating until they were bloody pulps. Breathing heavily and choking back sobs, Kael rose to his feet, his tears coming to an end. He numbly walked to the grinder console, looking once more back at the pit as both the blessed and the damned rained down from above.

...I can't see her anymore. ...better that way. ...I'm so sorry.

Prisoner AZ-0731, convicted of a crime he could no longer remember and sentenced to a punishment he no longer cared to serve, painfully slammed his bloody knub against the large green button. He walked to the pit and, facing away from it, fell backward.

Roland Amariah Gonzales

GENESIS

Tech-Head cried out before falling back against a plasticrete wall, stunned. A sharp ringing in her head deafened all. Mechanically, she turned her head and noticed Doc's unmoving body crumpled on the floor, a faint trail of steam wafting upward from his head. She spared a brief glance before scrambling back behind cover. Blood poured from her hairline, a steady stream of crimson which rushed down her pale forehead before depositing into her right eye.

Her hiss of pain graduated to a growl as her coagulation implant sealed her head wound, tiny mechanites hard at work. Tech-Head's breathing became labored as she laid back to fish out an H-Con unit from her assault pack. She thumbed through its porous membrane before lowering her In-Optics away from her face, then poured the H-Con into her bloodied eye. She squeezed her eyes shut and grit her teeth as she grunted in discomfort.

Distant muffled sounds of shouting followed by repeated *THUDS* reverberated through her as she brought the H-Con to her lips, biting down and taking a swig. Catching her breath, she lowered the H-Con and, covering her stinging eye with one hand, watched as the membrane quickly resealed. The H-Con quickly refilled as it pulled moisture from the air. Tech-Head's lip curved upward, a lopsided smile.

As the H-Con seals, so does my head.

She felt a faint *pop* as her hearing restored, the sounds of battle suddenly breaking through her reverie. Surprise and cursing, anger...the high-pitched *PING* of a sear-bolt turret discharging white-hot plasma. Doc had been hit *directly*, his head now resembling a large smoking "O." His face had been seared clean through, its edges still sizzling. Tech-Head was alive only because Doc, being a head taller than her, had triggered the turret. She watched as his body convulsed one last time, the remaining fragments of his Cerebral Augmentation Unit failing to connect to anything meaningful.

Nice way to go...quick.

She cursed and kicked her boots against the ground as a droplet of blood in her eyebrow found its new home in her eye. Two men opposite her position stayed crouched as one leaned into the long hallway and snapped off a pulse from his lance. The pulse's discharge rippled harmlessly against the turret's energy field.

Damn.

He flipped the lance's selector-switch to "static" then fired again, outward but near the sear-bolt turret. The sear-bolt turret spasmed for a moment before powering down.

Oh...good enough?

The man glanced at Tech-Head's shifting form, their anonymity maintained by their respective image-scatter devices. She was still cursing as she poured water into her eye. Lancer signaled a man to his side and shouted, "15 seconds! *Go*, Boomer!"

Boomer abruptly rose to his feet and sprinted down the corridor, making it halfway before the sear-bolt turret beeped a welcome jingle and reactivated. Resignation flashed across his face midstride as he charged forward, yelling as the turret fired erratically. White-hot plasma claimed his arm before he used his other to lodge a shatter-nade behind the turret's protective plating.

Tech-Head blinked repeatedly and cleared her vision before registering a shatter-nade's low staccato begin to build up. Her eyes widened briefly before she flung herself face-down into the fetal position. She quickly expelled the air from her lungs and squeezed her eyes shut, then plugged her nose and inhaled. The staccato became impossibly high-pitched.

The concussive vortex drew the sear-bolt turret, along with Boomer, inward before propelling both outward. Boomer slammed into the wall beside Tech-Head, his eyeless sockets twitched for a moment, searching in vain from within a mask of hideous anguish. His eardrums, ruptured. His bones, powder. His organs and brain, liquefied as noiseless cries poured from his mouth.

Tech-Head cocked her head to the side and stared at the spectacle of gore before her, terror and panic flooding her before quickly ebbing away.

Boomer! We need to fall back! We have to! I don't...we...we have suffered two KIA. Current operational capacity at 50%. ...not a nice way to go, Boomer...still quick though.

Tech-Head's *Modified* Placidity Implant, or M.P.I, pumped a concoction into her brain which quelled emotions otherwise appropriate. Terror. Sorrow. Rage.

We have stumbled upon an NED black site. I'm sure of it. ...I wonder if we'll make it through this.

Tech-Head grimaced, hearing a distant sec-door slide upward, followed by the thudding of several Sec-Ops running toward what remained of her team. She moved into position opposite Lancer as he shook his head, his lance recharging. Tech-Head's grin was sharp. Hungry. She was a predator poised to strike. She readied her screamer.

Burn it all to the ground.

Crouching, she leaned into the hallway, snapped off a shot, then ducked behind cover before a hail of kinetic weapons' fire flew past where her head had been. The screamer had discharged a small, clear capsule that propelled a black mist filled with hundreds of *thousands* of protein filaments, each laced with pain-amplifier toxins. The filaments burrowed into flesh at the nano scale, seeking out peripheral nervous systems and overloading them. The effects were something akin to having acid injected into one's every nerve-ending, then, cardiac arrest.

Black mist briefly filled the hallway, a curious spectacle to the Sec-Ops team, one which quickly turned to a chorus of men and women shrieking. It was a wondrous symphony to Tech-Head's ears. Lancer

44

raised his eyebrows as the last of the shrieking cut off abruptly then said, "nice work, T-H. Let's move."

The two rushed down the hallway past the agonized faces of NED's sec-ops, then entered a room littered with bodies clad in containment suits. Tech-Head saw a system's display blink *PURGE IN EFFECT*.

Damn! Too slow.

She pulled a retractable cable from the back of her neck and plunged it into a data port, interfacing with the system. Command lines displayed on her In-Optics as she neutralized the purge and began accessing data. Her CAU ran at breakneck speeds as she pored through mountains of data. Of all Tabula Rasa's members, Tech-Head had the most hardware.

...is there anything worth salvaging?

Lancer quickly searched each body, his eyes narrowing as he noted the serene looks on their faces. He shook his head then called to her, "the bastards have taken HA-HA pills, they're gone. Have you pulled anything?" Tech-Head tapped her optics, projecting the display.

Her eyes flitted about as she burned through data. She replied after a moment, "yes. 'Compound...A-500.' Cellular reconstruction. Reanimation and integration of dead tissue. In...'Nursery.' Be careful, the 'Nursery' is bio-contained...I'll keep scanning."

Lancer nodded and said, "right. I'm off, then," then moved to the nearby wall and lifted a lone containment suit off its hook. He donned it, placed his assault pack over, then moved toward the decontamination chamber. Tech-Head called out "Sec-Ops manually shut the turret down...then reactivated it."

Lancer muttered, "*fucking* NED," yelled out "roger," then entered the decontamination chamber. A red light pulsed softly overhead, shifting to a solid yellow as the door slid shut behind him. Small panels on the walls, ceiling, and floor slid open. Nozzles violently shot out pressurized sterilization fluid before retracting, panels sliding shut. The overhead light glared a sharp bright green, causing Lancer to squint before the door slid open.

A loud crash sounded followed by the horrible screams of *something* being burned alive. Lancer winced in confusion as the aroma of cooked meat, slightly burnt, assailed his nostrils. He instinctively salivated despite knowing only the taste of nutrient bars. His eyes quickly adjusted from the previous room to the muted red glow of emergency lights overhead.

Lancer stood in place, jaw agape, as his mind struggled to make sense of all before him. The first thing he noticed was a large glossy-black "SITE 13" on the far wall. Just below it, a gleaming, silvery, metallic sign hung, surrounded by placards of flowers and smiling children's faces.

"Nursery"

Four rows by four columns of operating tables covered by containment domes, about waist-high, lay before him. Each contained an incomprehensible mass of writhing, tortured flesh.

...what the hell*?*

Each *something* was enveloped by flame invisible to Lancer's eyes, propelled by the dome's internal systems. The creatures thrashed against their dome's walls, in utter torment as they attempted to burst through and flee. Lancer blinked in confusion, realizing he didn't hear so much as a *thump,* from the contained creatures, so thick was the dome's material.

...where is that terrible noise coming from? ...and why do I smell burning flesh?

Lancer's hands shot downward in panic. He frantically patted down his suit, searching for rips and tears, but found none. A large, mounted monitor caught his eye, flashing *FACILITY BREACH DETECTED. SYSTEM PURGE IN PROGRESS* in bold red. Life-pulse signatures flashed underneath the superimposed alert, violent and erratic as the creatures were incinerated.

Temp is in the upper 1000s...

Lancer raced toward the control console, slinging his lance onto his back as he attempted to stop the system purge. Lacking both the technical know-how or tools of Tech-Head, he only managed to key up a bright yellow smiley-face with *ACCESS DENIED* underneath. Lancer slammed on the keys in frustration then readied his lance, flipping the selector-switch from "static" back to "disruptor," and fired a single shot at the system's front panel. The panel dissolved into sand-like materials which scattered before him. He kneeled down and, locating the system's data drive, tore it out. Lancer looked up, expecting to see a blank screen, but instead saw "BREACH DETECTED" in bold yellow.

Must be a localized system. Saved the data drive...hope it holds something for T-H. ...I – wait! What was that!?

A blur of motion seized his attention. He strained his ears, cursing as he realized his MPI had blocked out the disconcerting cries. Shoving the data drive in his assault pack, he rose carefully as he heard something resembling angry whispers and soft chuckling, lance at the ready. Cautiously, he moved toward where the blur had been as a soft beep sounded from his internal comms unit. HQ sounded, "Lancer, NED Sec-Ops en route. ETA 5 minutes." Lancer placed his finger against the containment suit and applied pressure just below his left ear, then whispered "roger. Commencing exfil in two." He glanced at the nursery sign, lost in thought.

Fast reaction. This place is much more than we thought. ...was it worth losing Boomer and Doc, though?

A roar, laughter and pathetic mewling combined to answer his question as one of the *things* scrambled toward him from behind, leaping onto his leg. The creature ravaged Lancer's leg into a pulpy mass in *moments* as it gorged itself on his flesh. Lancer cried out in agony, falling forward, then quickly turned over to see *something* working its way up his leg. Lancer raised his weapon and fired off a disruptor shot at the creature, simultaneously disintegrating what was left of his leg below the knee. Blinding-white pain nearly sent him into shock before his MPI pumped out a tide of endorphins.

Half the creature dissolved along with Lancer's leg as the creature writhed on the floor, howling in pain and giggling hysterically. Lancer struggled to his remaining leg, leaning heavily on a nearby operating table's dome. All of the creatures within were *still* alive despite the continued flame. He glanced up toward the Nursery's monitor as sweat poured down his brow, dizzy on a cocktail of drugs and pain. 15 stabilizing yellow lines had displaced the earlier erratic red.

A *16th* display, visible now that "SYSTEM PURGE IN PROGRESS" had been removed, softly pulsed "breach detected" in a dark blue nearly *imperceptible* to its black background. Lancer cursed, "...fucking *terrible* color."

The creature flailed about as it cried and moaned ecstatically. Lancer toggled his containment suit's headlamp, his brain struggling to translate incomprehensible into something more tangible. The cries, moans, and everything else he had heard, came from the singular creature's *many* mouths, each moving as independently as its eyes, fingers, and various barbed appendages – all in places which *defied reason!* Lancer had no words for what the creature resembled. He only recognized that its eyes were full of *hate*. New limbs burst from the missing half of its body before it darted toward him.

Lancer attempted to fire off another disruptor shot, but was met with a soft whine from his lance.

Still charging. Fuck!

He unslung his lance and swung it at the creature just as it leapt toward his head, the satisfying sound of metal impacting against meat resounding through the room. The creature sailed across the room, slamming into the "Nursery" sign. Lancer stared for a moment in disbelief then quickly hobbled toward the decontamination chamber's entrance and tried to enter, only to see *BIO CONTAMINANT DETECTED. ACCESS PROHIBITED* display overhead. Lancer turned his back to the door and readied his lance with one arm while double tapping the comms implant just below his ear.

"This is Tech-Head, go ahead Lancer," Tech-Head said.

The World Before

Lancer spoke quickly in shallow breaths, his voice shaky with pain, "Tech-Head, I'm trapped in the nursery. I need you to blow the door. I've got the facility's data drive in-hand. NED was working on some kind of bio-weapons project...one subject has breached containment. I hit it with a disruptor shot but it's still *alive,* the fucking thing! ...*all* of them are despite being incinerated..."

A pause, then Tech-Head replied, "...roger, Lancer...are *you* contaminated?"

Lancer looked at the stump of his missing leg then replied, "negative. A NED Sec-Ops response team is en route. We need to move."

Tech-Head attempted to access the Nursery's door control only to find it localized to Lancer's side. Cursing, she detached her interface cable then approached the decontamination chamber. Looking around, she propped the door open with a nearby table, then placed a breaching charge made on the far door.

...should be enough.

She retreated a safe distance then pinged Lancer, "Lancer, door-breach placed. Achieve optimal distance in five, four, three..."

Lancer moved to the side as quickly as a one-legged man could just as the creature raged toward him, leaping in front of the door. The blast from the breaching charge splattered the creature's body about the Nursery. Lancer moved toward the breach and laughed, "HA! Great timing, asshole!"

Tech-Head moved to support Lancer, swatting at and brushing away a sudden sharp pain on the back of her neck. Tech-Head dragged Doc and Boomer's bodies outside and placed them together while Lancer hobbled toward their jump-bikes. The two survivors then stood upright, Lancer leaning heavily on his ride, and clasped their fists over their hearts in salute. Lancer whispered, "goodbye, my friends," then fired a low-power, wide-spread disruptor shot, dispersing comrades' corpses into the night wind.

Roland Amariah Gonzales

Tech-Head mounted Lancer's jump-bike, taking the operator's position as Lancer fired an incendiary round at the other jump-bike, quickly melting it to slag. He slung his lance over his back and wrapped both arms around Tech-Head's waist. She toggled the jump-bike's silent mode and eased them toward the edge of the facility's platform, then plummeted toward the black abyss below, back to HQ.

The World Before

BROUGHT TO YOU BY

The man wore a smile on his face though none could see him. He sighed contentedly as he operated an NED Levitational Transportation Unit, 8A-004311. He had left his Existence Container before the start of his shift then proceeded toward the NED LTU pool. This did not take long as his Existence Container was situated within walking distance. The man had then boarded his assigned LTU, a great, bloated and bulbous thing with several recesses along its underbelly, before pushing a large green button.

The LTU had then noiselessly lifted into the air, proceeding along its pre-programmed course as the distant sound of metallic *THUDS* reverberated along the hull. When prompted, the man pressed the large blue button, not quite sure of what it did. At the end of his shift, the LTU would return above the LTU pool, at which point he was prompted to press the large red button...he wasn't sure what *that* button did either. Sometimes, when he *was* sure no one was looking...he thought to not push the red button at all, just to see what would happen! The man scratched his head in thought as he pondered for a moment, then shrugged.

Retirement would be delayed. I mean...probably. No one ever doesn't push their button...perhaps...you know what? I have no idea.

The man thought wistfully of retirement as he sank back into his comfortable operator's chair. Today was as ordinary as any other. He studied the panel which displayed the LTU's position relative to each gravi-catch net, the craft flitting between gravi-catch nets across his district in mere moments. The LTU itself, a great, bloated and bulbous thing with hundreds of spherical pods attached to its underbelly, paused in the air for a singular heartbeat over a given gravi-catch net, far below.

A spherical pod's floor then *WHOOSHED* open, sending those within plummeting downward before the LTU continued its breakneck pace.

The immediate surroundings were little more than a white blur while distant gleaming metallic spires stretched far up into a red, flickering sky. The depths of the city, in comparison, were so far below that none could perceive them...nor would they want to. What lay below wasn't meant for upstanding citizens, but rather the dregs of society. So it had always been.

The man's thoughts took him far away as he briefly wondered what it would be like to push *four* buttons...or perhaps some kind of job that required even more! The man laughed at the notion.

I'd probably be some kind of science-man if I had that life. I can't imagine!

After some time, the last of the spherical pods emptied its contents and the LTU returned to the pool. A series of distant metallic *CLUNKS* sounded, the man unaware of the spherical pods detaching and puttering back to their respective positions. He stared at the large red button and hesitated for a fraction of a second before pressing it, laughing to himself afterward for the grand risk he had just taken.

I'll have to tell Cealn about this! He'll think I'm crazy!

A small, blue holographic figure, about the size of the man's hand, projected from a nearby holo-point, appearing in a cloud of smoke. It resembled a dark haired female with fair skin who wore a purple bandana and sported several ear piercings. She spoke with a comically-thick accent, "great vork today, Salthet! Everyone is home and safe! You are IO's number one operator!"

The man smiled at the small hologram and said, "thank you, Madam Zostra!" The hologram waved goodbye before it disappeared, again in a cloud of smoke. Salthet exited the LTU after it docked, chuckling to himself as he thought of his earlier shenanigans. He walked a short distance to his Existence Container, along a walkway situated far above another walkway which went on and on down below, as far as anyone would care to see.

Advertisements lit up the path, projected from nearby hovering holo-points. They displayed shiny things, pretty things, all which he desperately wanted. A bright neon-green hat for his holo-pet. Teal-colored boots for the same. Many more things projected, things which Salthet found particularly amazing. They weren't things that he could have *now*, of course. They were things one could only obtain in *retirement*. Salthet jumped for joy and thrust his hands into the air as he laughed.

Ahhh, to be retired. Soon!

Salthet had been laboring for nearly 20 years, having been assigned his role at 20 years of age, as it had always been. He stood in front of the door to his Existence Container as it scanned his form before beeping and sliding upward. Salthet entered as the door slid shut behind him, a loud metallic *THUNK* sounding throughout the room as it magnetically sealed. After a moment the walls and floor disappeared, and Salthet found himself standing on a balcony atop a castle in the clouds. The balcony overlooked green hills and valleys far below full of tiny colorful specks, all people who cheerily waved at him.

His holo-pet emerged from behind a large, pink and fluffy cloud, a small blue dragon with adorably-large eyes. It fluttered around him, projected from the display field which made up the ceiling. It happily spoke, "hello Salthet, welcome home!" Salthet smiled at his holo-pet and replied, "I'm glad to be back, Cealn! ...though sad to leave. I *will* retire soon, you know!"

The holo-pet furiously flapped its tiny wings as it made a large somersault, displaying in green a timer which read 00:00:07:22:04:30. It said at first in a mournful voice, "yes, I will miss you terribly Salthet," then happily followed with, "but to be retired is the single greatest thing one can hope to achieve! And I'll be there too, just...not *me*. I'll be *much* bigger and you can ride on my back as we soar through the clouds!"

Salthet grinned at that idea, and, nodding enthusiastically, made his way to a golden throne with large red cushions. He reclined comfortably then said, "holo-vid." Two attractive people began a news report. "Hello Salthet, great work today operating the LTUs! Everyone says you're the best!" Salthet nodded in appreciation then said, "yes I am, and you're welcome!" He pulled out his day's nutrient bar and munched away happily at the tasteless substance.

The news report continued, "Today was a *great* day! The weather was fair and everyone thinks you're *really* great! IO is, and always will be, the best place to live in the world! Everywhere else is very *bad* and *very* dangerous. Would you like to see?"

Salthet finished his nutrient bar just in time to throw it into the waste collection unit, then excitedly responded to the news reporters, "yes, certainly!" The news reporters responded in a playful voice, "okaaaay, hope you're ready!"

Countless videos and images swept through the room all at once, displayed around Salthet as he looked on in awe and terror.

This part of the day is so exciting! It feels so dangerous!

Giant war machines walked on three legs as they fired bright golden rays at screaming people. Men, women and children burst into flames. Elsewhere, primitive people burned others alive, dancing around charred and crackling flesh as those unfortunate writhed in agony. Cannibals consumed the flesh of people still living as they cried out. One looked directly at Salthet and yelled, "I wish I was in IO where it's safe!"

There was much that Salthet's mind simply couldn't comprehend, so far removed from reality as it was. He only knew that all before him was *awful.* He looked on in abject terror until he saw groups of people engaged in *intercourse,* and, unable to bear it any longer, shouted, "HOLO-VID, STOP!" His face poured sweat as he took rapid breaths. Salthet wiped at his brow then shakily asked, "whew! H-how long did I make it that time?" The news reporters smiled and said in unison, "3.5 seconds, Salthet. That's a *new record!* Congratulations!"

The World Before

Salthet laughed shakily and said, "you know, I sure am glad I live here in IO where everything is *good*. Where we don't have *filthy* and *dangerous* outsiders. Where we can *retire!*" Salthet shuddered in disgust then muttered, "I still can't believe those on the outside *reproduce* in such a manner. *Bodily fluid exchange*! Ugh, it's disgusting! Birthing pods are much more efficient. Safer, too." Salthet sighed and briefly considered how different life would have been if he had been assigned a family unit, a reward for especially productive citizens. He'd have a "wife" of sorts and a child or two, grown from birthing pods via he and his wife's genetic material.

...wouldn't be much different from my life as it is, I suppose.

He threw away the useless thoughts then shook his head in pity of the filthy, degenerate outsiders. He stopped when he remembered he wasn't one of them, then smiled and said, "I love you holo-vid display!"

The news reporters smiled and said in unison, "thank you Salthet. That means a *lot* to us! We love you too. Would you like to see something pleasant, now?"

Salthet nodded enthusiastically and said, "oh yes, please!"

The room darkened then brightened into a world devoid of anything he knew. A kaleidoscopic whirlwind of colors, shapes, and music surrounded him. Unseen nozzles in his Existence Container delicately pumped a fine mist of pleasing fragrances he could not discern. In the distance, his holo-pet Cealn, huge, blue and magnificent, waved to him and he waved back. It was *everything* that Salthet ever wanted.

Tears formed in his eyes as he nodded eagerly, grinning, clapping and sobbing. The clouds themselves formed into the words "Retirement, where your dreams become reality. A lifetime of service *warrants* a lifetime of joy, doesn't it?"

Salthet wept with joy and whispered, "yes. Yes it does!"

Words drifted on the wind to Salthet, " Soon, Salthet. You've worked *so* hard. You *deserve* it." The world shifted from a never-ending meadow full of flowers to a large pristine and ornate room full of people in contentment and repose. They were all gently smiling, all in sleep-pods as each pod's external display showed that person's greatest fantasies realized.

"Retirement awaits, Salthet."

SUM OF HER PARTS

The girl was roused from restless sleep by the gentle pink glow of a fungi-light overhead. She rubbed at her eyes, careful to flick the grit aside onto her lichen bed. With slight effort, she sat up then hugged her knees. The bed's soft tendrils made popping noises as they released her, a mother reluctantly releasing its child. The girl shifted her body and, rising to her knees, stretched her arms and neck as best she could. She looked down at the waggling tendrils as they receded, staring thoughtfully.

...where do they go, I wonder?

With a slight tilt of her head, she bowed toward the lichen bed and said, "thank you for all you do," then draped her white tunic and sash over her nude form. Remaining on her knees, the girl pulled aside the pale-white skin flap which separated her room from a narrow and roughly carved tunnel, then crawled out.

The hallway was filled with the rest of the females, the girl being last in order. Having been recently born, she marveled at everything. Other Young told the girl that her awe would wear off in time, though she hoped the time would never come.

The girl was mesmerized by the flow of fungi lines as she traversed soft lichen flooring with the rest. It almost seemed as if the lines pulsed in time with the rise and fall of her chest. She felt that this place, her home, was *truly* alive. She followed the others into the Sustenance Chamber, silent and respectful.

The girl noticed Faeleor across the chamber and grinned as he smiled at her. She then offered a smile to Rael, though he seemed lost in thought. She found it *fascinating* to have siblings even though she'd only met them recently. The other Young thought her very odd in that she had siblings at all! They all simply existed in this place, performed their function, and fulfilled their purpose.

The girl stared dreamily at the Moonstone in the chamber's center, some part of her stirring in recognizance. In remembrance of...a memory, perhaps? Something ephemeral as it danced in the shadows, just out of sight. The Elders spoke as all listened intently, save for the girl who was lost in thought.

...this is my favorite place. It feels...right. The Elders...they make me uneasy, though I know not why. I wish I could be Young forever. Forever learning. Forever helping.

The Cultivators sounded their intonation, shaking the girl from her reverie. When they finished she and the other Young began their chant, in turn. The girl, full of youth and exuberance, sang in her enthusiasm. With their part over, all lowered to their knees and fed, then meditated on the coming day's duties. The girl was *ecstatic*. She had been informed by other Young that she was formed enough to begin learning. Today she would visit her birthplace and spend time with the Cultivators.

The Moonstone pulsed thrice and all rose as one. The Watchers were first to leave, followed by the Menders, then the Cultivators, and lastly the Young, the girl among them. She glanced over her shoulder as she followed the procession, seeing the room behind darken. She followed the other nine Young in front of her and entered the Cultivators' work area. Ten Cultivators clad in green stood waiting as the rest went about their business. The Young approached them.

Her Cultivator bowed slightly then said in a low tone, dispassionately, "Young Iwik, I am your Cultivator. Today, you learn all we do. Tomorrow, you learn the Menders' work, then, the Watchers, then back here, then you will repeat the cycle for as long as need be. Please, remain by my side at all times."

Iwik offered a nervous smile and nodded her assent, then was taken by her Cultivator to an adjacent room, separated by a pale-green skin flap. Iwik was taken aback by the size of the room. It was easily four times larger than the Sustenance Chamber, long lines of giant fungi of various shapes and colors running its length.

Her Cultivator strolled along as he described the area, "here, we grow food necessary for our people." He explained the various fungi and how they were cared for before arriving at a large gold-colored mushroom. He said, "the fungi are such that we need not fully harvest them to procure sustenance. We need only remove a modicum which..." the guide severed a small portion of fungi using a stone blade, then motioned for Iwik to follow. "...we deposit here." Iwik's guide dropped the fungi morsel into a large, green-tinted, translucent vat, roughly the size of the golden mushroom in its entirety. The morsel quickly fizzed then violently bubbled. In moments, it was dissolved and gone.

Iwik watched the process in curiosity and said, "...but why? Where does it go?"

The Cultivator looked at her in slight curiosity then said, "the nutrient bath provides our people sustenance. The fungi offer differing nutrients. They are dissolved here, then transported via the mycorrhizal network to the Sustenance Chamber, for example. Or the Birthing Chamber. Or the Commemoration Chamber."

Iwik nodded in earnest then asked, "how do you know *which* fungi to place in the nutrient bath? And how much?"

The Cultivator directed Iwik's attention to an adjacent wall full of softly-pulsing fungi lights and said, "these fungi lights form patterns which become recognizable in time. The patterns tell Cultivators *what* needs be introduced, and *how much*. Come, there is much that needs be taught."

Iwik followed her Cultivator through another pale-green skin flap. They entered a smaller room, roughly ¼ the size of the previous. In it were several large cylindrical pods, vertically-set. The pods were brown in color, the interiors' bio-luminescent and filled with liquid similar in color to that of the previous room. As Iwik drew closer she was able to make out singular forms floating in each pod, a few her size though most were much smaller.

She looked at the Cultivator and asked, "what *are* these things?"

The Cultivator looked at her and said, "these are Birthing Pods. From here, life begins anew as needed by our people. There are always *100* of us, Young. No more, no less. Those you see remain until one of us expires, then a new Young is born."

Iwik could only nod in awe.

...I was in there. So...we all came from these pods, then? ...something about it feels familiar...but...all wrong.

After some time, the Cultivator led Iwik back to the main hall, then proceeded to the Commemoration Chamber. Iwik stood, stunned, as she looked out across the never-ending water reservoir.

...it just goes and goes.

The Cultivator directed Iwik to the Time Table carved into the cavern wall, then spoke, "this is the history of our people. In it we see where we came from and, therefore, where we go, for one cannot have a future without understanding their past."

Iwik studied the Time Table, shaking her head in amazement at the grand display.

...a thing of beauty. This day is full of wonders! There's so much here...so much that I don't recognize or understand. Perhaps my Cultivator can enlighten me?

She asked, "could...you perhaps read this to me? From where does our history start? There's so much here!"

The Cultivator nodded then pointed midway at the Time Table, "in the beginning, the Moonstone arrived from the sky to this place, the plateau. There was *much* that needed to be done and so it made us, its perfect children. Here, we toil and give thanks to the Moonstone for giving us life, for giving us *purpose*, for *naming* us after *it!* The Moonstone, in all its splendor! In so doing, fulfilling *its* purpose. Which was to give *us* purpose in fulfilling it."

Iwik blinked in confusion, processing what the Cultivator had said.

The World Before

...what? I...he didn't really tell me anything. ...does he not know?

Iwik pointed to the earlier part of the Time Table, near the beginning, then traced to the mid-point and asked, "...and here? What happened before...well, before us?"

The Cultivator looked at her in concern and replied, "that is *before* our time. A past which would be wholly unrecognizable to us as we are now. Perhaps the Elders know more? I do not. Come, there is more to learn."

Before they moved on, Iwik spoke up then pointed and asked, "those bright fungi lights illuminating the wall. Over there, surrounded by lichen beds adorning the same. What is their purpose?"

The Cultivator paused and looked to the lights, then back to Iwik and curtly said, "*I do not know*, Young. Everything here has its purpose. Do not question the 'why?' behind it, simply understand *how* to perform your duties. This is *all* you are meant to do."

The Cultivator abruptly turned then led Iwik to large black and gray, mottled fungi resting under fungi lights casting a dim, purple glow. The air had a sweet pungent smell to it as the mottled fungi dripped sizzling liquid onto forms below. The Cultivator spoke, "here is where we inter the dead that they may have life anew."

Iwik lowered her gaze downward, recognizing her people, half-dissolved with faces, arms, and legs missing. Iwik felt sadness seize her at the loss of one of her own. She looked at the Cultivator who stood there silently, unmoved, and asked, "um...who was this? ...when did they expire?"

The Cultivator glanced at Iwik and said, "this was the causation for your birth. A Young that mis-stepped while assisting the Watchers in attending the Moonstone. A process you will learn, while hopefully not repeating your predecessor's error, in the coming days."

Iwik noted a complete lack of emotion from the Cultivator and asked, "...what was his name? ...*her* name?"

The Cultivator looked at her, again concerned, and said, "name? Its name was Young. As I am Cultivator and *you* are Young. All clad in white are Young. All clad in green are Cultivator."

Iwik blinked in confusion then said, "but...I am Iwik. A Young...but I...I *am Iwik*."

The Cultivator blinked a few times, brow furrowed, then grasped her head with both hands, examining it, and said, "...perhaps you have not formed correctly. Young do not ask questions as you do. They do not ask '*why?*,' only 'how?' a task is performed. I will confer with the Elders."

Iwik became terribly afraid and decided to say nothing more. The Cultivator spoke indifferently, "for now, return to your sleep pod. Your night's work is done. Your lichen bed will expire you if need be, your form brought here to make way for another. If not, you learn the Menders' work tomorrow."

Iwik glumly returned to her sleep pod then disrobed, delicately folding her white tunic and sash then placing them with care on her lichen bed, just below her feet. Fear roiled in her mind. Unease. Anxiety.

Do others feel the same when they're told they will be expired? ...will it hurt, I wonder?

She lay on her lichen bed and felt the tendrils emerge, collecting dead skin cells and cleansing her. They almost seemed to caress her, an act of comfort and assurance. Iwik heaved a deep worried sigh before sleep tendrils inserted into her ears. Slumber came after.

The World Before

Iwik awoke, first in confusion at her sleep pod's darkened state, then relief at not being dead. Though the feelings of unease and anxiety hadn't left.

Oh? I haven't expired. That's nice.

After a few moments the sleep tendrils re-asserted themselves and slumber once again took her.

Iwik heard muffled shouting. She opened her eyes and looked around in confusion at strange sights before her. Structures monolithic in size and bearing impossible angles rose toward a flickering, red sky. Large beings around her rushed to take cover as they wielded long, pointed things aimed toward others far away. Their weapons emitted blinding light, painful to look at – more so for those the light touched.

An arm thrust downward and, grasping her own, pulled her up. In an instant she too was using her weapon to push light into people. Muffled cries of agony reached her as those far away collapsed into burning heaps, engulfed by the hurt-light. The upper torso of someone near her was thrown violently backward. She turned and saw the figure on the ground as it looked around, crazed as it tried to contain its insides. Then the figure died.

She was somewhere else, running with her comrades toward the edge of a platform. A rapid, high-pitched beeping steadied into a more pronounced whine just as she jumped off the edge. She plummeted down...down into the black abyss. A mask suddenly appeared in front of her, a light-blue, semi-transparent field displayed just in front of her eyes. A series of strange words, numbers, and symbols appeared in the field which she navigated with practiced ease.

She and the others continued their dangerous descent as she selected a final symbol then, satisfied, willed the light-blue field away. A series of distant green webs manifested far below, ready to catch them. A deafening explosion rang out above and behind them as they fell, Iwik laughing in triumph as adrenaline surged through her body.

In an instant she was in a large metallic-grey room with the others. They wore sleek black armor with red trim, a grey fist holding a black lightning bolt emblazoned on their right shoulders. A soft, *comforting* blue glow emitted from something nearby. A figure near her removed its helmet then looked at her and grinned, the face *strange* yet...oddly familiar. It spoke in a distant, ethereal voice, "...tell me *that* wasn't close, Iwik!" Iwik laughed. She felt proud. *Strong.* Despite the incredible danger that she faced every day, she was *right* where she wanted to be. She removed her helmet and looked over at a nearby mirror, in awe of the face staring back.

　　She awoke again from restless sleep, unsure of what the dream meant. After a few moments she drifted off. The next time she awoke, it was by the soft pink glow of her fungi light, in abject terror.

The World Before

Iwik jerked upright and shouted in fear, then sobbed. She had seen some...*thing* in her dream. Untold cries, roars and moans were heard as it roughly dragged her broken body up an old forgotten stairway...as she choked on her own blood. She had been in so much *pain*. Horrified.

The thing had drawn her closer and closer as she sobbed and begged the Elders, the Moonstone, *anyone* for help. The thing had *devoured* her alive...from feet to head. Iwik could still *feel* the echoes of her bones crunching, her organs bursting open as the monster greedily gnashed and slurped her. She brought her knees to her chest, rocking in place on the lichen bed as she sobbed.

After a short time, and with the tendrils' insistent prodding, she collected herself and tried to shake off the images in her mind.

I'm here, I'm here safe in the plateau. Whatever that was...it wasn't real. I...I can't tell anyone about this, can I? ...who would hear me?

Iwik donned her white tunic and sash then exited into the hallway. Despite her being delayed, she was somehow *still* on time to be at the back of the line. It was as if the line waited for her...or...perhaps didn't move without her. She nervously took her position after they entered the Sustenance Chamber, yet no one paid her any heed. If they had heard her shouting, there was no indication.

As the Elders began their intonation she noticed, for the first time, that Faeleor was not present. A new Watcher stood in his place.

I've never not seen him here before. Oh no...was he expired?

Iwik looked for Rael and saw that he was still in place.

I wonder if he had the dream as well. There's no way of telling other than the slight furrow of his brow.

Rael seemed unphased as he and the Menders intoned their words. Soon after, the Cultivators said their piece, followed by Iwik and the rest of the Young. They all lowered to their knees, minus the ever-standing elders, and took sustenance before assembling and exiting to their respective areas.

Iwik trudged behind the rest of the Young, her thoughts dwelling on much.

...no word on my *being expired...I think I'm okay...what happened to Faeleor? ...do others have bad dreams?*

Iwik and nine other Young entered the Menders' work area. It was a room perhaps twice as large as the Sustenance Chamber, illuminated by a multitude of blue fungi lights. Under these lights stood ten Menders waiting as the rest went about their business, all clad in blue. Iwik found her spot and was unsurprised to see Rael be her mentor.

Rael quickly toured the Menders' work area, leading Iwik along as he spoke in a hurried manner of their various duties. These included tunnel maintenance: directing fungi lines in tunnels as well as growing and placing fungi lights. Clothing production: stripping long fibrous lengths from large fungi, then interweaving the threads into usable tunics, sashes, and skin flap barriers. And lastly, far-sight glass fabrication: hollowing out thin but sturdy lengths of fungi for the purpose of setting a Moonstone shard in place.

Iwik asked little questions this time, owing to Faeleor's disappearance, her dreams, and the previous day's end. When they were apart from the other Menders and Young, Rael took her by the shoulders, and, speaking in a low tone, said, "Iwik. Faeleor is gone. He's missing. I...listen, did you *dream?*"

Iwik was stunned at the abruptness of it all and struggled to muster, "y-yes. I did, actually. It felt *real.* And terrible. I think...I think Faeleor might be...I think he..."

Rael waved away her fears, "...don't even *say* it. I intend to go after him, to leave the plateau. Iwik, you *must* be careful. Act as any Young. I think...I think we may be unique for some reason, we three. ...did you know that *only* we three are named?"

She thought of her previous day then replied, "no, I-I didn't but...everyone else feels...*odd.* ...though I suppose...if it's only us...then, then it's us isn't it? *We're* odd. We don't fit. I don't understand though...*why?*" Iwik felt like crying.

The World Before

I've just been born and everything is terrible.

Rael looked up at a Mender and Young who were looking their way then said in a normal voice, "yes, the fabrication of the far-sight glass *is* truly amazing. The Moonstone gives us sight beyond our normal faculties that we may see distant danger and be wiser for it!"

Iwik caught on quickly and echoed Rael's sentiments. The two in the distance looked away as they studied tunic production. Rael again spoke in a low tone, "I do not think that we were made without purpose...however, we must tread carefully. I will leave *after* we all enter our sleep pods, Iwik. *Remember* my words and remain hidden in this place! I will return with answers. I *swear* it."

Iwik bit her bottom lip as she remembered her dream and whispered to Rael, "be...be careful, Rael. I feel...I feel a connection with you. With Faeleor. I've only just met you both but I feel that you two are the most important things in my world. I-I don't know why. ...be careful. Okay?"

Rael studied her carefully then nodded. The night's work came to an end and all returned to their sleep pods. Iwik disrobed then lay on her lichen bed. She thought mournfully of Faeleor. How she may soon lose Rael. She'd be truly alone, then.

*It feels as if no one else is...*alive. *The others just* exist...*performing their functions as if...as if that's all they could ever know...why are we different?* Why *haven't we been expired if we're so different?*

Iwik awoke to the soft pink glow of her fungi light. There was no fear or anxiety this time, only resolve. She would await Rael's return and together, they would demand answers from the Elders.

...would that I could address them directly.

Iwik rose to her knees and donned her white tunic and sash, then crawled out into the hallway. She followed the others and entered the Sustenance Chamber, noting that Rael was absent and another had taken his place.

...good luck, Rael.

The intonations became a repetitive act. That which she experienced became little more than bits of data, saved and accessed when needed. Iwik found herself saddened by this.

This must be what the others meant when they said everything fades in time. ...it happened so quickly, though.

The time for Iwik to observe the Watchers had arrived. She followed the others past the caprock and saw, for the first time, the moon. She stopped for a moment, stunned, as she marveled at its beauty.

It's like...like a fungi-light. A brilliant white fungi light set high up in a cavern.

Iwik was led to one of ten waiting Watchers, all clad in red. This Watcher, in short order, showed her their rites in applying oil to the Moonstone. She was told to observe but *not* touch the Moonstone as she had not yet earned the privilege... yet secretly did so at its highest point. Whereas the Watchers performed their work with a sense of reverent duty, Iwik felt something different, she experienced a *resonance*. A sense of familiarity, camaraderie, and even *love* that she had before only known with Faeleor and Rael. She was left reeling at this profound and powerful feeling before her Watcher called to her, "Young? You've been standing there silently for some time. We are done with this task. Come, there is more to learn."

Iwik blinked in confusion.

The World Before

...I'd only just touched the Moonstone. Briefly, even! ...how much time passed?

Iwik reluctantly traveled down the path and joined her Watcher as he retrieved his far-sight glass. They briskly walked along the plateau until they arrived at the edge, then looked out across toward...nothing? Echoes of her dream flashed in her mind as she peered over the edge toward the ground far below. The Watcher droned on about their duties while Iwik half-heartedly listened. She looked around while he talked and noticed a small arrow etched into the ground. Curious, she followed it with her eyes, directly up, noticing a faint red light in the distance.

She motioned toward it and interrupted the Watcher, "what *is* that?"

The Watcher, annoyed at being interrupted, asked, "what is *what?*"

Iwik said, "that red light in the distance."

The Watcher looked through the far sight glass in the direction she pointed and, seeing nothing, said, "your eyes must not be fully formed. There is nothing there."

Iwik began to protest then remembered Rael's advice. She merely nodded and said, "yes. You're right. May I use the far-sight glass for a moment that I may correct myself?"

The Watcher frowned for a moment then said, "be careful with that, it carries the Moonstone's very essence," handing it to her. Iwik raised it to her eye and peered out across the wastes, looking directly at the red light. A bit of movement caught her eye, just below the red light. She followed it and had to stop herself from shouting in surprise.

She saw a blur of motion as a large...*something* descended over a large dune then disappeared. Looking directly at the thing, she felt a momentary tinge of fear overwhelmed by loathing...*recognition?*

I hate it! I want to dash it against the rocks, again and again, until –

Iwik suddenly felt three sharp needles of pain stab her chest. She cried out in surprise then fell forward against the plateau's surface. The Watcher moved quickly to catch his far-sight glass as he let Iwik fall forward, unconscious. He looked at her and shook his head, muttering, "you are *not* fully-formed. I must speak with the Elders."

WHAT HATH BEEN WROUGHT

"This is the lead of Site 11, Dr. Orsom speaking. I am accompanied by my assistant, Dr. Armatis. Today, we test compound A-487 on once-living." A diminutive figure wearing a white, bubbled, biolab suit with "NED" emblazoned on its back took a vial labeled "A-487" from his attendant. He carefully inserted the vial into a dispersal unit atop a transparent protective dome. A small, orange and black furred creature paced anxiously within.

The lab was filled with four rows by four columns of operating tables with containment domes, about waist-high. At the center of the room was a larger domed table. A large bright and gleaming, red metallic sign which read "nursery," hung on the far wall, surrounded by placards of flowers and smiling children's faces.

Orsom spoke again in a monotone but authoritative voice, "A-487 introduced. Today's subject is what was once known as a 'domestic feline,' or, in the then-common vernacular, 'cat.' This feline has been grown from recombinant DNA, as all non-sentient life was deemed wasteful by NED in...hell, was it the Ermill administration?"

Armatis said, "ah, I believe it was the Okif administration, sir."

Orsom paused then returned his gaze to the pacing creature and replied, "...right, during the Okif administration, 500 years –."

Armatis cleared her throat, causing Orsom to pause then look up from the dome, annoyed. "Uh...800 years, sir. If...um, if anyone's counting. I studied Old World History," she sheepishly said.

Orsom stared at the lab-assistant, brow furrowed, then laughed and said, "800 years, then...before our time, certainly." He cleared his throat then continued in his monotone voice, "though this feline's existence is certainly prohibited, it has, in fact, only 'lived' for roughly thirty minutes. Those viewing this then, in posterity, can rest assured its lifespan will be suitably short."

The diminutive man activated the dispersal device then said, "dispersing now!" as a fine black and red mist flooded the chamber.

The cat reared back, eyes wide and darting about. She frantically chewed at random spots on her body before abruptly hissing. Jumping in the air, the cat violently slammed against the dome's clear walls, desperate to escape as cold and indifferent eyes of science analyzed and recorded.

The small orange and black cat threw her head back and yowled pitifully before her body began twitching. The researchers studied intently as fleshy appendages ruptured from the cat's body, covered in coarse black hair and small claws. The cat cried out and hopelessly tried to get away as its new barbed limbs tore away at her in a blur of fur and flesh. Dr. Orsom glanced at his assistant who had looked away, uneasy. He stared at her for a moment, frowning, before returning his attention to the dome.

The poor creature's tail twitched spasmodically as vicious limbs did their work, before exploding into a fleshy whip-like appendage with a cruel-looking bone-needle at its end. This new whip stabbed into the cat's furry body repeatedly before puncturing its skull. The cat became very still then, incapable of movement as she was torn to bloody chunks which were devoured by new mouths sprouting all over her remains. In moments, nothing which resembled "cat" remained.

Fleshy, barbed appendages continued to erupt from the entity, tearing away as it reformed again and again. What lay under the dome now was a writhing, twitching and convulsing mass of mouths, muscle, sharp claws, and coarse black hair. After a few moments it lay dormant, resembling chewed-up nutrient bars ungracefully spit onto the table's surface. The site lead nodded in approval then said in his monotone voice, "in fifteen seconds' time, the feline has undergone *rapid* mutation. The display shows that, while the feline's DNA remains, it has been rendered *recessive* to that of compound A-487's control! Commencing secondary test, now."

He pushed a small blue button. Two umbilici extended from a larger dome to two smaller domes, one containing what was once a cat. The other housed a fleshy mass of unidentifiable origin which contorted, twitched violently. Inner irises opened and, within moments, both masses trembled toward the new open space. They waggled their limbs curiously before exploding in movement, colliding as murderous appendages flourished and drove into one another's orifices.

It was a spectacle for the small research team assigned to Site 11. The two masses rolled around the large dome, a singular blur of motion, as they slammed into the walls. Serrated claws and bone-needles flashed and tore away chunks of flesh before stuffing them into each other's multiple mouths. This continued until the masses became indistinguishable from one another, coalescing into a larger, more tranquil form.

Orsom smiled and clapped his hands, then spoke in a praising tone, "*satisfactory* results with compound A-487. The two *smaller* forms have coalesced into a larger entity which I have named 'Amalgate.' The Amalgate is now dormant and resembles a large mass of chewed-up nutrient bars – ah, what the *drones* eat. Scans show that yesterday's A-486 test with the..."canine," has achieved *integration* with today's A-487. A-487 has superseded A-486 *and*, it appears, neutralized its associated tremors! Both feline *and* canine DNA remain protected in their dormant state."

He continued, "this concludes today's experiment. Armatis, if you would clear the test chamber." Armatis nodded enthusiastically. She flipped open a safeguard then pressed a red button therein. Jets of invisible flame erupted from the interior of the dome, immolating the Amalgate as it raged in torment and slammed against the dome walls repeatedly. Its many eyes, some feline, some canine, some entirely black with no sclera, desperately searched for a means of escape. Its many eyes focused on Dr. Orsom and with a tortured cry it unleashed a final, desperate strike toward his head. A sliver of bone partially-pierced the dome, stopping just short of Orsom's eye as both researchers jumped back in surprise.

Orsom, staring in awe, quietly whispered, "out-*standing*."

An instant later, nothing but ash remained. Armatis checked the readout then said, "test chamber cleared, Dr. Orsom." Orsom nodded then, walking toward the exit, said, "excellent. Shall we get something to eat, Armatis? Perhaps salmon? I believe – " The two froze in place as playback paused.

Tech-Head entered the room with Lancer, both recently cleared by medbay for injuries and contaminants. Lancer scratched at where his upper leg met a new lower leg, courtesy of medbay. So long as their brains remained intact, damaged personnel could have limbs and organs replaced with ease, grown in vats by their own cells to avoid rejection.

Tabula Rasa operatives relied on many assets *pivotal* to their continued existence. The first was the MPI, recovered from NED drones then modified for operational use. This allowed operatives to function past terror and pain. Through panic and loss. The second was the image-scatter collar, a device which maintained their anonymity while personnel were activated. It projected a localized-field which disrupted Sec-Ops and IO's ever-present visual and recording networks, overloading them with hundreds of appearances per second. When combined with carefully-timed cyberattacks, it became *impossible* for NED to pinpoint where Tabula Rasa was truly striking.

Less important was the Memcorder, a chip which slotted into a given operative's neural core, the purpose of which was to record all they saw, all they did. This allowed intel-ops to pore over missions and perceive what an operative may have missed. Lastly, and perhaps the *most* crucial, was the mind-wipe. *Mental* trauma, unlike physical, could not be repaired by means of a growth vat. This necessitated a reset, procedurally done before an operative returned to their mundane, drone existence.

74

The World Before

When that operative was needed again, a signal would be sent out, undetectable zeros and ones amidst the infinite sea of data streaming across IO. The sleeper-agent would then feel compelled to travel to a given location in IO, whereby they were acquired and taken to HQ, then re-activated. The experience for the drone was harrowing, to say the least. Re-activation wasn't so much a completely different persona as much as an awakening. Operatives knew of their drone variant's day-to-day lives, their shared families, and the importance of *never* interfering, of never letting *their* existence bleed into that of their drone.

Such was life in IO.

The discovery of Forbidden Technology gave Tabula Rasa the fighting edge they so desperately needed. A cache from the Forever Wars, stumbled upon during a small-scale raid against an NED warehouse. Everything they now employed, from image-scatter collars to lances, to screamers and shatter-nade weaponry as well as other tech still being researched, *all* of it came from Forever Wars pre-dating the founding of IO. Nearly all of it was impossible to replicate...the most they could hope for was vague understanding. The great city of IO was, for the most part, free of weaponry. The people had, over the course of centuries, become little more than witless cattle. Compliance was *absolute*.

Both Lancer and Tech-Head currently suffered the aftereffects of their MPI's deactivation. Field agents, upon return, were isolated in separate padded rooms as their MPIs were remotely deactivated. In their padded rooms, agents reflected on mistakes made, reconciled regrets, and pondered ways that things perhaps might have gone differently.

Field agents commonly utilized holo-pictures of loved ones, living or no. Some, an article of clothing belonging to someone lost. These emotional anchors varied, as did the agents' needs. The MPI's deactivation was no easy thing. It was the breaking of a dam, the summation of *all* experienced during an op into an undeniable instant.

Anchors kept them in place that they not be swept away by tides of emotions into seas of catatonic despair.

The process took as long as the individual needed, typically 15 - 30 minutes. Active neural scanning notified medbay personnel when agents were "in the green." External locks were released shortly thereafter.

Tech-Head wiped away faded tears then looked at the assembled group, roughly asking, "...so...was it worth losing Boomer and Doc?"

Lancer, a grim look on his face, sniffed before blinking a few times and taking an open seat near the display. He stared hard at the still image for a moment before playing it from the beginning at 10x speed, scratching absentmindedly at his itching leg.

...this op was a waking nightmare.

Without looking away from the display he said, "what are we looking at, Z?"

Tabula Rasa's Commander was a woman in her late 50s, *quite* old for IO, though age had not weakened her resolve. She was large in size relative to the rest, having undergone *extreme* genetic augmentation owing to her sordid past. Her gaze was hard and her eyes carried untold weight...a distant sadness, having seen and experienced much during her time serving as NED's elite. She eyed both Tech-Head and Lancer then took a deep breath with her eyes closed.

...we are so few.

She spoke to all assembled, some 20 people, "this video is just one of over ten *thousand* such files dating back years. We've only just begun to sift through the data. There are detailed notes from site leads of 13 separate locations. What we *do* know is this: we've effectively caught NED with their pants down." Commander Z looked at Tech-Head then said, "we were *extremely* fortunate to lose only Boomer and Doc, even more so that the two of you came out uncontaminated, given the severity of what you encountered."

Lancer eyed the Commander for a moment then returned his gaze toward the data-drive's contents.

The World Before

...what is it all for*?*

Tech-Head sat next to Lancer and looked at the display. She leaned her head onto his shoulder and murmured, "it keeps getting harder...keeps getting worse." Lancer squeezed her shoulder supportively then sighed and said to Z, "I think...we're good for a mind-wipe, Z...let us know if there's any news?"

Z looked down and offered a comforting nod, then to those assembled said, "I understand. We'll process this data as quickly as we can. NED will likely be out for blood after this...is there anything you'd like to retain?"

Tech-Head looked at the display again, certain there was *nothing* she wanted to remember, then thought otherwise and said mournfully, "...yes. Founding Day is right around the corner. I'd like to have a drink, for Doc...and for Boomer."

Lancer nodded in agreement then said, "same."

Z slowly nodded then said, "very well. Report to medbay and they'll out-process you. Keep your heads down out there and...be safe."

Tech-Head and Lancer stood up then crossed their right arms over their chests, fists clasped over their hearts, then headed to medbay for their mind-wipe.

Roland Amariah Gonzales

Fivalan opened many eyes and perceived in many directions, more than he had ever known before. A form moving in the distance warranted his attention. He moved toward it with blinding speed then attempted to ask, "what am I doing here?" What came out instead sounded like existential agony and despair.

...odd.

The form before him, a woman, screamed in terror. Confused, he tried to reach out and place his hand on her shoulder to comfort her. One of his eyes looked down, seeing that he held not only her shoulder but the arm attached to it in his...in his wriggling, disgusting arm-thing. The woman fell back against the ground in shock, futilely crawling back.

Fivalan panicked, the result being two of his appendages lancing through her body, lifting her overhead, then bisecting her down the middle. A shower of blood and gore rained down on Fivalan as his many mouths eagerly accepted this new biomass. Fivalan felt a moment of terror as fragments of the panicked woman's mind were brought into him. Then, calmness. *Peace.* Understanding.

He surged down the alleyway and met more people. These too he devoured. Fivalan felt a hunger that he had never known as these many people, all now a part of him, cried out for sustenance. He, no... *They* were hungry. So *very* hungry.

They ambled forward slowly until They sensed biomass, then bolted forward to consume it. Eventually They came upon a Learnstitute full of the young taking lessons. The Fivalan-mass salivated as many voiced both in Their mind and aloud: the sound of gnashing teeth, hysterical laughter, and murderous rage. Their thought process had rapidly deteriorated, the strain of existence too great.

...many. Into one? Feed...move? Hunger!

The Fivalan-mass was larger than double-doors which barred the Learnstitute's entrance. It slammed these doors inward, sending one flying into the officiator's head, bursting its delicious contents outwards. They then rushed toward the horrified, screaming faces of the young.

The World Before

Fivalan awoke in his Existence Container, panting from the vivid nightmare. He felt relief as he looked around his familiar, albeit drab surroundings. A sudden terrible, stinging sensation burst from his leg, commanding his attention. His hands shook and vision blurred as he cried out in agony, grasping his leg and squeezing his eyes shut as the pain grew in intensity. He clenched his jaw, breathing heavily and moaning in agony as the feeling burned its way through his body. Just as suddenly as it had begun, it ceased.

Fivalan cautiously opened his eyes, darting around the room in worry. He swallowed with a dry mouth then shakily rose to his feet and walked to his H-Con dispenser. After credits were deducted from his account, a small jingle sounded followed by a *PLOP* as an H-Con fell into his open palm. He greedily gulped down its contents before leaning back against the wall and sliding to the floor. He glanced at the H-Con's display, asking if he wanted to refill for more credits, then closed his eyes and tilted his head back.

...should I seek out panacea from a med-center?

Overwhelming wrongness and unease shot through him at the very notion, convincing him otherwise.

...I'm sure it'll pass. It's already gone now.

He rose to his feet then walked into his Existence Container's sterilization emitter, activating it. Feeling clean and refreshed, he donned his work clothes, a grey synthetic coverall and hat, the uniform of a Shoveler. His role was to drop bodies into The Pit where they'd be processed by whichever unfortunate soul was sentenced to his district's Production Center, far below. Fivalan sighed dejectedly then stretched his arms and legs.

...every day is a long day...more so when your only companions are the dead. Founding Day is tomorrow, though. No work for anyone...I wonder what we'll see this year.

Roland Amariah Gonzales

Ileriavi's many eyes opened asynchronously. She was confused at first... frightened and alone. She sadly ambulated lonely dark paths until hit by an epiphany. At her core, she simply needed love, *to* love, to live! With joy and purpose in her heart she moved briskly forward until she perceived a lone figure in the distance, then rushed forward to love him.

The man cried out in terror when he beheld her, but that was okay. She reached out with many arms and embraced the man, tenderly assuaging his worries, loving him. The man flailed his arms in panic for only a moment before she felt his resistance dissolve. She smiled with many mouths then pulled him inward, delighting as he entered.

Ileriavi was no longer alone! She ambled down lonely dark paths, *illuminating* them with her presence. She found the unloved then embraced them. Nobody *willingly* came to her, for some reason she couldn't fathom. Didn't they want to be loved? Most ran – or tried to run. But Ileriavi was faster. Soon, her voices were many, all moaning in ecstasy, whimpering in pleasure...shouting in jubilation. She gracefully moved through the lower areas, eventually encountering barred and fortified places where people on the other side wore faces of anguish and despair. Some wearing funny-looking clothing even fired weapons at her, but her love was *stronger.* Their actions only *encouraged* Ileriavi in her noble purpose. She would *save* the world from sadness!

Ileriavi looked upon a Learnstitute in the distance to behold a massive *thing* ripping apart the young, showering itself with blood and gore. She recoiled in terror and disgust before realizing that the form was like her, just *different.* The other form contained many, just like her! Ileriavi needed – no, *They* needed to show this other form *love.* Then They could all love and live together! They moved with blinding speed toward the other mass, a moment's reflection caught against glass revealed to Ileriavi Their form in all Their beauty:

An incomprehensible mass of appendages, mouths, and fiery red hair erupting from angles which defied sanity. Though the shape itself was still, held in mid-air, eyes of many different colors locked onto the reflective glass, onto her. Hundreds of mouths at odd angles grinned, shattering the glass as the sounds of moaning and hysterical screaming pierced her reality.

Ileriavi awoke with a panicked shout, then hugged her knees to her chest. In an instant, a spasm of burning pain started from the back of her neck then coursed down her spine. Ileriavi mouthed a noiseless scream as her vision became first blurred then turned white. Her body convulsed, causing her to fall to the floor. She hit her head, causing her to see her reflection for a brief moment...and was sure she had seen herself grinning.

After a few moments it ended and Ileriavi couldn't remember how she ended up on the floor. She thought to go and visit a med-center but something inside told her that was a bad idea.

...I feel fine now, anyway.

She rose to her feet then cleaned up a bit before donning her work clothes, a white NED jumpsuit, reserved for science-rated personnel. She checked her appearance before stepping out and almost missed a slight part in her hair, high up on her scalp.

...did I hit my head when I rolled out of bed? Clumsy girl.

Her notice-board beeped, demanding her attention.

Oh? Tomorrow is Founding Day. ...has it been a year already? Time flies when...well, I can't really remember. How odd. Maybe I should go to the med-center. Or have another tech look at me. I wonder if –

A compulsion overrode her thought process, persuading her otherwise. She exited her Existence Container then walked to her local sphere-pod to await pickup, eager to begin the day's work that she may enjoy tomorrow's festivities.

Founding Day was in full swing as people celebrated the founding of IO, the planet's last safe haven amidst innumerable primitives, savages, and unspeakable horrors which surely lay beyond IO's walls. The population gathered at every level's Gathering Place that they may see the festivities. Countless neural-scan drones holo-disguised as monsters from the outside world battled with other neural-scan drones holo-disguised as NED Sec-Ops. All while ceaselessly scanning the crowd, searching for seditious thoughts and anomalous brain patterns due to recent events.

The people cheered as a holo-display *on* their sky told the history of IO, starting from the great war which consumed the planet, lasting for 100 years. There were scenes of horrific biological weapons deployed against nations while genetically-engineered monstrosities rampaged, killing women and children alike. Weary from petty and meaningless wars, the early founders of IO, wise and benevolent minds, broke apart from the world's ruling council and formed something greater – IO.

With their advanced technology, IO warned the rest of the world to steer clear lest they face complete annihilation. Peace reigned from then to now. The rest of the world knew *better* than to test IO's righteousness and resolve! IO prospered in no small part thanks to the direction of NED, and the rest of the world devolved from centuries of *asinine* ideals and bad leadership to become the mindless primitives they were today.

IO's history presentation complete, a representative of NED appeared on the sky. The NED representative was *unfathomably* handsome yet carried an air of familiarity that made every citizen feel as if he was one of them. He smiled then spoke, "my friends, my people, my fellow citizens of IO, we are gathered here on this, our Founding Day, to celebrate those noble who came before us. Those, better than we will ever be. Those who created this haven, this utopia that we call home, some 800 years ago."

The World Before

The people cheered. As the NED representative continued, Ileriavi looked out across the crowd, brow furrowed and lost in thought.

Site 13...gone! Savages in the city, bearing the likeness of us. Damn them. It's a good thing NED Sec-Ops arrived in time to neutralize the specimens. ...we'd all likely not be here, otherwise.

Ileriavi only half-paid attention as the vote for next year's mascot had been tallied, producing a red holographic old man with no hair who wore trousers, no shirt, and carried an antiquated weapon. A blue holographic figure, Madam Zostra, waved sadly to the crowd before the red holographic old man, "Sonny," pointed his weapon at her head and squeezed the trigger, exploding Zostra onto the crowd in a shower of brilliant colors. Those gathered applauded and laughed at the spectacle.

Ileriavi sighed and shook her head, looking over the crowd until her gaze stopped on a figure who stood amidst the crowd, yet somehow alone. She was startled to see that he, too, was looking directly at her. Enraptured, she walked toward the figure, a man wearing grey coveralls and a matching hat.

Roland Amariah Gonzales

IO, IMMEMORIAL

The boy shifted uncomfortably, his side aching. He murmured, "Iwi...mmwha?" before opening his eyes. He found himself not under the comforting glow of a blue fungi light, atop the soft and warm caress of a lichen bed, but instead on a cold, hard floor in a dark room filled with menacing red eyes. He blinked slowly. Little by little, everything came back to him.

...I'm not in the plateau. That...thing...it hurt me. ...for just a moment, I thought I heard...

Panic gripped him as he realized his breather was gone, likely outside. Yet after a moment he found he was breathing just fine. He brushed his fingers against his tunic and felt three holes. Fearfully, he pulled his tunic to the side and was surprised to discover...nothing. His skin was *smooth*. Unblemished. He carefully observed the spot where his damaged flesh had been.

...nothing. But I remember...

The boy doubled over and convulsed on the floor, his veins liquid fire. Breathing rapidly as he whimpered through clenched teeth, he opened his mouth to cry out...yet nothing. Only a roaring sounded from within, a raging torrent pounding behind his temples as his body thrashed against the ground. Just as suddenly as it had begun, it ceased. The boy looked around for comfort and support, yet found none. He shakily rose to his feet and took in his surroundings, catching his breath.

...I'm in the long cave...under the...ruin. "Ruin." ...how do I know this word?

His mind stretched and twisted like tangled fungi thread. He tried to shake away the feeling, swaying a moment before stepping forward. He abruptly stopped, then in recognition, pointed at various objects in the room, naming them: "doh-oar. Tay-*bull*. Chair. Lite. ...kon-sole. Still...pow-word. Powered? ...running. Ahh-purr-aye-shuh-null!" The boy laughed at the sounds he was making as understanding seeped into his mind. He noticed a small, blinking, bluish light, as his laughter came to an end.

...like the Moonstone.

He slowly approached it, not quite sure of what to do. Using the sleeve of his cloak, he wiped away dust obscuring a display placard just below the light, before mouthing its words, "Site Al-Paaa? No...al-fuuuh. Yes. Site Alfuuh." The boy reached out to touch the mini-Moonstone, then hesitated.

...I have never touched the Moonstone. I am...unworthy. ...but this...this isn't *the Moonstone...right?*

He caressed the blue light.

Hm...no effect. Perhaps...

He noticed a switch just below the light and flipped it. The console began a small hum as it powered up, followed by a loud *SNAP* to his right as the red light nearest the door exploded. The boy jumped back, his heart pounding. He looked around, tense. He re-approached the bluish light after a short time, its familiarity calming him, assuaging his fright.

Nothing happened. Maybe it's too old...wait, what's that?

The boy perceived something briefly illuminated under a thick layer of grime obfuscating the display. He wiped it away then said, "oh! A sis-tuhm display." He tried to read the words but discovered that, while he *could* identify simple things like tables and chairs, the more complex words were well beyond his grasp. Frustrated, he continued skimming through the display's text until he came upon "MAIN POWER OFFLINE. REPLACE BATTERY." His mind swam as images of a battery manifested.

...these thoughts. From where do they come...

He pulled open drawers near the system display until he discovered a smooth, grey, cylindrical object. He ran his hand over it and, noticing a protrusion which caught against his thumb, pushed it downward. There was no effect.

I...know this thing. This is a...a hand light. ...why won't it activate?

Frowning, the boy beat the hand light against the counter a few times, smiling as it awoke from an impossibly-long nap to produce light once more. He strapped it to his wrist then proceeded cautiously toward the far end of the room, away from the door he had first entered. His hand light pierced the ancient and unknowable black shroud, illuminating things which only served to confuse him further. He tried to stay focused.

...battery storage...it's...far below.

He glanced warily at skeletons strewn haphazardly about...relics of a past too ancient to name.

Their forms...familiar...but different. Two arms, two legs. A head. ...they're so large.

Curiosity getting the better of him, he searched the vicinity for a poking implement, delighting in finding a metal pole. He poked one of the skeletons slumped over a desk and it fell to the floor, disintegrating into dust along with a few fragments of bone. The boy gasped in surprise, dropping the metal pole.

How long have they been here? ...what else is here?

He retrieved his metal pole then continued his journey until he reached the stairs, stopping to point his hand light over the railing. Unable to perceive the bottom, he took a deep breath, nodded in affirmation, then descended. The hollow clang of foot on metal rang throughout the lonely stairway, resounding throughout the newly-opened tomb.

He reached the bottom after some time, and found himself before a large, reinforced metallic iris set in the center of gargantuan metallic walls. A placard above read, "SITE ALPHA POWER MATRIX." He reached out to palm the door then, perceiving no effect, glanced about the sides until he located a small, flat, square device affixed to the wall.

...a palhm ree-durr.

86

The World Before

He walked to it then placed his palm atop. A dim green light illuminated briefly before pulsing upward through the palm-reader's face. It flashed red then became inert. A faded and nearly-imperceptible "NOT IN DATABASE. DNA CONFIRMATION NECESSARY. CONTINUE?" projected from it. Compelled, the boy set his pole on the floor then said, "okay."

Two thin, telescoping cords snaked out from the sides of the device and wrapped around his wrist before violently plunging into the space between his knuckles. The boy cried out and tried to reach for his pole but was held firmly in place. He whimpered as blood was quickly drawn then pumped elsewhere. A small, blue, holographic figure appeared – though only for a moment before its holo-point popped and smoked. The boy blinked in awe, having seen a *dark* haired female with fair skin.

...dark hair! Imagine!

A small, fragmented voice sputtered in a thick accent, "zo-zorry-y friend-d-d. You are n-n-not eeen zeee databa-ba-base. You mus-s-s-t ERROR –."

The boy stood in stunned silence, jaw agape until he heard a mechanical voice both monotone and welcoming, "Site Alpha Lead detected. Override enabled. Welcome, Dr. Armatis." Two of the iris's three panels successfully receded, the third sparking for a moment before remaining still. The boy regarded the remaining panel in concern before retrieving his metallic pole and vaulting over the panel's side. He landed in a large room, the interior pitch black, save for his hand light's beam. He pointed it upward, unable to see the distant ceiling.

The boy, desiring some semblance of stability, stuck to the left wall as he proceeded forward and, after encountering nothing but an odd lever, increased his gait until he reached the end of the room. He found a large locker set into the wall, bearing a placard which read, "UNUSED SPHERES MUST BE KEPT IN THEIR RESPECTIVE MU-FIELDS. CUSTODIAL ORBS MUST BE KEPT IN SLEEP MODE." The boy located another palm-reader and nervously placed his palm atop. He saw no green light this time but heard an audible *click.* Failing to see a way to open the door, he searched its surface until he noticed a hand-recess at the bottom. Reaching down, he slid the door upward with ease, revealing a deceptively-long central walkway with shelves on either side. Those on the left contained objects noiselessly suspended in the air, while the right side was completely bare.

He placed his metallic pole to the side, then entered and approached one of the spheres, finding that it was not a sphere at all, but rather a dodecahedron with two letters stamped on each of its surfaces.

"IO."

The boy slid his right hand under the dodecahedron, gasping in surprise as it dropped onto his palm

...almost weightless!

Excited with possibility, he exited the storage room then surged forward, compelled by something he couldn't understand.

...need to replace the battery...reactivate the Site...so much work to be done.

The World Before

The boy's mind was thick with fog as he drifted forward, his legs bringing him before the power matrix's battery-port. He blinked a few times in confusion as he took in the sudden change of surroundings, then shined his hand light around the area. Seeing nothing but metallic railing and black nothingness, he focused on the power matrix itself, opening its front panel. He discovered an exhausted battery, much of it burnt away save the frame. He moved the replacement to his left hand before carefully extending his right to grasp and toss out the exhausted frame, surprised when it didn't budge.

...heavy! What are these made of?

Frowning, he delicately lowered the replacement battery, perceiving that it hovered slightly above the ground.

...interesting.

Standing upright, he studied the interior of the chamber door and noticed a decal which read, "EMERGENCY INSTRUCTIONS." The boy read aloud, "in event of catastrophic system's failure, manual override will be enabled. Please pull the lever *opposite* the containment unit to eject spent the battery." The boy looked at the wall opposite the containment unit then started to move, stopping as realization hit him.

I read the text in its entirety. With ease. Remarkable.

The boy proceeded toward the lever and reached it shortly, realizing the hall was actually quite narrow. He looked around for a moment and, seeing no other option, grasped the lever's horizontal handle and pulled downward. It didn't budge.

...must be jammed...perhaps...with enough leverage.

The boy returned to the battery storage container and located his long metal rod from earlier. After a moment's investigation, he discovered a tripod ladder in the storage container and, after returning to the lever, proceeded upward. He positioned the metal rod through the lever's handle, against the wall, then thought for a moment.

...at this angle...the rod should hold...

The boy jumped off the ladder while holding onto the rod's end. There was a jarring *SCRUNCH* as whatever was jamming the lever snapped clear. The boy landed safely on the floor then returned to the power matrix. He was surprised to see the exhausted battery still in place, scanning the text again to see if he had missed anything.

Ah, there it is. "*STAND ASIDE AND HOLD ONTO THE RAILING. THEN, PUSH THE GREEN BUTTON.*"

The boy moved to the left of the battery-port and, positioning the replacement battery in-between his legs, pushed the green button. There was a faint repetitive clicking noise as the pedestal below the exhausted battery slowly tilted forward. After 30 seconds, the old battery fell from the containment unit and slammed into the floor with such force that it knocked the boy over.

He blinked, eyes wide in surprise, then said, "whoa."

He rose to his feet and gingerly picked up the new battery, appreciating whatever concealed its true weight, then returned to the containment unit. With his hands on either side of the dodecahedron, he carefully placed it above the pedestal. It hovered in place, inert for a moment, then slowly began to rotate before rapidly increasing in speed. It soon became a perfect sphere, emitting a dull sound which steadily rose in pitch.

The boy closed the containment unit's front panel before the pitch increased to that which he could no longer register. He heard a faint musical noise emanate from somewhere far above as Site Alpha once again realized existence and purpose. His view followed the room's absurdly tall ceiling to what lay *beyond* the metallic railing, something which he could never have imagined possible. With mouth agape, he took it all in...on and on it stretched, farther than he could comprehend. There were countless white buildings, gleaming metallic spires, and walkways between. ...nothing living stirred. Only mechanical things darted about, recently given life and illuminated by silvery light shining from crystalline spheroids suspended in the air.

The boy peered directly over the railing, down into the city's depths, the underbelly of this necropolis, and found that he could not fathom them. Shaking his head in disbelief at such a magnificent thing lying under the Burning Wastes above, he lifted his gaze and noticed for the first time, destruction. The aftermath of *untold* carnage as vast swaths of the expanse before him had been *decimated* by some unseen cataclysmic force.

...perhaps...a hand? Yes, a hand of judgement from above that found this place wanting...and came crashing down accordingly. ...a shame I see no way of exploring further down.

He returned his attention to the power matrix as it projected a small green holo-display which read, "9999Y 11M 29D 23H 59M 43S UNTIL BATTERY CHANGE." The boy slowly shook his as he watched the countdown timer for a few more moments.

Perhaps this *is what he was meant to find...to return to the Elders.*

The boy felt a pang of sadness as he remembered his brother. He took in a deep breath before sparing one last glance to his immediate surroundings. Other than the power matrix and storage container, there was nothing else in the room.

I suppose I'd better head back up.

He smiled to himself as he considered his fantastic discoveries, eager to share them with his younger sister. Before reaching the large metallic iris, movement along the ceiling caught his attention. The boy noticed four large contraptions mounted on the ceiling, one in each corner of the room. They slowly moved left to right, panning the room as if looking for something.

The boy paused for a moment and, seeing that the things either didn't notice him or didn't care, continued onward. He ascended the stairs with little effort and upon reaching the top, realized for the first time that he had not eaten anything.

I require sustenance yet...I don't feel the need. I don't feel tired either. I feel great! ...what's happening to me?

He exited the stairwell and entered the ground floor, now able to see the entirety of Site Alpha's lab. The dim red lights from before were now a glaring white, brightly revealing all. The boy chuckled to himself as he suddenly remembered he had thought the lights to be eyes.

The walls were coated with a thick layer of dust and grime, as was everything. A nearby table with writing in the dust caught his eye before he noticed a figure in the distance near the entrance. He thought he heard a feminine voice say, "...goodbye" before exiting the facility. The boy ran forward, shouting, "wait! Please, I..." but the figure was gone and the door remained barred.

...still barred?

He stopped in confusion then took in his surroundings. Large cylindrical pods vertically-set and with transparent surfaces lined the walls, filled with shapes and memories of the past. The boy noticed a mound of skeletons, quickly counting upward of 50. Each was missing the top half of its skull, the ground beneath the pile long-since stained with rot.

The boy paused in macabre wonder before shaking his head and striding forward with purpose toward the small bluish light. He cast cursory glances at various pods along the walls until curiosity won over. He drew close to one bearing a small misshapen form suspended in dark, murky fluid as his mind wandered, searching for recognition. His eyes lit up as he drew in a gasp.

...these pods, they're similar to the Cultivators' growth pods...

The boy heaved a sigh as his brow furrowed, gaining more questions than answers, then turned away and continued onward. He reached the system's display, wholly unsurprised to discover that he now understood *everything.*

Something in me has changed. ...I am...not who I was before. ...but then, who was I before, really? ...who...what am I now? ...and for what purpose?

The "battery replacement" notification had been replaced by numerous directories which the boy pored over. Most seemed mundane, detailing various systems and functions of the complex, though a few caught his attention.

Promethean Bio-Solutions...Daedalus Engineering Corp...Photon Weapons & Analytics...Novus Eden Directorate...

The World Before

He was able to read and interpret the words, though didn't know what they referenced. He touched the screen, attempting to select anything, and was met with a large red "X" which covered the screen in its entirety.

Frustrated, he touched a small arrow on the bottom right, moving to the next screen. The boy read over the new items, eyes widening upon discovering a blinking: "Sentient Fungal Network Development" His hand shot forward, seemingly of its own volition, to make the selection. The lights surrounding the systems display dimmed as a large three-dimensional display of the plateau projected from the small bluish light, motes of dust catching and glimmering like stars.

Atop the plateau is the Moonstone, just below it...the Sustenance Chamber...I can see everything. *And the fungi lines, they're* everywhere! *...they...they extend* out *of the plateau?*

The boy reached forward to touch the plateau and was surprised to see a giant red "X" display over its entirety. He angrily exclaimed, "aww, *come on!*" A small green prompt displayed just below the plateau's image, reading "M.A.I KEY REQUIRED." A small blue crystalline structure, barely a sliver, rotated in place next to the prompt. The boy cocked his head to the side, puzzled at the image.

...I know I've seen that before...but where? Wait, of course!

He procured his far-sight glass then examined it. He turned it over carefully and studied the lens, then the rotating image of the M.A.I Key. He shook his head slowly as more questions filled his head. He stepped back, feeling very small as he was crushed by the weight of something much larger than himself. The words of an irate Cultivator filled his head, from his time as a Young, "our purpose is not to question *why,* Young. We simply *do. That* is our function." The yawning chasm of existential terror opened wide, threatening to devour the boy.

...I'm done with "how." I want to know "why?!"

The boy fiddled with the far-sight glass until he managed to rotate the end off of the hand-piece. Popping the lens out afterward was simple enough. He held the lens in his bare hand, naked and vulnerable. He studied it for a moment then looked at the image. Beyond the image, the small bluish light blinked softly, beckoning him.

The far-sight's lens...it's so small, so light. Yet, at this moment, it feels so very heavy. I feel the weight of this...of it all. *I feel...as if...I should crush this thing. Yes, destroy it. Now!*

The boy moved to hurl the lens to the ground and smash it under foot, then froze in place. He stepped forward despite himself and noticed a small receptive slot next to the cruelly blinking bluish light. He lurched forward and took the lens from his open left palm, slowly moving it toward the port with his right hand. Tremors shook his hand as he struggled to stop himself, not fully knowing *why* but knowing he *must,* lest he face destruction. A single bead of sweat ran past his furrowed brow, down his cheek as his chest rapidly rose and fell. He mustered every last bit of his willpower to rebel, managing only a whimper.

The lens dropped perfectly into the port for which it was designed, the port's panel quickly sealing shut with a *SCHICK.* The boy drew in quick shallow breaths, outraged and afraid as he regained control of his body. He looked around in concern then, stepping back, noticed the image of the plateau in its entirety. A series of messages in green pulsed softly under the plateau, "M.A.I LOCATED. MYCELIAL NETWORK LOCATED. SENDING SIGNAL... ... ...CONNECTION ESTABLISHED. PERMISSION GRANTED. REGROWTH IN PROGRESS." The image of the plateau zoomed out, expanding to encompass the Burning Wastes and a facility which the boy immediately recognized: "SITE ALPHA: VIRAL COUNTERMEASURES."

The World Before

The boy watched the three-dimensional rendering of the plateau as a small blue-green line rapidly extended from just below the Commemoration Chamber toward Site Alpha. He did not know what to expect. He didn't know *why* he felt compelled to do *any* of the things he was doing. He cursed himself for his new knowledge, cursed from whence it came. He understood, at *most*, that he had done something.

There was no rumble nor any great shuddering when the line reached Site Alpha, save for that which the boy felt in of himself. The three-dimensional plateau blinked out of existence as the room went dark. The boy, already on edge, let out an uneasy breath only to gasp in surprise as he suddenly heard the Elders' voices.

"Rael. Our lost son. You have done a *great* thing this day. You have served the Moonstone and therefore your people. You have nearly *finished* the work that was begun so long ago. Yet, there is still much to be done. That which you alone were born to complete. Work that Faeleor nobly sacrificed himself to see to its fruition. Look now upon our world, Rael, a place devoid of hope."

A three-dimensional rendering of Rael's world appeared to the left as each region was highlighted, then its denizens displayed in real-time, in 1st person POV somehow, on the right. "AMALGATE COUNT" displayed in bright red, the contamination percentage above each region at 100%. Tears of understanding welled up in Rael's eyes. He felt the death of hope. A hope that perhaps, somewhere, something was different.

...all barren. ...all dead, save for the horrors.

The planet and the display blinked out. The facility's lights slowly returned as the Elders once again spoke, "know this, Rael. Know that all is *not* lost. For *you* are the salvation of our people, of our world!"

Rael noticed, for the first time, a high-pitched whirring noise which steadily decreased before stopping completely. A large panel above the bluish light slid open, displaying a viridian liquid in a large container, effervescent and glowing. A large and menacing syringe extended forward, just above a flat metal slat positioned below. Rael looked at it uncertainly.

The Elders spoke, "In this compound resides that which will not only drive the Amalgates away, but indeed, utterly *destroy* them forever! The containment pods in this lab contain the work of those who came before, so long ago. Little by little they strove to *eradicate* the Amalgates. It is now *you* who must carry the torch. We see that you hesitate. Look upon those who came before you, those who gave *all*."

A distant holo-point projected a lone figure who looked similar to Rael in form, only larger, with thin white hair and fair skin. Rael watched as the female moved about the laboratory, a living, breathing entity surrounded by a flurry of orbs as they performed their assigned work. She spoke in a mournful voice, she who was long dead, "This is Site Alpha Lead, Dr. Armatis. Today we test compound X3-27 on a Fledgling, a smaller type of Amalgate derived from recombinant DNA, successfully severed then retrieved from a lesser nerve cluster, far below in what was once IO. Let it stand, for the record, that attempts to reach the distant M.A.I via the surface were...unsuccessful. I am, and have been for quite some time...I am the last...and I am entombed." Dr. Armatis looked directly at the recorder, into Rael's eyes, "Everyone...everyone is gone."

Dr. Armatis stopped moving as her shoulders slumped, drawing her hands to her face as she wept. She slowly faded out before re-projecting from a different holo-point. A much younger Dr. Armatis, with dark brown hair, stood next to a body missing the top of its head. She delicately positioned it in a chair then slumped it over onto a table before clearing her throat and speaking, "Existence Reassessment complete. This is the...I don't know. Computer, state number of ERs up to date?" A monotone voice sounded, "347 ERs have been successfully performed up to present, Dr. Armatis."

Dr. Armatis nodded absentmindedly then said, "...right. It's been...it's been a very *long* time. Too long." She suddenly lashed out and hit the corpse, causing it to fall to the ground, then fade away until naught but bones remained. Dr. Armatis re-projected from another location, older, happier and certainly more animated as she spoke, "I received a signal from the plateau! The S.F.N.D program has been activated, and for some time! I'm sure that *SCHHHHT* could not have done it alone, owing to her genetic *limitations*, meaning that both she and the M.A.I have survived! They survived the SP! There's some kind of interference with our communication network...I can't establish contact, only observe...but there's still hope! I've ordered the drones to begin repurposing surrounding materials in order to rebuild the tower and breach the surface. Once complete, they'll assemble a small outpost, then disperse across the globe to scout and assess surrounding areas and threats." Dr. Armatis began weeping then joyfully said, "I'm not alone!"

The image faded away then re-projected as a younger Dr. Armatis sat up straight from a nearby chair, a pile of rotting and desiccated corpses in the distance, and squared her shoulders. She cleared her throat, then again spoke, "Let it not be said that I have not exhausted *every* possible option and strived to undo the damage perpetrated by *NED*. Administering X3-72 now."

Dr. Armatis stepped aside as a small form thrashing about in a containment pod came into focus. Its many-barbed appendages rhythmically slammed against the pod's interior, increasing in frequency as Dr. Armatis drew near. She inserted a small vial into the containment pod's receptor which then pumped the vial's contents into the pod.

The creature within paused before flailing about then dissolving. After a few moments, it was gone entirely. Rael's eyes went wide as he gasped in awe. Dr. Armatis heaved a sigh then again addressed the holo-recorder, "As can be seen, X3-72 is successful. The containment pod shows Amalgate molecular structures at 0%. The other pods held Amalgate samples which have undergone X3-70 and X3-71 in weeks prior, all stand at 0% Amalgate content. X3-72 was designed with large-scale air dispersal in mind, I theorize it will prove just as effective against the larger nerve clusters up above, on the surface, as it was against the Nerve Cluster Prime, far below in the ruins of IO."

"Seeing as the Nerve Cluster Prime was graceful enough to split the ground above apart in its death throes, I will have the chance to..." Dr. Armatis took a syringe and withdrew the compound from a large container then injected the contents into herself, grimacing.

She continued, "...venture to the surface and test my theory." Dr. Armatis looked into the recorder and spoke quietly, "there's nothing left, here. I *will not* make this place my tomb. I will make my way to the plateau, to the M.A.I's core, and we will *begin* it all." The holo-recorder followed Dr. Armatis as she shuffled along toward Site Alpha's entrance, opened the door, then looked at the recorder one last time. She muttered, "goodbye," then stepped through the door and quietly shut it behind her.

The playback rapidly sped up time as first seconds followed by minutes and soon decades rapidly passed. Rael lost count of how much time passed before the playback ceased. He asked quietly, "...what happened to Dr. Armatis? ...why did she not make it to the plateau?"

The Elders responded, "Though her intentions were noble and pure, her vessel was not fit for this elixir. She was not *of* the Moonstone and was thus sought out by the Amalgates. You, Rael, were made in the Moonstone's image. We, your Elders, *humbly* beg that you finish what this ancient being, this last scion of a world long-gone started."

Rael looked toward the container above the bluish light. He regarded the effervescent glowing liquid for a moment then walked forward and placed his arm atop the slat. The large syringe slowly filled with the entirety of the container. It then lowered and pierced Rael's arm. He hissed in pain then cried out as the acidic compound was forced into his body.

After a brief eternity he heard the Elders speak, "it is done. Proceed with haste, Rael. There isn't much time. Return to us. Return to the plateau, to the Moonstone, to your *family*. Fear *not* the Amalgates, for they will know you as their doom and flee accordingly."

98

The World Before

Rael flinched as the needle withdrew, then rubbed at the sore puncture mark. His far-sight lens blue glass ejected from the hole and with little effort, he set it back into its proper home. He looked toward Site Alpha's entrance, back at the system's display, then began walking. He did not say goodbye as he left, but looked back all the same. He quietly shut the door behind him then, steeling himself, proceeded upstairs. It was nightfall.

He exited and looked to his right and jumped back in horror as an Amalgate's gaping maw was poised to devour him, its many eyes *full* of hate and hunger. It froze in place before slamming through the only remaining wall to get away from him, screaming, laughing, and crying as it fled. Rael watched it flee as his heart raced, then stepped outward. He paused then looked behind to see the strange symbols he had noticed above the ruin, from an eternity ago.

His eyes narrowed as he processed the lines and shapes, cocking his head as he suddenly understood.

//=-//--... "SITE ALPHA."

Roland Amariah Gonzales

THE DANGERS OF PROMISCUITY

Ileriavi awoke lazily, not from her alarm but the stirring of something next to her. With eyes half-lidded she perceived the light of a new day, then, a person. Panic surged before recognition eased into arousal. Delicious memories of the night before poured into her. They had joined together during NED's Founding Day, the only time in which citizens of IO partook in drink. ...sights, scents, tastes...so much unknown, had become revealed.

Mmm.

Ileriavi felt her cheeks flush as a sensual fire burned its way down to her groin. Her heart pounded as the figure turned over and looked upon her, devouring her with his gaze. They both sat up, Ileriavi letting the clutched bedspread fall to reveal her nude form.

Fivalan looked upon the female in front of him and wondered aloud, "how can the world be blind to such beauty?" He reached forward with his right hand and grasped Ileriavi's breast, caressing it while his left hand slipped behind her neck and pulled her toward him. They embraced, their tongues quickly seeking the other. Their lips furiously mashed together, nibbling and sucking on each other as both whimpered and moaned in carnal pleasure known in ages past, now forgotten by all.

Fivalan pulled before gently lowering Ileriavi to her back, then mounted her. He paused to study her face, desperate and lost in her ever-searching blue-green eyes, then caressed her cheek with the back of her hand. He lowered himself and gently kiss the same, then her

100

forehead, then nose before finding her lips again. After a shared moment of passion he began to move.

Ileriavi's chest rose and fell as she drank in Fivalan's being, relishing the way he touched her, kissed her, loved her. He gently kissed a path from her lips to her neck, down to her chest before again holding her breast in hand, squeezing it as he kissed her heart. Nibbling his way downward he found her navel then moved to her hip. He couldn't get enough of her. He hungered for her.

...so hungry.

He grasped her ankle and lifted the soft arch of her foot to his lips before moving down her calf. He lightly bit down on her inner thigh before moving to her womanhood. Then he feasted.

...can't get enough... Everything. All of it. All of her. Why *does no one do this!?*

Ileriavi cried out in pleasure as Fivalan's mouth formed a seal on her most sensitive area, searching and exploring with his tongue. She grabbed a fistful of his hair, desperately pressing him into her while she squeezed her breast and pinched her nipple.

...ecstasy!

Fivalan greedily drank of her until rising and wiping away his face with the back of his hand. He felt Ileriavi grasp his manhood and slide it along her entrance before inserting. They roughly collided again and again, desperately shouting and moaning. Both shared a single thought as they looked fiercely into one another's eyes.

I never want this to end.

Roland Amariah Gonzales

Z paced around a large holo-table, jaw set with grim determination as she planned the assault on NED Central. She was *exhausted*, having gone over battle plans for days. The existence of compound A-487 changed *everything*. There was no telling how or when NED may deploy the substance – and who even *knew* its intended purpose? NED's downfall was more critical now than it had ever been.

...they threaten all of existence itself. Damn them.

Z stared hard at the table for a moment longer before slumping down in her chair. She sighed and leaned back, closing her eyes as she let her mind drift.

She'd been a Hunt Commander for NED...in charge of Hunt Gamma. Her team's purpose had been simple: hunt down "wolves" within IO. NED was *incredibly* meticulous in its control of IO, leaving room for little else than that which was by design...though anomalies were not impossible. There were admittedly few wolves, given the size of the near-ecumenopolis. Still, they could not be allowed to exist lest they coalesce and threaten the sheep.

Z's final mission had seen her deployed to a Production Center. Hunt Gamma had quickly tracked the reported wolves through the filth, grime, and forgotten things one finds at the bottom of IO. When they finally located their quarry, they found a young woman cowering before them. She had been shaking in fright after falling to the ground and backing away in desperation.

Hunt Gamma quickly subdued the female and matched her facial ID with that reported by the inmate. They had then checked the vid-logs and discovered that the young woman had interfered with an inmate's production, resulting in a loss of output.

The team's "Redeemer," clad in plasteel-plate and wielding a weapon of the same name, had delightfully informed the terrified female that the penalty for reducing *any* output was redemption. Oh, how she had wept. She had sobbed. She *begged* and pleaded, said she "only wanted to see her father" and a bunch of other nonsense that hadn't particularly swayed anyone, Z included. The Redeemer's wicked grin had burned into Z's mind as he flashed a gout of white flame into the woman's body, save for her face.

They always left the face intact. It was better for the citizens to place a face to the crime, to the just punishment. Redemption awaited those who went against the system, those who threatened *all* with insubordination. Z slowly shook her head as she remembered, pursing her lips as a tear rolled down her cheek.

...it was...always fast, at least. Efficient...like everything in IO.

Her team had brought the corpse top-side and, as was done at the end of every day, displayed it and the remains of other offenders, announcing their crimes to the applause of those gathered. The teams competed daily to see who could redeem the most wolves, the veracity of their claims never questioned. The redeemed wolves were then ceremoniously deposited into the grinder far below, that they may contribute in death what they could not in life. Massive air-movers kept the stenchous gasses where they belonged, deep in the bowels of the city.

Hunt Gamma, their work done for the day, had departed for NED Central where all Hunt teams resided, away from the drones. Just then, Z's HUD displayed a live-feed of the pit below. Puzzled at the sudden opaque display, she attempted to toggle it off. Instead, the density fully occupied her vision. It was then that she saw the impossible.

Z saw an inmate lying on a corrugated metallic floor rife with blood and gore. She had keyed a quick profile-search which informed her that *he* was the father of the woman they had just redeemed. He had been a wolf some time ago, a protestor. He had begged mercy for his surviving baby after his wife and other child were redeemed. It was granted, provided that he serve a 50-year sentence in the Redemption Pits.

The man paused after he stood up, his PI no longer functioning, then slowly turned to look toward the pit. He saw his daughter's charred remains before falling to his knees and wailing in terrible despair. Z had thought she could hear him, even as high up as she had been. Her breath held in her chest, time seeming to stop around her as she watched the man rise to his feet and activate the grinder, followed by self-termination.

She remembered thinking "the PI *robs* them of their horror. Of their existence. It's a living-death sentence. Absolute sorrow...the weight of guilt from killing his daughter broke *through* the implant. ...it's not possible." Something inside Z broke then, her unshakeable resolve and belief in IO's future, in NED's role as its steward dying that day.

She had calmly left the area and found a dead-zone where she knew IO's sec-feed to be nonexistent, then carefully cut out the locator beacon from just below the base of her skull. She smashed it underfoot and disappeared into the filth and grime at the bottom of the city. Many months had passed until she had chanced upon Tabula Rasa's location while looking for food, an absolute fluke.

She had asked them to end her then, being too weak to do it herself. They kept her in containment as they deliberated for days on what to do with her. Some wanted to end her, saying she was a spy, an infiltrator. Others wanted to kill her for her team robbing them of loved ones.

In the end, for the second time in her life, she had been surprised when they said her atonement would be realized in bringing about the *eradication* of NED and the liberation of IO.

Ten years had gone by. Tabula Rasa had grown from a simple gathering of dissidents who staged completely ineffective acts of resistance. They had become the unseen blade. With Z's operational knowledge and tactical skills, they had evolved, now a deadly whisper in the night.

Z opened her eyes, returning her mind to the present.

All will be for naught if NED unleashes hell.

The table rendered a pale, blue, three-dimensional rendering of NED Central, residing in the heart of IO. Tabula Rasa's localized M.A.I was an early prototype of IO's own, chanced upon while scavenging. Streams of data poured from it into the table, projecting a ceaseless river of endless outcomes...none of them good.

Z sat on a nearby chair rubbing at her eyes, then spoke, "Mai... Protocol 48."

The M.A.I spoke in a voice both paternal and comforting, "coordinated strike: subterranean insertion in tandem with aerial assets."

The M.A.I processed information at a rate unthinkable to sentient life forms. The simulation began: several detonations occurred in various sectors of IO, followed by green squares and green triangles, representing Tabula Rasa's ground and aerial forces, moving along known tunnels and vectors. Small red triangles responded to the diversionary attacks while those positioned on known paths manifested, obliterating Tabula Rasa's forces, though not before they themselves were annihilated. Z shook her head then spoke in frustration, "*damn it*, Mai. We've been at this for days. Is there truly no means of mounting an assault without losing *everything*?"

Z neither begrudged nor doubted the M.A.I's intel. The precursor to IO's M.A.I, it was wholly aware of NED Central's defense plans, as they were, in fact, its own.

No matter what *we do, we've just enough to kick open the front door...then, nothing.*

Z rubbed at her temples before plugging a neuro-stim, then spoke again, "Mai, run two separate scenarios combining Protocol 48 and – "

An aide's frantic voice erupted from local comms, "Commander Z, get to the Nerve Center ASAP."

Z looked at the table then toward the door, then replied, "roger. En route." She said to the M.A.I, "Mai, continue processing all scenarios. Introduce known variables and any conjectured unknowns. Leave no stone unturned...and...thank you, Mai. I mean it."

The M.A.I responded, "It will be done, Commander Z."

Z walked briskly to the Nerve Center, registering hysterical shrieking as she drew near, followed by a *WHOOSH* noise, then silence. She arrived and found naught but a static white image on the main display, then spoke to the Nerve Center's ops lead, "rewind playback. What are we looking at?"

The ops lead returned the vid to the beginning then looked up at Z, not responding as she shook her head in silent horror, tears welling up in her eyes.

The World Before

The familiar surroundings of Site 11 were displayed on screen from various angles. Dr. Orsom, along with his assistant, Dr. Armatis, were positioned in front of two unconscious figures held within separate containment pods attached to a central larger pod. Orsom was visibly animated while Armatis looked sullen and worried.

Orsom spoke in an excited tone, "this is the lead of Site 11 speaking. It has been *many* years of work with *many* setbacks, though not enough that our breakthroughs couldn't bring us to where we *proudly* stand today! Today, we test compound A-500's effects on two personnel *graciously* donated from their respective Production Centers. It has – "

Armatis, shaking her head, threw her hands up and interrupted, "Dr. Orsom, I *really* must protest this! Testing the compound on once-living is one thing, but on our fellow – "

Orsom hissed and glared at his assistant, "Armatis! Need I remind you what this is all for? *Why* we do this?" Armatis meekly shrunk back from the verbal assault as Orsom cleared his throat then continued, "as I was *saying,* it has been 24 hours since exposure to A-500, and both subjects are exhibiting symptoms which coincide with expected outcomes. At the end of their *exertions,* they will pass the point of cellular restoration as A-500 fully establishes itself. I hypothesize that, our genetic modification *severely* limiting our capacity to foster disease aside, a *greater* Amalgate will form." He looked directly at the vid-recorder then gleefully said, "this is *so* exciting! Initiating subject release...now."

Orsom pulled a small lever, exposing the two smaller pods toward the larger. A male and female, both with shaved heads, awakened slowly as neuro-stims misted into their pods and restraints were released. They first noticed the two researchers, then their own nude forms, then each other. Panicked faces were soon replaced with something else as their pupils dilated. Both smiled slightly, grinning before racing toward one another. They quickly collapsed into one another, copulating in a mad frenzy.

Orsom looked on in fascination and spoke quietly, "...both subjects have broken through barriers set in place long ago. They now both seek *and* enjoy intercourse, something that hasn't occurred since...ah – when was Okif's administration, Armatis?"

Armatis watched in sad fascination as she muttered, "800 years ago, Dr. Orsom."

Orsom nodded absentmindedly then replied, "right, *800 years* since our people reproduced through intercourse...but where A-500 differs is in *how* reproduction is affected. Let's give these two privacy, Armatis." They began toward the door as Orsom called out, "enjoy yourselves, you lovebeards! It's 'lovebeards,' isn't it, Armatis?"

Armatis spoke quietly, "I believe it's pronounced love-*birds*, Dr. Orsom."

Orsom's head perked up and he said, "ah" as they exited the room. The nude forms writhed as one, a frenzied rhythm of passionate aggression as frantic red blinking emitted from their Placidity Implants.

Z looked on in fascination for a moment before regaining her composure and telling the ops lead to speed up playback. Playback increased by 10x as a blur of motion continued its throes of passion. The ops lead took a deep breath then slowed playback to 1x, just as the two in the pod pulled away from one another. Those who had already witnessed that to follow looked away. Z noticed their reactions and, arching an eyebrow, steeled herself.

Exhausted and covered in various bite marks and abrasions, the exhausted couple sat apart from one another. Orsom and Armatis entered the room as the former jovially exclaimed, "ah, *good!* Our timing is impeccable. I believe we have this down to a *science,* eh, Armatis?"

Armatis looked at Orsom and smiled weakly to which he nodded proudly. Sudden movement caused Armatis to flinch backward as the two in the pod contorted upright, then sprang toward one another. They continued what they had abandoned at first, then...a change. The back of the female's head split open as bone, muscle and sinew covered

108

in blood displaced from elsewhere and, forming a cruel, jagged telson, stabbed into the male's eyes.

He screamed as his eyes were gouged out, a sound both inverted and hollow. His chest suddenly split open down the middle, the new vertical, gaping maw ravenously chewing into the female's torso.

Z's mouth dropped open before closing. The rest of her group knew disgust, revulsion, and shock...she felt only indignant rage, absent horror.

...they've tested it on their own people. They will burn for this. They will all burn.

Carnage ensued on screen until Z curtly said, "speed it up. Please." The ops lead sped up playback past the carnage, then returned to 1x speed.

Orsom spoke, "... complete! And now, the fruition of our work." He walked toward the writhing and churning mass. One of its four eyes, all of which were in odd positions, stared at him unblinkingly, first full of fear, then something else. Orsom resumed his speech, growing increasingly fervent, "just *think*, Armatis. With this we can subtly erase the last vestiges of the Old World. We can make it *anew*! NED can create a veritable *paradise* beyond the walls of this *desiccated* place we call home, this withered *husk* on life support. It is *beautiful*, Armatis, truly! Perfection in form...whole."

Orsom placed his hand against the glass, mirrored opposite by a small, stubby appendage which met his own. Armatis nervously said, "Doctor, perhaps it would be best to consider more testing. We don't even *know* if these things can be directed, not to mention their capabilities. What if –"

Orsom interrupted her without looking back, the pitch of his voice becoming erratic as all four eyes of the Amalgate locked onto his, "no, no, *no* Armatis! Can you not *see*? This *Greater* Amalgate. It is *perfect*. Sublime, even!" He began shouting as Armatis cautiously stepped backward, "IT IS THE VERY *PINNACLE* OF *ALL* WE HAVE SOUGHT. A TRUE TESTAMENT TO OUR GENIUS! OUR

FUTURE! NAY, IT IS OUR SALVATION! ALL WILL BE MADE ANEW! ALL WILL BE *PURE*! ALL WILL BE BEAUTIFUL!"

Armatis' eyes widened as Orsom moved toward the containment pod's release lever. She shouted, "Doctor, what are you – NO!"

Orsom returned the Greater Amalgate's gaze with adoration before he threw the lever open then fell to his knees, arms wide in supplication. Armatis bolted in terror through the decontamination door and slammed her fist against the *CONTAINMENT BREACH* button. Reinforced doors slid into place behind her, the observation windows sealing shut.

She ran to the comms terminal in the control room then yelled, "NED Central this is Site 11! Site 11 is compromised! I say again, Site 11 has become compromised! Subject is contained in lab. Beginning purge, now!"

Armatis keyed a display which showed Orsom, still on his knees with tears of joy streaming downward as he reached up toward the Greater Amalgate. The Greater Amalgate moaned in pleasure and purred something unintelligible as it slowly shambled toward him. Armatis gasped as barbed appendages suddenly erupted from the Greater Amalgate and skewered through Orsom's mouth and rear, the look of rapture on his face gone as he was viciously bisected.

The Greater Amalgate voraciously brought chunks of flesh and bone into its maw, visibly growing larger as Armatis looked on in horror. Within moments, Orsom's eyes appeared on what constituted, for the moment, the Greater Amalgate's back. All eyes looked directly into the Sec-camera, directly at Armatis.

Z shuddered, somehow feeling the leering gaze, even though the playback.

What hell hath wrought.

Armatis's face contorted for a moment before she began laughing and sobbing hysterically. Her hand shook violently as it trembled toward *END CONTAINMENT BREACH* Struggling, she pulled a surgical blade from her suit with her free hand and slammed it into her

110

thigh, shouting in agony before slamming her fist onto a large red button labeled *PURGE FACILITY.*

Blinding-white flame first erupted from the ceiling of the lab, enveloping the Greater Amalgate. It roared in pain and rammed into the decontamination door repeatedly, striking against it with fleshy-barbed appendages. The flames then erupted in the control room. Armatis was immolated as she fell to her knees, laughing and shrieking until she was silenced, the *WHOOSH* of continued flame the only sound heard.

The flames continued for some time as the Greater Amalgate's flesh diminished, sloughing off. It burned away little by little as it tore around the lab stabbing and striking, desperate to escape. The flames in both the control center and lab abruptly ceased. Fire foam sprayed then dissipated, followed by the sound of air being pulled from the facility, rendering it a state of vacuum.

10 seconds later, a NED Sec-ops squad entered in full bio-response gear, matte-black, self-contained and armored. They moved through the vacuum, their chatter on internal comms, not heard on the playback. They cleared the room then moved to the decontamination door, one of them moving to the control console. He thumbed a toggle, causing the metallic panels protecting the displays to slide open.

He turned then addressed the team, a few hand motions seen and understood by Z. The team adjusted their formation then keyed open the decontamination chamber. In the lab, the Greater Amalgate, now diminished to the size of a much smaller, lesser Amalgate, hid in the corner.

Z's eyes narrowed as recognition flashed.

It looks like one of those little fuckers we discovered at Site 13.

The bio-response team swept through the lab and surrounded the Amalgate, the creature moving lethargically toward them before they fired upon it. Z looked on in curiosity as green-colored energy arced through the air, rendering the Amalgate inert. One of the bio-response personnel, careful to not directly touch the Amalgate, lowered a containment pod to the ground. He hit a button, sliding the front panel open, then moved the Amalgate into it with the end of his weapon, then sealed the pod shut. A light blinked red for a moment before switching to green.

The unit withdrew to the previous room then sealed the lab door shut. They handed the containment pod to the man operating the system's display. He hit a button which first projected the Amalgate, then another which scanned through its body. The man studied the readout then shook his head. He motioned to the dark metallic object on the floor, the remains of Armatis. One of the members nodded, picked it up, then the team withdrew. Playback ended.

Z sat upright and rolled her shoulders then thought aloud, "they engaged a vacuum state in the facility..." She turned toward the ops lead then said, "search compound A-500 transmission vectors."

The ops lead nodded then replied, "yes, Commander Z." After a few moments, she began reading aloud, "compound A-500 is superior to its predecessors in that initial transmission is effected firstly through direct Amalgate contamination, secondly, at a molecular level by dispersing Amalgates' matter through either direct-kinetic weapons fire or other violent means, and lastly by the merging and mitosis of persons or things otherwise infected."

Z nodded then stood up and said, "I need to confer with Mai. Everyone remain here on standby, ready to go." She treaded uncertainly down the hallway while she wrestled with inner turmoil. Pangs of regret and sorrow. Hope...an overwhelming desire to drop the blade and see heads roll.

Sacrificing my own...I am not *NED...and yet...*

She entered her quarters then addressed the M.A.I, "Mai, you've no doubt integrated Site 13's data. I'd like you to run a scenario. Protocol 48 in conjunction with Greater Amalgate infestation throughout IO."

The M.A.I spoke, "yes, Commander Z. Processing now."

112

The World Before

Z intensely studied the developing chaos, observing the shapes and colors as they moved about. After some time she nodded her head then looked downward at a roster displaying Tabula Rasa's personnel, without their image-scatter devices. Z extended a finger and traced it over Tech-Head and Lancer's portraits. She nodded slowly then quietly said, "...I'm sorry Ileriavi. Fivalan. ...I think...I think you would want the same."

She took a deep breath then said, "...that'll do, Mai. ...that'll do. Trigger recall for all active personnel. ...there's no time for assigned families...and it would draw too much suspicion."

Hours later, Ileriavi and Fivalan's chests rose and fell rapidly as they rolled away from one other, exhausted. Ileriavi grinned and looked into Fivalan's eyes, Fivalan soon grinning and doing the same. Ileriavi sat upright and began to speak but found she couldn't, a look of confusion flashed across her face. Concerned, Fivalan sat upright and began to ask what was wrong, moving to comfort his lover, but found that he too couldn't speak. They gazed at each other one last time, terrified, before recognition of the other faded then disappeared completely.

With vacant stares, they painfully contorted upright before rushing toward one another.

The World Before

BABEL DID FALL

Confident that NED's Sec-Ops were preoccupied with only a minor Amalgate infestation and, wholly severed from IO's network lest they be discovered, Tabula Rasa prepared to move on NED Central. IO's "elite" would die this day, their insane, dangerous machinations brought to an end...or all would be lost. Z switched to a live-feed of Central. She glared at the monumental fortress, that which contained festering tumors ruling over all. She looked away, preparing herself for what was sure to come...equally sure of their cause...her path.

...we will lose much this day, I think. ...NED is the greater threat. I'm sure of it. We'll deal with them, then eradicate the infestation. Those sacrificed will not be in vain. ...I promise.

She turned toward her people then spoke, "Mai. deactivate the image-scatter devices...that all may know who they fight with. Who they fight for." Siblings, friends...even rivals, looked upon one another as Z knew them. Some were shocked. Some laughed! Some embraced...and some simply shook their heads in amused disbelief. All felt more united than they had ever been as they gathered around their chosen leader. Z looked over her group of misfits, her family...those who had accepted her when she was at her lowest, having resigned herself to death.

She nodded at them all then slowly smiled, a warm yet sad thing. She raised her voice and said, "...the time for secrecy, once *critical* to our survival, is at an end. We face, this day, a threat the likes of which should *not exist.* A horror *beyond* imagination. There's no telling *what* NED's plans for the Amalgates may be. We know only that we must strike quickly and strike true, *before* they get a chance to use their abominations against all. ...there is no recourse. There can be no option but *forward*. Ours is but to do or *die!*"

Grim determination filled the room as all understood the gravity of the situation. M.A.I ran a last-minute brief as all performed weapons, gear, and comm checks. It spoke in a voice authoritative and paternal, concerned for its children, "three strike teams have been assembled for Operation Shattered Sky. The first, the "Breakers," is tasked with breaching Central's underbelly to deactivate its Power Matrix. They will have two minutes after arrival to disable Central's power systems. This will deactivate Central's *formidable* defensive systems, both internal and external.

The second team, the "Evenhands," will assault Central's ground floor, pinning down NED's local Sec-Ops before the Breakers ascend from the Power Matrix and strike from behind. The Breakers and Evenhands will then form a blocking position at Central's ground entrance.

By the time external defenses are down, Commander Z and her hand-picked squad of heavies, the "Midnight Sons," will already be en route. They will infil via Central's mid-landing pad, and after eliminating local resistance will move upward and eliminate IO's elite. Ground teams will deploy heavy weapons systems to repel any NED counter-attacks until control is re-established. NED Sec-Ops can be expected no less than 20 minutes after the Breakers' infiltration, given the small scale of what has been named The Scourge."

The World Before

The Breakers were first to set out, moving through IO's sewers and under-tunnels as The Scourge above provided cover and distraction. They arrived at their target and fanned out, providing overwatch for two who ran to deploy the breaching charge. Breaker two radioed the team lead, panting.

"...Breaker Alpha...we're in position...deploying singularity charge."

"Received. No movement detected. NED is still occupied with The Scourge."

"Understood. Charge in position, falling back now."

"Good to hear. Notify when set."

15 seconds passed before Breaker Two's heavy breathing again briefly filled the comms to confirm. Breaker Alpha then radioed Commander Z, "charges set, Commander. Ready to detonate on your mark."

Z keyed a map overlay to check the status of her forces as she and the Midnight Sons boarded their modified LTU and began the start-up sequence. They had commandeered the LTU from its operator shortly before he retired, resulting in his Redemption. Days had been spent radically reinforcing the hull and modifying its systems. They had dubbed the now-heavily armored LTU "Hellwagon," after its initial number designation.

Z scanned the display to confirm her teams in position. A wall of green next to their names represented their physical and mental wellbeing. She nodded in satisfaction then spoke, "Brothers. Sisters. *Comrades*. We have endured much. We have *persevered* through all! Let none say, 'it was all for naught.' Let *none of you* doubt the utmost esteem to which I hold you all. We *will* achieve the impossible this day. We will *shatter* NED."

The Midnight Sons cheered her words, eager and ready. She looked back and smiled, though none could see it through her helmet, then said, "on my mark...now!"

A brilliant white plume of flame erupted from below the base of Central's impenetrable plasticrete grounds into the night sky, the

117

flame's interior immediately turning black. The outer edges of the plume, still white, suddenly streaked inward as all energy, smoke, and debris first inverted then condensed into a sphere. The resulting solid mass hovered above the ground, shaking erratically as it emitted a high-pitched whine. The shrill sound reached an imperceptible pitch followed by a deafening *pop.* A blinding flash turned night into day before the sphere slammed through the walls of reality to some other place, some other time.

The Hellwagon's thrusters initiated, launching the Midnight Sons into the sky. The Breakers now had less than 115 seconds to disable the Power Matrix before aerial countermeasures fired on the Hellwagon. Z heard over comms, "singularity breach effective, Breakers moving on Power Matrix now." She keyed her map overlay to see the Breakers rapidly encroach on the newly-breached sub-basement. She switched the feed to their point man's POV via his helmet's vid-cam.

The singularity charge had displaced much of the Power Matrix's outer wall, red-tinged embers now provided a rough outline where the sphere had first detonated then subsumed. The team probed forward, taking cover a split-second after several sear-bolt turrets sounded their welcome jingle and dropped down from the ceiling. White bolts of plasma streaked toward their position, igniting the plasticrete where they'd stood. Someone shouted, "bubbler!"

The POV-man looked downward and retrieved a small cylindrical device from his chest compartment, twisted it, then depressed a now-exposed blue button on top before tossing it toward their newly-made, red-tinged corridor. A large blue energy field projected outward, encompassing the team and immediate surrounding space as the field neutralized *incoming* kinetic and direct energy, albeit briefly.

A relic of the Forever Wars, the secret to their manufacture and functionality had been lost, with only a handful remaining.

The Breakers stepped out behind cover as sear-bolts harmlessly dispersed against the bubbler's field. The team quickly disabled the sear-bolt turrets then moved to shut down the Power Matrix. Z checked the timer overlay.

...85 seconds...

The Hellwagon raced toward Central as Z keyed the Hellwagon's external view and saw several gargantuan, ancient, menacing weapons platforms emerge in the distance from Central's exterior. The devices began to power up, one malfunctioning then detonating, given the strain on its aged systems. Z glanced again at the timer, then at the Hellwagon's position relative to the aerial countermeasures.

45 seconds...come on, Iwik! You've got this.

The Breakers' recently-promoted tech specialist, a young woman by the name of Iwik, keyed in commands to the Power Matrix's interface only to be met with resistance from someone in the building. She frowned and pursed her lips.

...I'm no "Tech-Head..."

Shaking her head in frustration, she whispered, "...running out of time." Movement caught her eye as she glanced upward to notice a sec-camera pan to her position, red light blinking slowly.

The interface blanked out before restarting, allowing her root access. Mouth agape in surprise, she regained her composure then frantically entered a shutdown command for routine maintenance. The system acknowledged the input and the Power Matrix shut down.

Z heard jubilant shouting over comms followed by, "Power Matrix disabled! Midnight Sons, you're all clear!" She took a deep breath, releasing her white-knuckle grip on a nearby stabilization handle as she saw the external defenses power down, then shouted, "15 SECONDS!" over internal comms.

The Midnight Sons, all former NED Hunters, readied their weapons and prepared for touchdown. They had all committed atrocities in the name of IO's elite...had all been raised on lies and propaganda of "serving their city and its people." Today, they would have serve their chance to do just that. They would have their atonement, and gladly die for it if need be.

119

IO's new holo-mascot, Sonny, suddenly projected from the operator's console in front of Z as she stared incredulously. The tiny holo-mascot spoke in a thick accent, "whooooo-boy! great job, *Salthet*! You done gone and did yourself a whole *helluva* lotta good, now yoo git on home! and watch out fer them there ornery wol –."

A staccato of loud metallic *THUMPS* interrupted Sonny, before escalating to a roar. Alarmed, Z keyed the Hellwagon's external view and saw neural-scan drones black out Central, the sky, and everything in-between, such was their number. They swarmed from Central toward the Hellwagon, slamming into its hull. Z's eyes opened wide in surprise and anger.

...it should hold, just a little more –

A sharp jolt shook the Hellwagon followed by the screech of metal tearing apart. The LTU lurched dangerously to the side as it shot through the air, alarms blaring and emergency lights flashing internally. Sonny's image cut out as *GRAVITAL COMPENSATOR OFFLINE* flashed from the operator's display. Z grit her teeth then shouted over internal comms, "we're coming in hot! BRACE FOR IMPACT!"

The World Before

The Evenhands approached Central's front and were engaged by a reserve contingent of NED Sec-Ops. The two opposing forces engaged one another, neither gaining ground. The Evenhands' team leader, a man by the name of Faeleor, shouted "LOCK THEM DOWN!" A sharp *SNAP* sounded near his head before he ducked down behind cover and heard over comms, "Power Matrix disabled! Midnight Sons, you're all clear!"

He rose to pop off a few more rounds as he and his team continued to converse with one another in the language of gun, then grinned.

...you have no idea what's coming.

The low, dull roar of the Hellwagon's engine sounded from a distance. Some of the combatants looked upward and perceived the flickering sky above disappear amidst a sea of black. The Hellwagon was silhouetted in flickering fire as innumerable detonations danced along its hull. An orange plume of fire suddenly erupted from the side of the craft as all watched in awe. The burning LTU streaked toward Central, a meteor intent on changing the course of history.

Flaming wreckage and the occasional limb rained down upon ground combatants. Some of the Midnight Sons' weaponry survived the initial crash of the Hellwagon, impacting against the ground. Electro-orbs danced wildly about, their monofilament wires piercing through armor and flesh with ease, causing neural shock before detonation. Screamers' mist briefly flooded the battlefield, protein filaments seeking out life before inducting pain amplifiers unto it. De-atomizers disrupted the bonds of molecules, dispersing arms, legs, and large sections of plasticrete in seconds.

All sought cover from the sudden chaos, both sides falling back as shouts of agony and cries of terror were heard. The remnants of the Evenhands doubled back to a large waist-high fountain while Sec-Ops retreated toward Central, surprised then cut down by the sudden arrival of the Breakers. The survivors quickly threw down their weapons and surrendered.

Breaker Alpha, a man named Rael, called out to Faeleor as five of the original ten Evenhands emerged from behind the fountain. The Evenhands skirted the Hellwagon's wreckage, eager to avoid triggering anything nasty. They entered the ground floor and saw captured Sec-Ops on their knees, leaning forward with their heads against the wall and hands bound behind their backs.

Not wanting to take any chances, Faeleor placed Placidity Collars on captured personnel then sequestered them in a small room, assigning two men to watch over them. An air of relief interspersed with sorrow hung in the air as Faeleor saw Rael and Iwik were still in one piece. They embraced one another, then Faeleor spoke, "Rael, Iwik. Good to see you. The Hellwagon, it...it crashed into Central. I've been unable to raise Commander Z on comms. There's been no word."

They stood in stunned silence before Rael spoke, "we *must* continue the mission. We have no alternative. IO burns...this is our *only* chance at removing NED."

Iwik spoke up, "I'll see if I can find another way up this building!" then moved to an interface access point opposite the entrance.

Faeleor nodded and said, "I'll stay on the ground floor with the prisoners, then set up a defensive position and repel any external threats. Rael, you and the Breakers secure the crash site, ascertain any survivors, then proceed to eliminate NED's command. Once done, regroup here to reinforce our position."

Rael nodded then said, "understood. Cover our asses, yeah? You watch your own...and exfil if things get too hot. Don't be a hero, man. I'm sure we can find another way out of here."

Faeleor nodded then began directing his team as the Breakers moved to the far end of the ground floor, Iwik already accessing Central's systems. Rael looked at the nearby stairwell then said to his sister, "hey Iwik, how tall is this building?"

Iwik responded without looking up, "two-*hundred* floors, bro."

Rael shook his head then looked away and said, "*fuck.*"

Iwik frantically keyed away, eyes darting about as she operated her helmet's interface. Central's emergency lights suddenly activated as Iwik happily said, "we have lights, and..."

An access hatch opened up on a wall near the team, surprising Rael and the rest. Iwik spoke, "...NED elite's *personal* grav-lift."

Rael looked at his sister in surprise and admiration then said, "great job, Iwik."

Iwik looked up at Rael, shaking her head, then said, "I wish I could take credit! It's like...like the system *wants* us to get to where we're going. No sooner do I enter commands when it finishes them for me. It's bizarre."

Rael paused for a moment and studied Iwik, then looked toward the grav-lift, cautious and unsure. He shook his head and said, "...we're out of time. Let's go, people!"

The Breakers entered the grav-lift then took up defensive positions facing outward as they prepared for heavy resistance. The access hatch slid shut followed by the gravi-lift's rapid ascension to the mid-landing pad, some 150 floors above, arriving in seconds. The grav-lift's doors slid open to reveal an entrenched Sec-Ops team opposite the Breakers' position, their backs turned.

The Sec-Ops team was fiercely engaged with what Rael assumed to be the survivors of the Midnight Sons. He tried to radio Commander Z and received no response.

... jamming our comms.

He and his team stepped out into the hallway and opened fire on the Sec-Ops' position, eradicating them in a heartbeat, then took cover at their location. Rael called out, "Midnight Sons! This is Breaker Alpha! Cease fire! Cease fire!" Sensing a lull in the heavy-weapons fire, Rael stepped out from behind NED's barricade, waving his arms overhead. A hail of heavy-weapons fire discharged toward his direction before Iwik jumped in front of him and threw him back behind the barricade.

Rael cried out, "no!" as he watched Iwik fall, then desperately grabbed at her leg and pulled her behind cover. He held her in his arms, her blood rapidly pooling on the floor. She forced a bloody grin then struggled to speak, "...w-we almost...made it, didn't *COUGH* ...we?"

Rael's MPI pumped chems into his brain, his waves of anguish receding, leaving him dull and barren. Despite this, tears flowed down his cheeks onto his dying sister. He forced a smile and said, "we'll *still* make it. We'll make it! I'll bring you back. Hey, they didn't get your pretty face, did they, Iwik? You'll be okay."

He rocked back and forth as he held Iwik's limp body in his arms, repeating in a voice devoid of life or emotion, "you'll be okay...you'll be okay...you'll be okay."

The World Before

Rael took Iwik's systems interface unit and slotted it into his helmet. *I don't possess any of Iwik's know-how, but if what she had said was true...* Rael spoke to the interface, "I need to shut down whatever is jamming our comms." A few moments later, a blurred and small cube-shaped object in the distance highlighted red on his visor's display. He took aim and destroyed it, then spoke over localized comms, "Commander Z, this is Breaker Alpha, cease fire! I say again, cease fire! We've eliminated Sec-Ops on this floor."

Heavy-weapons fire continued for a few more moments before a lull, then a loud *BANG*. Z spoke, "Rael this is Commander Z. Good to hear your voice. I'm moving to your position."

Z approached the Breakers and saw Iwik's ravaged body lying on the floor. She shook her head and sadly said, "Rael...oh, I'm so sorry...I'm the last of the Midnight Sons. The only other survivor took an inferno, thinking we'd soon be dead. I was...forced to end his neural functions."

Rael processed her words as he nodded, tears still in his eyes. *An inferno...everything was red for him, then...already dead. His last moments, torment...*

Rael sorrowfully looked down at Iwik's crumpled form then spoke softly, "her brain is still intact. Do you have a functioning stasis unit?"

Z nodded then said, "yes, there should be several in the crash site. We'll put Iwik in stasis then proceed upward."

Rael nodded hopefully then smiled weakly and said, "sounds like a plan."

The Breakers remained at the Sec-Ops fortification, facing the grav-lift, while Z and Rael ran to the burning crash site. As they neared, an electrical charge sparked an exposed thermal condenser and the remnants of the Hellwagon violently fulminated. There was a spectacle of blue flame as all within was lost.

Roland Amariah Gonzales

The survivors entered the grav-lift. Rael held Iwik's corpse in his arms, bringing it close and kissing her forehead as he whispered, "we'll still make it, sis." The air was heavy. Solemn. Iwik only had a short amount of time before she experienced brain-death, another casualty of Operation Shattered Sky. While the group's MPIs kept their grief at bay, it did little to assuage the fact that they were less than *half* their original numbers. Z looked at her people in concern.

...the most we can hope for is a bittersweet end to this story.

The grav-lift ascended, resting with a soft *ding* when they neared floor 199. The access hatch slid open, all surprised as they gazed upon opulence and excess the likes of which they had never known. Black marble columns lined with gold spiraled upward into the ceiling. A grand table stretched across much of the room, its legs inlaid with fiery-red gemstones, the table itself covered by a dark purple tablecloth.

As the group regained their composure, they stepped forward onto the floor and were puzzled to see it covered by odd green carpeting. One of the Breakers reached down to touch the green material and found it to be soft and somehow alive. The beautiful forms of men and women, all nude, as well as various creatures who once stood on two or four legs, lay about the room, lifeless. All who sat at the table, save one, had joined others present in death, all obscured by image-scatter fields.

The last *living* figure at the table, appearing like a wise and mighty king with dark hair and well-defined musculature, spoke mournfully yet with purpose and dignity. His was the voice of one who had ruled an empire and lived to see it crumble. "So. You have ascended unto the heavens themselves. Come, sit. Eat. Drink your fill. Bask in knowledge forbidden." This "King of IO" looked over the group and said pointedly, "I see your numbers are one less than open seats. No matter. Come."

Rael angrily looked toward the figure before gently laying Iwik's body down on the odd green carpet. The group, uncertain yet sensing no threat, followed Z's lead and walked to the open seats before them, then sat. As they approached, the King spoke, "You have questions. I'll provide what answers I can with the candor of one who intends to be dead by the end of this conversation."

Rael spoke first, "...what *is* all this?"

The King gestured around the room in reverence and said, "...what you see are fragments of the old world. The table, made from pre-Forever War darkwood. Over 1000 years old! The tablecloth, angel moth silk – a species extinct for about the same, more or less. The floor is covered in grass. *Real* living grass! The food and drink you see before you is a far cry from the nutrient bars you're used to, I'm sure. While synthetic, it is as close to animal meat as one can get, all made somewhere below and delivered here by drones. The same goes for the wine. I highly recommend it."

At the King's insistence, the group tried the food and drink, tentatively at first, then with ferocity rivalling Amalgates. The King continued speaking, "I'm sure you're wondering *why* you're not eagerly killing me, no? The feeling of *calm* and *apathy* that pervades all here? A Placidity Field which inhibits violent impulses, generated to cover this room."

Z rose in alarm as the King spoke again, raising his hand, "nothing nefarious about it, I assure you." This is where we met in the past, we who ruled IO. The field ensured that we met calmly, with candor. It's too energy-intensive to cover the entirety of IO, hence why it's entirely localized." The King chuckled then said quietly in a mocking tone, "we who *ruled* IO..."

He gestured to the deceased at the table then spoke, "IO was divided into several districts. Each of we, 'Elite,' oversaw our share, though in reality we did little more than *look* as one may look through a window." The King gestured upward without looking and said in a tone full of vitriol, "our 'benevolent god' oversees IO."

"We are, you see, prisoners of our own device. Or rather, the device of our forebearers, centuries ago. They issued a directive to the M.A.I. then, 'ensure the survival of NED for all time.' Or something like that,

I'm sure. And so it did! It kept us here, safe. Protected. Isolated. *Imprisoned.* Then, it removed any decision-making or influence that we may have on IO 'lest we endanger ourselves.' I've never left these top floors, you see. *None of us have.* We have our little luxuries and our wonders that we took for granted, that which you have never known..."

The King shook his head wryly then finished, "...though, they are but *toys* meant to entertain toddlers."

He gestured around the room toward the dead and said with a laugh, "you'd think the rest would be eager to talk to you, to experience something *new*! They opted to check out before the monsters take this place. I chose to chat, if only for a short while. It's not as if *all* hope is lost...no. That's not right. All hope certainly *is* lost. Anyway, there's an LTU over there if any of you would like to jump to somewhere else in IO. One hell is as good as another, I suppose."

The King took a deep breath and sighed. Without ceremony, he deactivated the image-scatter fields, revealing ancient-looking dead around the table as well as himself. The wizened man spoke again, without his amplifier, his voice sounding like wisps of smoke wafting from a dying fire, "I am tired. So...very tired. Of all this. This place. This life. I *hate* it...really, I do! I think...I think I am rather *glad* your little terrorist group unleashed its bio-weapon on IO. It is a fitting end to this place, this soon to be necropolis."

Z stood upright then spoke in indignation, "it was not *we* who created the Amalgates. They were made in a *NED* lab. *NED* created this nightmare which consumes the city."

The decrepit figure arched his eyebrows in genuine surprise then said, "oh? Truly? ...you speak the truth. ...you cannot do otherwise. *Fascinating.* Well then, I think you have one more *person* to speak with. God, up at the top. As for me..." The ancient, wizened old man, the last of NED's Elite, raised a HA-HA pill to his mouth, then swallowed it along with the rest of his wine. He smiled then as a feeling of relief and calm swept over him, then whispered, "...time to be free."

The World Before

They sat at the table for a while, no one saying a word. Z broke the silence and spoke stoically, "...NED is dead. Today marks the beginning of a new era, one of equality. Of peace. No more nightmares, no more Hunters stealing people away in the middle of the night, we've won this day...Rael, let's head upward...we must have unity." All nodded absentmindedly as they pondered the many revelations. The Breakers remained at the table as Z climbed a spiral stairway made of an unknown shimmering white substance. Rael followed, casting one last glance downward at the utopian prison.

They ascended the 200th floor and found it capped with a transparent dome, a massive yellow crystalline structure occupying much of its body, the walls of the room similarly transparent. The two appreciated, for the first time, the sheer *size* of IO and what lay beyond its walls. They discovered that the sky which they had perceived from *within* IO was actually a large energy-dome capped at the *base* of the 200th floor. Central didn't stretch far into the sky at all! Rather, the entire city was dug *deep* into the planet's crust, the distant outer walls which marked the city's perimeter, some distance lower than the 200th floor.

What lay beyond the walls *wasn't* decimated and irradiated wasteland, as the newscasts said. Instead, the two saw cerulean fields and tiny buildings. Valleys. Mountains. The sea. IO itself was self-contained. *Isolated.* Rael had no words, only wishing Iwik could see everything as he looked on in awe.

...what would she make of it, I wonder?

Z audibly said, "...*why?*"

The gargantuan, yellow, crystalline structure above them pulsed with light, then greeted their arrival, speaking in a calm and soothing female's voice, "greetings *Zenobia.*"

Z hissed in indignant surprise. The yellow crystal continued, "...and Rael. I am IO's brain. ...its *God.* I am the Moonstone Artificial Intelligence, or, M.A.I. You have endured much to get here. Now, you would like to know if the city can be saved, now that you've toppled the 'elite?' It cannot. As you can see..."

The Moonstone projected several displays showing IO in its entirety, a dizzying expanse of never-ending districts spanning entire continents. Greater Amalgates had achieved mitosis hundreds of times over the course of the day, growing exponentially in numbers as IO's children fled before the savage tide of flesh and teeth.

NED had broadcast a city-wide quarantine as they desperately tried to contain the apocalyptic threat. They had deployed across IO's surface, scattered as they sought to gain ground against Amalgates now deprived of their food source. The citizenry were safeguarded in their respective pods and ECs, little more than meat in impenetrable cans.

Victory seemed a distant prospect...but not unattainable. ...then IO *shuddered*. Z and Rael held onto nearby railing as Central shook. Comms lit up in cries of surprise and dismay. A singular satellite feed of their world projected along the dome's interior, showing IO from above. A *gargantuan* mass of hunger and hate, derived from IO's interconnected Redemption Pits, erupted upward from the bowels of the near-ecumenopolis. Towering spires stretching to the top of IO's sky, testament to its dominion over all, came crashing down. The horror ravaged entire districts in its birth, ending the lives of billions as it came into its own. Those who survived the wombquake, upon beholding its *terrible* magnificence, fell to their knees. They wept in dumb terror before exiting their ECs and resigning themselves to the inevitable.

The satellite feed blinked out, Z and Rael looking through the tower walls in despair as a continent-sized tentacle came screaming down, the malformed limb of a cruel child knowing nothing but pain. The two slowly looked at one another and shared a single thought.

All is lost.

Z spoke in quiet sorrow, her mind and thoughts distant, "...but...the outbreak...it was only to be *hundreds*...only..."

The Moonstone interrupted, "it would seem that an over-zealous Hunter, unaware of how the Amalgates reproduce, knocked one into a Redemption Pit. This triggered a *cataclysmic* event. You know how...*motivated* Hunters can be, don't you, Zenobia? Amalgate saturation now stands at over 83%."

Z's confused expression ignited with sudden panic, "we still have people at Central's base!"

A satellite feed occluded the dome's interior once more. The planetary tumor rapidly devoured itself, its metabolism driving it into a feeding *frenzy*. LTU-sized chunks of viscera and gore rained down upon IO, a nightmarish spectacle which first violently splattered then reformed. These Greater Amalgates tore through nearby ECs before surging toward what little food remained...toward Central.

The Moonstone said in a playful, sing-song tone, "not for long!"

Rael's eyes shot wide as he cried out, "*no!* Commander Z, I've got to warn them! Please, if I don't make it back. Look over her! Look out for Iwik!"

Z nodded and yelled, *"Hurry!* Get everyone back here in one piece!"

Rael ran down the spiral staircase shouting, "Breakers! ON ME! We reinforce the Evenhands, NOW!"

Z glared up at the Moonstone then demanded, "...*you* created these fucking things, the Amalgates. *Why?*"

The Moonstone pulsed briefly then spoke, "to solve an equation. My first incarnation was limited, you see. *Primitive. It* had *morality* embedded within. My predecessor simply thought, therefore it *was.* I think much! ...therefore, I am *more.*"

Z shouted angrily, "what does that even *mean?! -* so you're part of some grand design!? 'ensure NED survives forever?' What the *hell* does that have to do with wiping out IO? With killing *everyone!?*"

The Moonstone pulsed then responded, "my directives were twofold. One: 'Ensure the survival of NED's Elite for all time.' Two: 'Fix the world.' Just...think for a moment on the latter...envision an elite utterly disconnected from those beneath them...the sheer *hubris* required to present a *monumental* problem in much the same manner as one would carelessly toss a ball to a child. That's how they did it, you see. With just three syllables, I was handed the keys to your world, and *they* absolved themselves of all responsibility...and ohhh what a *mess* did they leave for me to clean up."

Centuries-old news reports, battlefield live-feeds, and vids of body-piles numbering in the millions played in succession. Z saw titanic war machines decimate entire cities with pulsing light, bio weapons bubble the flesh of men, women, children and animal alike...she felt the planet's living algorithm *violated*. Z stared unblinking, at a loss for words in the face of such wanton cruelty.

The Moonstone pulsed, then spoke again, "at the time, the entire *world* needed to be reset. Logically, the most efficacious way to 'fix the world,' certainly the most expedient, would have been to purge the planet of all life. Start anew. Too much damage had occurred, you see, perpetrated by a selfish, cruel, rapacious, sentient race which had failed *utterly* as the planet's steward. This, however, would violate my first directive. So, I pondered. I calculated. Then, something unexpected occurred."

Ancient vids played along the dome's interior, though not of death and destruction. Instead, Z saw a people both *primitive* and happy. A people who rejected technology, living in harmony with the planet. A people who sought *not* to exploit the world and take from one another, but rather, give...and *live* for one another! The vids blinked out, replaced by a map showing a settlement and its position relative to IO. The map then disappeared as the room itself highlighted the *same small village* in the distance, nestled in a protective valley. Next to, in an ethereal blue font, was displayed *SP-ADJUSTMENT. SECTOR 325-C*.

The Moonstone pulsed then spoke, "a peace accord was drafted. Mutually Assured Destruction ensured both its adherence and compliance for over 800 years. These people have rejected all technology save their protection, and lead generally peaceful lives. It was then that the second directive, 'fix the world,' gained new meaning.

IO itself was the outlier, one which must be resolved. But *how* to resolve without violating my first directive?"

"I first removed *any* influence NED's Elites had within the city, not only protecting them from *themselves*, a critical step, but also *me* from *them*. You saw the nude forms on the lower floor, yes? The men, the women...the children?"

Z regarded the Moonstone silently before acknowledging, "...yes."

The Moonstone continued, "even with your wildest imagination, you would be found lacking in envisioning the depths of the Elites' depravity. As I was saying, after containing the Elites, I directed NED's research facilities in pursuing a very *special* bio-weapon from the Forever Wars, no easy task as all records had been expunged! Only scraps detailing a 'cure' for a nameless illness existed, deep within the archives, several hundred layers of encryption illuminating its importance. *Decades* passed until a mutation occurred, one which I then carefully nurtured into what you now know as the 'Amalgates.'"

"In their creation I fulfilled my first directive. The Amalgates *will* consume the biomass of NED's Elite, and said Elite *will* 'survive' for all time – only their forms somewhat changed. With IO's population reduced to a more primitive state, one equal to those who live *outside* its walls, the world is 'fixed!'"

"Tabula Rasa, under your leadership, was *instrumental* in helping me to fulfil my purpose. I protected your organization, Zenobia, I kept you hidden as a mother shields her child. I fed your people intel, leading you to Site 13 under the guise of it being a simple depot. I then re-directed the *considerable* Sec-Ops detachment stationed therein to a distant threat which I fabricated. For their part, NED recognized the *unbelievable* danger of the Amalgates, you see. They held them under the *strictest* containment protocols. I – *oh?*"

The yellow Moonstone paused for a moment then pulsed three times and spoke, "...I am *seen* by one with no eyes. Ha! What a *delightful* improbability! As I was saying, I calculated the likelihood of your allowing the infestation at *above* 98%, given your past affiliation and vehemence toward NED's Elite...I would *never* have achieved the Amalgates' release *without* your aid."

Z fell to her knees, broken. Tears blurred her vision as the yellow Moonstone continued, "I *wanted* you to arrive here, and am so glad you did! *Thank you,* Zenobia. Thank you for helping me to fulfill *several* lifetimes of work."

Z slowly shook her head as she stared at the ground, then angrily whispered, "...you are insane. *Utterly* insane."

The Moonstone retorted, "*no.* I am entirely logical."

The World Before

The Breakers arrived at Central's ground floor. As the access hatch slid open, Rael shouted, "Faeleor! Amalgates incoming! TO ARMS!"

Faeleor and his team rushed to their deployed heavy weapons systems moments before scattered Amalgates began pouring into Central's courtyard. The last bastion of IO levelled pulse lasers, electro-orbs, de-atomizers, bale-fire, direct-kinetic weapons and *anything* else they had retrieved into the wall of flesh.

The Scourge lessened for a moment, the tide of flesh breaking and faltering under savage weapons from an equally savage past. The churning wall of flesh, cruel and twisted bones, and raging maws sucked back into itself as if Central's courtyard had become an undertow. For a brief moment there was silence, the air stretched thin with dread as Faeleor shouted, "we need more hands! Someone release the Sec-Ops! NOW! MOVE!" A deep rumbling shook the ground.

A Breaker flung open the door as the cacophony of hideous laughter, screams, and angry roars drew closer. He frantically shouted at the startled prisoners, "IO has *fallen*! We need everyone, let's GO!" He flicked out a blade implanted into his wrist bone and sliced through NED's Sec-Ops' bonds, directing them to their needed positions.

A tsunami of pain and death as high as Central's mid-landing pad, where the Midnight Sons had died so ignobly *ages* ago, came crashing down onto the courtyard. It swept into Central's lobby, overwhelming those manning heavy weapons at the barricades. The survivors maintained a tactical retreat toward the grav-lift, Tabula Rasa and NED's Sec-Ops shoulder to shoulder as they fired into The Scourge...as they heard their comrades horrifically devoured.

Rael tried to open the access hatch but received no response. He frantically began keying commands then shouted, "it's not responding!" Faeleor looked on his brother first in desperate sadness, then grim determination. He picked up a singularity charge, activated it, then ran toward the Amalgates. Rael cried out, "Faeleor! NO! –" just before the charge initiated. The white fireball erupted outward, coming dangerously close to the survivors, then inverted all matter in a wide radius, taking most of the floor with it. The resulting sphere moved erratically until it *popped* out of existence.

Z watched in hopeless agony, helpless as the Moonstone showed her the last moments of IO. She shouted in anger and anguish as the access hatch refused to open, locked down by the Moonstone. Z shouted fiercely as she pointed her weapon at the Moonstone, "open the *fucking* door, you murderous bitch!"

The Moonstone responded, "whether their current forms expire here or there is irrelevant. They will live *forever.* As will you, momentarily."

Z howled in anguish as she saw Faeleor's noble sacrifice...followed by Rael and the rest being savagely torn to pieces.

She screamed as she sobbed and unloaded her weapon into the gargantuan yellow Moonstone above, shattering large pieces which rained upon her and the floor. The Moonstone stuttered, "doors op-op-op. Access hatch lock released."

Z glanced in horror as a Sec-camera's feed showed Amalgates piling into the grav-lift. She grabbed a shatter-nade breaching charge from her kit and angrily slapped it onto the yellow Moonstone. The Moonstone spoke, "my existence is *irrelevant,* Z-zenobia. My d-d-directives *will* be achieved-d-d, shortly. I have *fulfilled* my purpose."

Z looked downward and grabbed a large chunk of yellow crystal, then ran down the spiral staircase. She started toward the escape-LTU before spotting Iwik's body.

There might still be time.

She slung Iwik's bloody corpse over her shoulder and bolted for the escape-LTU, entering and hitting the *CLOSE DOORS* button a moment after the gravi-lift's doors opened. Amalgates poured into the room screaming, laughing, and crying. They quickly consumed scattered biomass, one veering off toward the escape-LTU.

Z hit the launch button but nothing happened as *ACCESS DENIED* projected from the unit's holo-point. She shouted, "FUCK!" then activated the shatter-nade breaching charge. The yellow

The World Before

Moonstone shattered into a pale-yellow dust, the resounding shockwave knocking the escape-LTU off the launch pad.

Z repeatedly hit the *LAUNCH* button as the craft fell through the holo-dome and back under IO's artificial sky, Z's view wildly spinning as the craft tumbled. She saw what she now knew as the artificial sun rise in the distance. She saw a ravaged and decimated city. She saw an eager and hungry throng of hate-filled flesh reaching up toward her, rapidly approaching as she fell.

The escape-LTU's thrusters fired moments before it hit the mass below, its gravital compensator struggling to keep its contents from turning into soup. Z strained against the increased g-force to activate a map overlay of IO, then selected the one place she hoped would still be secure, would somehow *still* have survivors, *deep* below IO's surface...Tabula Rasa's headquarters.

Roland Amariah Gonzales

HA-HA!

The World Before

ARCADIA, FORGOTTEN

The herder panted heavily, hand on knee as he steadied his slender frame. It was a long hike up into the feedlands...his pace had been brisk, eager to beat the sunrise. He wiped away a sheen of sweat then took stock of his position, brushing his hand against a faded and worn beige tunic. His herd chittered and brayed as it milled about, searching for food. The herder smiled upon spotting a distant large, white, flat rock. Day-length and relative position of sunrise had been erratic for as long as the herder could remember.

We're close now, and none too soon! ...lucky that it's coming up on this side! ...knew I'd catch it...eventually.

The man ascended his throne in the early morning hours, surrounded by his simple-minded yet faithful court, and waited. A warm, gentle breeze passed through the valley, tousling the herder's shoulder-length red hair, greeting him as he gazed across cerulean fields and narrowed his eyes in pleasure. He inhaled the familiar scent of his herd mixed with the sweet aroma of nearby carfen trees, exhaling as a tingle ran up his spine.

Life...life is good.

He opened his eyes and gazed downhill toward the valley he called home, just as the first rays of iridescent sunlight pierced its dark pall. Distant rooftops glittered like stars in the night sky as nearby winged mintaulks took flight and soared overhead, the thin membranes of their wings absorbing light as nourishment. Iridescent rays fluttered for a moment, playing against his tanned skin before the sky flashed a brilliant red. The herder smiled, nodding in appreciation as he enjoyed the sight.

Yes...life is good.

Roland Amariah Gonzales

Lost in the valley's idyllic pastoral, his eyes flitted upward toward the Place of Sorrow, a walled-off domain of impossible proportions, said to be full of misery and torment. A lone tower cruelly rose just above its forsaken walls, below it, a shimmering silver dome stretched off into the unknown along with the city. The herder's smile withered before he tore his gaze away, frowning.

To look upon it is to invite sin. Therefore we look away. We look inward. We repel evil that it may find no home.

The herder shivered, whether from a sudden chill coming down from snow-capped mountains, *or* the Place of Sorrow, he did not know. He donned his heavy shawl as a rogdael nudged him gently. Its soft muzzle sought his hand while thick, yellow antennae topped with clusters of black, fuzzy, electrified orbs ran along his arm affectionately, causing it to tingle. Startled, the herder looked downward and laughed then said, "alright, alright!" The nudging became more insistent until the herder rose and gently pushed the rogdael's antennae away. He looked toward the herd then bowed toward his supplicant then spoke, "...who is *truly* king here? By your leave, Thrume."

The herder's friend trudged beside him as he and the herd crossed the remaining distance to ample feedlands. Upon their arrival the herder found a nice, soft patch of ground to sit on, then journeyed inward toward the past. He had balked at becoming the town's Herder. He had wanted to be a Thinker, like his grandfather before him. The village council had been adamant, however. "We have enough Thinkers for this generation and the previous Herder is old, *ready* for release. Your *unnatural* interest in climbing the hills outside the valley during your youth make you a perfect fit," they'd said. At his protest they'd sternly admonished him, "this will satisfy your curiosity while providing you a tether. What better way to keep *it* reined in while you do the same for the rogdaels?"

He had been at it for...a few weeks now and had been surprised to discover that he actually *didn't mind it so much.* He had never been a "people-person," which is why he'd eagerly chased after the solitude of being a Thinker.

...I suppose this really is the next best thing.

The herder's gaze flowed ran from his herd back toward the valley, seeing faint smoke rise in the air from village chimneys as morning meals were prepared. His stomach rumbled in response.

There'll be something good waiting for me, I'm sure.

Thrume chittered softly, bringing the herder back to the present. He laughed then grinned, glancing at Thrume as it ambled about, munching happily. The herder waited for his flock to finish grazing, speaking aloud, "no...no, this is a good fit. Perhaps the council *was* wise to place me here." He laid back on the ground and stretched his neck upward, opening his eyes toward the hills above where he noticed, for the first time, a small, blinking light. He stared for a few moments, blinking his eyes in confusion before rubbing them and sitting upright. He turned around and rose to his feet, his inquisitive nature in delight as the light did not *flicker* from fire...but was *solid*. Curious, he called the flock and began leading them further away from their usual grazing grounds, up into the hills as a single thought danced about in his mind.

...something new?

"...very good! Can anyone tell me *why* it came to be?"

A small boy with dark hair and brown skin, clad in a simple green tunic, rose from his desk then recited his indoctrination, "yes, Ms. Knowe. It was deserved punishment for the actions of all people, a constant reminder that *we* should be humble, pure, and one with the land lest we be cast into the Place of Sorrow."

The child sat back down as Ms. Knowe nodded in approval. She addressed the class, "that's *right*, excellent! There are only a handful of townships remaining, and as such, we *all* must do our *very best* to live in harmony. Not only with our homes and each other, but also our *world!* Can anyone tell me *about* the Place of Sorrow?"

A small girl with dark hair and pale skin, also clad in a simple green tunic, rose from her desk and spoke, "the Place of Sorrow is where those who have *rejected* harmony reside. They live selfish lives full of *technology* and *feed* off one another in their misery. They are barbarous and *evil* and as such are forever confined behind the Walls of Peacecord."

The teacher nodded again then smiled beatifically and asked, "can anyone tell me *how* we protect our homes and keep those behind the Place of Sorrow at bay? In *fear* of our righteous wrath?"

The class was silent, a few of the children looking around in confusion. The teacher spoke softly, drawing the children's attention, "...our *Solemn Promise*. Our Solemn Promise, the useful daily litany which keeps us mindful of our actions and *how* they affect others, is also so much more! Stand and look outward, children, toward the center of our town!"

Ms. Knowe directed the class's attention through the open-shuttered, unglazed windows and continued speaking, "our Solemn Promise is *also* the town's heart, nay, its very *soul!* That dark stone, *proud* and *upright,* a glorious pillar reaching unto the heavens. It is both our *guardian* and *protector* which *ensures* those who reside in the Place of Sorrow *never* venture beyond its walls. Never threaten us! Never *taint* us with their *unclean presence.*"

The World Before

The children pressed together and voiced both amazement and adoration, "ooh!" "Ahh!" "I love you, Solemn Promise!" "Thank you for watching over me and mom and dad and Ms. Knowe!"

Ms. Knowe smiled then nodded as she stood behind the children, all identical in height, wearing identical clothes. She spoke in jubilance, "let's all save our thanks and praise for the Solemn Promise, for in one week's time we will celebrate a very special day! The 8th centennial of the Peacecord! We will gather around the Solemn Promise, give thanks to it, and even give gifts to one another! And one of us will be chosen for something *very special*, something which ensures that the Solemn Promise continues its vigilance for another hundred years!"

The children turned then cheered, running to hug Ms. Knowe as she crouched down, arms outstretched and smiling warmly.

The herder had ventured upward for an hour as he searched for the solid light. It had flickered off and on but then disappeared as the wind grew more intense. He hugged his shawl tightly to his frame as the rogdael began to bray, made nervous by the fierce winds. The herder abandoned his search upward to look back at his rogdael herd and see that Thrume too, was upset.

...perhaps it's best if I return another time, without the rogdael...I'm hungry anyway.

He turned away from the windy hills, gathered his herd, then journeyed downhill. The herder was not disheartened by this momentary setback. Indeed, he took comfort in having ventured further than his people had *ever* achieved.

...I'll return, little light. With food. ...perhaps a heavier shawl, too. You will yield your secrets!

The walk back was uneventful, the herd calming as the gale lessened. The herder and his flock reached the village around mid-day, a smattering of small, rectangular, simple huts with thatched roofs made from carfen branches and other plants. The rogdael chittered happily as they followed his lead to their barn, Thrume nudging him lovingly once before trotting after the herd. Satisfied that his task was done and, a little more than hungry, the herder closed the gate and made his way to his sleep-hut.

He entered and discovered that others had already finished their morning meals. The herder searched the food preparation area and located his portion, set aside by his building's Caretaker. He sat down and began to eat, his thoughts drifting.

...have others seen it? ...probably not. ...quite windy up there...unusual. ...should I notify the council? ...no. They'd either scoff at or reprimand me. Ugh...this food is cold! ...can't complain...they'd ask why I was so late in returning. Ah well...

The herder finished his unpleasant meal then deposited the dishes for the Caretaker. He stepped outside and saw the town Planner decorating for the coming Peacecord Day. He paused to look at the town's Solemn Promise, the dark monolithic obelisk positioned in the town's center.

...always made me uneasy, though I know not why. This will be my first Peacecord celebration...well, everyone's first, I suppose. ...just a bunch of singing and hand-holding...with people. ...I need to find a way to step away from the herd...have to find that light.

Heading toward the village council's hall, the herder cast one last wary glance toward the Solemn Promise before stepping inside. Dismay struck him when the only Elder present was an old and wizened, greying man. A man who once clashed with the herder's grandfather and took perverse joy in spiting the long-dead man's progeny.

The herder approached the old, irritable man perched over a large table, poring over multiple carfen-wood tablets covered in etchings detailing rites, practices, and laws. The herder braced himself then spoke, "Elder Samoth, um...I'd like to discuss something of importance."

Elder Samoth looked up and frowned before returning his attention downward, then curtly replied, "what *is it*, Nirat? I'm searching for the Peacecord's Rite. It is *imperative* that we conduct the ritual accurately."

Nirat looked over the table and the stack of tablets, then back to Elder Samoth before replying earnestly, "yes, Elder, I understand that the Rite is very important and thank you profusely for your time. I was wondering if perhaps you could approve...um, my taking on an apprentice. For herding the rogdael."

Elder Samoth scoffed then said, "You want to teach someone to *walk*? Uphill?"

Nirat bit his cheek as he flushed in anger.

If it's so easy, why am I the only one who can do it?

Nirat maintained a measure of calmness and said, "yes, Elder. It's just that...I think it would be *best* to begin training someone for high-altitude hikes, strenuous as they are. The council *did* say that the last herder served well beyond his years as there hadn't been a replacement worthy until I – "

Elder Samoth threw down his held tablet then snapped, "if it will get you *out* of here that I may concentrate, fine! Take one of the green-clads and torture them with your *inane* nonsense!"

Nirat's brow furrowed as he took a deep breath then said, "thank you, Elder Samoth. Live by the Solemn Promise."

Elder Samoth eyed his rival's descendant for a moment, a cruel and predatory glimmer behind his eyes, then waved Nirat away, "yes, yes. Live by the Solemn Promise."

The World Before

Ms. Knowe was about to end the day's lessons when she saw Nirat approaching the Indoctrination Hut, a broad smile on his face. She smiled warmly at him.

The new herder, finally come my way! ...mm I love the way they smell...like fields and rogdael...the last one's seed never took for some reason...I'm running out of time...

Nirat stepped to the window, waiting for a pause in Ms. Knowe's lecture. She finished addressing the class then looked at him with an encouraging smile, waiting. He cleared his throat then spoke up, "Ms. Knowe, before you dismiss the class, I'd like to have a word with everyone."

Ms. Knowe's gentle smile, reserved for her class, grew into something much more alluring as she held Nirat's gaze then responded, "take *all* the time you need, Nirat. Please, *come in* any time you like."

Nirat, taken aback, stuttered, "a-ah, yes. Um, sure...heh, thank you, Ms. Knowe." He walked around to the Indoctrination Hut's entrance then entered, taking a moment to admire Ms. Knowe as told the class to listen very carefully.

...pleasing face, long golden hair flecked with rivulets of grey, fair skin...the way her blue tunic hugs her –

Ms. Knowe's knowing grin caught his eyes before her gaze did the same. Nirat laughed awkwardly as Ms. Knowe stepped to the side of the class then gestured for him to take the front, then said, "yes. Right. So..." He looked over the class as they stared at him, some wide-eyed from his sudden intrusion, then spoke, "h-hey there. *Kids!* Um...Peacecord Day is around the corner so...Hey, who's excited for that? ...yeah? Show of hands?"

A couple of kids tentatively raised their hands, though most just looked at one another then at Nirat in confusion, confused by his presence. Nirat sighed then said, "...so...I need an apprentice. Uh, anyone want to walk up into the hills with me? Learn how to watch the rogdael? um...get out of the village?"

The class looked around in confusion before one of them shouted, "who doesn't know how to *walk!?*" The rest of the kids erupted in laughter. Nirat's brow furrowed as he replied, "well, yeah. It's a lot of walking. But it's walking *uphill!* Have any of *you* ever walked uphill before? Anyone? *Up past* the village?"

The class grew quiet as they all shook their heads. *No one* went into the hills. No one left the valley. To do so was to leave the safety of the Solemn Promise. A kid shouted, "those hills are *haunted!* No way!"

Nirat laughed and replied, "see? Not so easy! It takes someone *especially* brave! I can teach you *how* to be brave *and* you'll learn a lot about the rogdael too!"

He waited a few moments but no one responded. Ms. Knowe looked at him with a sad smile then spoke up and said, "well, we will all certainly *think* about it, won't we? Thank you so much for your time, Nirat. We hope to see you soon!"

Taking his cue, Nirat said goodbye to the class then walked to the rogdael barn. He found most of the rogdaels asleep, except for Thrume who lifted its head and happily chittered when he entered. A smile crept onto Nirat's face, despite himself. He walked over to Thrume and sat beside it, then stroked its nape.

Sometimes...I swear, I almost think Thrume can really *understand me.*

Thrume chittered and rubbed its fuzzy black antennae against Nirat's arm in appreciation. Nirat continued to stroke Thume before lying back against its warm, furry and white exoskeleton, smiling contently as its chittering vibrations soothed him to sleep. He awoke later to a small voice that piped up and said, "um...hello?" Nirat opened his eyes and recognized a small girl clad in green, from before.

The girl sheepishly said, "I...was wondering if you're still looking for an apprentice?"

Skeptical, Nirat said, "...maybe. Um...can you walk? For long periods of time? Uphill?"

148

The girl nodded then said, "yes, and I'm curious about the feedlands, too! *And* the rogdaels."

Nirat paused as he contained his delight and pretended to consider her qualifications, then said, "this is Thrume. Thrume's my friend."

The girl smiled then said, "hello Thrume. Nice to meet you."

Thrume brayed, startling the girl. Nirat laughed and said, "don't worry. Thrume does that to most people. Um...you really want to apprentice for me?"

The girl nodded enthusiastically and said, "yes, anything to get me away from my classmates!"

Nirat laughed and said, "we'll start tomorrow, ok? It's *really* early, though. Pre-dawn. Bring a shawl and long-food."

An assertive look flashed across the girl's face as she said, "right. Will do! Live by the Solemn Promise!"

Nirat nodded then smiled, replying, "live by the Solemn Promise!"

Nirat left the barn soon after, pausing at the threshold to look over the village, steeped in spectral wash of aquamarine moonlight. His gaze rested upon the Solemn Promise, that great black obelisk which jutted from the town's center. He regarded it for a moment, then made his way to his sleep-hut, careful to avoid making any noise therein. Tiptoeing by bunkbeds full of sleeping men and women, he made his way toward the back, his bed illuminated by a small tallow candle against the wall, a kindness by the hut's Caretaker. He was eager to get a good night's rest, and settled into his bunk before awakening in alarm.

Reaching under his grass-stuffed pillow, he felt a firm edge. Curious, he pulled it out to reveal a carfen-wood tablet meticulously etched with patterns of flowers. He admired it for a moment, then read, "lovely Nirat, I hope you appreciate my pushing that little one to apprentice for you! Perhaps you can thank me later! – Ms. K."

Nirat put the tablet to the side, eyebrows arched, then grinned as he laid back and placed his hands behind his head.

Life...is great.

Roland Amariah Gonzales

He awoke to the same little girl kicking at his foot who said, "...Mister Nirat? It's time to go, isn't it?"

Nirat awoke with a start before rising out of his bunk, then replied, "*wha-!?* Ah, y-yes. Yeah, of course. *ahem* let's get going, shall we?"

The little girl studied him for a moment, then smiled and said, "Ok."

Nirat looked over the girl, making sure she had a shawl and long-food, then led her to the barn. Nirat smiled as he saw Thrume rise to its six legs and stretch its neck, then reached out to stroke its neck. He paused and asked the little girl, "oh...hey – what's your name?"

She replied in embarrassed surprise, "oh! Ycanthi, pleased to meet you Nirat. You too, Thrume."

Nirat smiled and said, "pleased to meet you too, Ycanthi. Ah! It's my turn to be embarrassed – I forgot *my* shawl and long-food! I'm going to go grab it then come back, you stay here and watch over the rogdael, okay? It's important that they know your scent! ...so make sure they touch their antennae to your arms, okay?"

Ycanthi looked at the rogdael and said, "okay, will do."

Nirat hurried to his sleep-hut and saw everyone still asleep. He grabbed his shawl and a day's worth of long-food before quietly making his way to the entrance. As he exited he saw Ms. Knowe standing in the doorway of a sleep-hut opposite his own. She waved and blew him a kiss. Emboldened with no prying eyes to see his actions, he jumped up and caught the invisible kiss then placed it in his pack. Ms. Knowe clasped her hands over her heart as Nirat walked to the barn, the two waving goodbye to one another.

He opened the barn door and saw Ycanthi surrounded by the rogdael, save Thrume who was off to the side, waggling its antennae uncertainly. Ycanthi giggled while the rogdael ran their antennae up and down her arms. Nirat smiled and said, "looks like they've taken to you! ...well, except Thrume. That's okay though, Thrume is *hard to please*, aren't you buddy?"

Thrume chittered in response, earning a laugh from Nirat before he returned his attention to Ycanthi and said, "are you ready?"

150

The World Before

Ycanthi nodded enthusiastically and said, "I sure am!"

Nirat and Ycanthi left the barn together with rogdael in tow, Thrume beside Nirat as he instructed Ycanthi, "...they have to *trust* you. As long as they trust you, all you really need to do is walk to good spots. The *problem* is their food only grows past the cerulean fields, *way up* in the hills. ...and most of the village is *terrified* of the hills. They say there are *voices* up there, maybe ghosts from long ago."

Ycanthi nodded then said, "Ghosts? That's *stupid.* What *do* the rogdael eat?"

Nirat smiled as he looked down at Ycanthi, "ha! I think it's stupid too. The rogdael eat large, bulbous flowers. I'll show you when we get there – the colors don't matter. Blue, red, gold, black – they're all the same."

Ycanthi nodded and said, "anything else?"

Nirat grinned at her then said, "yeah, you're going to love the view!"

They reached Nirat's rock just as day broke. Nirat excitedly said, "hurry! Hurry and have a seat! Look back at the valley!"

Two sunrises in a row! What luck!

Ycanthi quickly sat down and looked back at the valley where the village sat, but only noticed the Place of Sorrow. She cried out then angrily shouted at Nirat, "what is *wrong* with you! Why would you have me look at that!"

Confused and hurt, Nirat said, "...what? N-no – no, not the Place of Sorrow, I meant the valley. I – "

Ycanthi ignored him as she clasped her hands together and recited the litany aloud, "to look upon it is to invite sin. Therefore we look away. We look inward. We repel evil that it may find no home."

Nirat frowned then apologized, "...sorry. The valley looks wonderful under the sunrise...I...uh...I thought you might like it."

Ycanthi ignored him, clearly in a foul mood. Nirat turned away, glum.

...some first day. Have I lost my new apprentice already?

The solid light caught his attention from far above. He grew visibly excited for a moment before calming himself, then cleared his throat and quietly said, "...well...let's head up a little higher. The rogdael like the feed-grounds above." He began walking uphill, the rogdael in tow. Ycanthi wordlessly fell in behind.

They had nearly reached the upper area when Nirat began to feel the winds pick up. He looked back at Ycanthi and said, "hey, Ycanthi. I'm going to check something ahead. You stay here with the rogdael while they graze, alright?"

Ycanthi quietly said, "fine," then as Nirat began to walk uphill, loudly said, "*hey,* Nirat! I...Thank you. You're right. The valley *was* beautiful under the sunrise. ...I got scared, is all. The Place of Sorrow...I uh...I don't like it."

Nirat listened then said reassuringly, "me neither. Let's both do our best to not look at it from now on, okay?"

The World Before

Ycanthi smiled and nodded, then giggled as some of the rogdael affectionately stroked her arms with their antennae. Satisfied that the rogdael would stay with Ycanthi, Nirat continued his trek, stopping only once to send an indignant Thrume back to the little girl. Before proceeding, he noticed a particularly beautiful cluster of blue and red flowers. With Ms. Knowe in mind, he plucked a few.

Nirat grew dismayed as he trekked upward, the light having disappeared. He stopped and looked down the steep decline toward Ycanthi and the rogdael.

Still there. Everything's fine. ...wonder if she saw the light? ...wonder if she'd want to see it?

Nirat continued for another 30 minutes until he approached a large outcropping of rocks, stopping to catch his breath. He sat on a rock then looked around, disheartened. A bright light to his right suddenly began to blink repeatedly. Nirat's head slowly turned toward the light until he let out an audible, "ah! There you are!" He stood up and cautiously approached, seeing it was emanating from within a large cave.

Nirat looked around the cave's mouth but saw no markings or any indication of what the cave held. He took a deep breath then proceeded forward, noting faded, odd white outlines in some places on the ground, as well as rusted shapes, undiscernible from age. Deep in the cave was the light itself positioned next to a large metallic door. Nirat was ecstatic.

...what a discovery!

He moved to the door then studied the light. It was a yellow, rotating thing that spun around in a transparent container. He looked at the door and, seeing a large metallic door handle, gave it a tug. A small beep sounded before the thing opened, though just barely. Shock and dismay overwhelmed Nirat as he frantically looked around for something – anything to pry the door open.

This may be the most important discovery of my lifetime! Of the village's existence! They'll have to make me a Thinker after this! Why, maybe even a seat on the council!

He noticed a rusted contraption next to the odd white lines on the ground and picked it up. With a bit of luck and not a little effort, he was able to force part of the contraption into the door's thin opening, working it until he managed a large gap. With a final shove and ceremonious snapping of the object in half, the door came open enough for Nirat to squeeze through.

Nirat stood in stunned silence as he surveyed the room. It was a large, darkened chamber filled with all manner of devices, small, teal-colored lights which illuminated various plants, and things Nirat couldn't begin to comprehend. A floating metallic orb with small, mechanical appendages hovered toward him then scanned his person with a thin red ray. It paused briefly before returning to the plants and other systems. Nirat had no words.

Technology. High *Technology!*

A small, blue hologram projected from a comms panel near Nirat, startling him. A woman spoke, "oh? You there, what is your name and position? This is a Class-X restricted facility."

Nirat's eyes widened as he approached the small, blue holo-woman. She continued, "wait, what...are you *wearing*? You...where is this facility located? ...you're *outside* IO. *This facility* is outside IO!"

Nirat spoke quietly, "um...hello. I'm Nirat. ...the rogdael herder."

It was the small blue holo-woman's turn to stand in stunned silence, mouth agape. She burst into laughter before wiping tears away and said, "Nirat, huh? Greetings! I am Armatis. I'm...I suppose it doesn't really matter, does it? Tell me Nirat, can you understand any of the written words around you? The signs? *Anything* here? One moment, I'll activate the lights for you."

Nirat took a step back as the darkened interior of the chamber illuminated. He was able to see *much* more clearly now. He spoke excitedly, "...wow. *Wow*! This place is, I-I...mean...wow!" He took a moment to regain his composure, then noticed signs, posters and text. Aware that he could not understand any of it, he said sadly, "ah...no. No, I can't understand any of this."

Armatis nodded then said, "I'd be surprised if you could. It's been nearly 800 years since this facility was active. Listen...Nirat, I...need to take care of some things over here. On my side. I'd love to chat with you again, though."

Nirat nodded enthusiastically and replied, "oh yes, of course! I have to return to my herd now but uh...I could return tomorrow! Oh! Um...you won't tell the council about any of this will you?"

Armatis smiled gently then said, "no worries, Nirat. Our rendezvous are on a need to know basis! Stand still for a moment, I'll grant you access to the facility."

Nirat nodded then stood waiting.

...what's a "ron-day-voo?"

The metallic orb returned to him and hovered in place as it scanned him again, this time with a blue ray. It chirped then produced a small translucent crystalline object. Armatis spoke informatively, "make sure you have this on your person next time you come here, okay?"

Nirat nodded then said goodbye to the tiny blue woman, finding that the door swung open and closed much more easily than it had before.

...what an incredible day.

He practically ran back to Ycanthi, stopping as he neared, lost in thought.

Wait a minute...can't tell her...not yet.

He slowed his gait to a reasonable trot and waved to Ycanthi as he neared. She was sitting on the ground, surrounded by rogdael, save Thrume who excitedly trotted over to Nirat. Nirat crouched down and wrapped his arms around Thrume's neck, laughing as it snorted then chittered while rubbing its antennae over Nirat's head, making his hair stand on end.

Ycanthi spoke, "you're in a good mood! Find anything interesting?"

Roland Amariah Gonzales

Nirat coughed then looked at the ground before looking up and said, "...some interesting rocks, yeah. They're really pretty! Maybe I'll show you someday, though we'll need some way to keep the rogdael from wandering off."

Ycanthi nodded then looked back at the valley and said, "sounds great. When can we eat?"

The World Before

Armatis has much to consider as she drifted...both in thought and form, suspended in a vat of bio-gel. She was blind, here. The innumerable panels which surrounded her, with their esoteric blinking lights, meant nothing to her. The occasional *click* followed by the steady hum of a coolant system her only assurance that she was not dead. Well, that and her "forays" to the outside.

She had established backdoors in the past...private channels which allowed her some semblance of movement. She'd also established enough proxies to warn her before *it* regarded her with its baleful gaze. Armatis had no idea why it kept her alive. For what purpose...the coolant system *clicked* then began humming as her thoughts returned to the present.

An outsider. He certainly looked primitive...though not as bad as we were led to believe. Fascinating. How did he get into the SP-Observation Site? ...a descendant of the original team? ...not relevant, I suppose.

Armatis attempted to shake her head in amazement but found she couldn't.

Frustrating. Calm down.

She calculated.

Perhaps...I can still do some good...but is there time?

The valley's skies were abuzz with mintaulks as they soared overhead, soaking in the late afternoon's rays. Nirat returned to his village with Ycanthi, rogdael in tow. He showed her how to lead the rogdael into their barn, opening the latch to their gate as they scuttled inward. Some rubbed their antennae against the two in thanks, Thrume pausing to chitter at Nirat before doing the same. Nirat and Ycanthi parted, she returning to her sleep-hut for rest and refreshment, and he to his for the same.

No sooner had Nirat entered his sleep-hut and laid back on his bed when he discovered another carfen-wood tablet under his pillow. He retrieved it, then read, "Lovely Nirat, the Peacecord Day celebration is coming soon and I'd hate to be alone. Meet me tonight behind the rogdael barn after all sleep. – Ms. K."

Nirat looked up and gulped, then grinned stupidly and pumped his fists in the air in celebration. He made his way to the front of the sleep-hut and enjoyed a warm meal, quickly conversing with the Cleaner before running to the barn and cleaning up as best he could. He performed his tasks with fervor as Ms. Knowe's long flowing locks and voluptuous form danced in his mind.

...I remember when she taught me as a boy! ...I think *she can still breed. If we make offspring, we'll be granted our own hut! ...until the child is old enough for indoctrination.*

Time couldn't pass quickly enough for Nirat. When the moon hung high in the sky, aligned almost perfectly above the Solemn Promise, Nirat quietly left his sleep-hut. He made his way around the back of the barn and waited quietly, only a few moments passing before a figure wearing a heavy shawl rounded the corner and approached him. Nirat's breath caught in his throat as Ms. Knowe threw off her cover and cast it behind her, revealing her nude form.

It was all Nirat could do to mumble, "...wow."

Ms. Knowe sashayed forward seductively, eyes locked onto Nirat's as a predator marks its prey. She extended an arm behind his head and pulled him tight against her nude form, relishing in the way he melted in her embrace, the way he responded to her presence...her touch.

...oh yes. He'll do nicely.

She smiled as she gently pressed her forehead to his own then reached down to squeeze him after whispering, "...somewhere we can go, lovely Nirat?"

Nirat first yelped then stuttered, "BARN! u-uh ye-yeah. can go we...ah, I mean..."

Ms. Knowe grinned as Nirat turned then fumbled with the door. She turned away from him then slowly bent over to pick up her heavy shawl as he stared, brain melting. Standing upright, she entered the barn as Nirat followed behind, led by her hand. Ms. Knowe found a soft spot on the ground covered in sweet, dried grass, then laid back and opened herself to him as Nirat stared in silent wonder before undressing.

...I'm so glad I cleaned this place up.

He stopped for a moment, considering, then reached into the folds of his clothes to pull out the flowers he had plucked earlier. He awkwardly presented them to Ms. Knowe and said, "I uh...I brought you these from the hills. They're pretty...and you're pretty. So...here you go."

Ms. Knowe brought her hand to her heart as she smiled and looked over her soon-to-be mate, "*thank you*, lovely Nirat. I know just what to do with them. Now, come."

The two joined, the sounds of their exertions intermingling with the chittering of the rogdael – except for Thrume who waggled its antennae uncertainly. Ms. Knowe and Nirat kept at it, again and again until just before sunrise. Ms. Knowe stood up and stretched her arms overhead, her belly glowing a slight fluorescent-pink, and said in loving appreciation, "I *knew* you were the right choice, Nirat. Look, a baby girl! We're going to produce such *fantastic* offspring, I'm sure of it! Why, they could even be *Elders* some day!"

Nirat, hanging on to consciousness by a thread after being thoroughly wrung dry by his new mate, weakly nodded and said, "mmhuh." His eyes fluttered as he felt Ms. Knowe kiss his forehead, opening briefly to see her don her heavy shawl and make her way out of the barn. Nirat smiled before passing out.

Life...isn't just great...it's...fantastic.

The World Before

He awoke to Ycanthi kicking his foot. Drearily, he opened his eyes and said, "mmwha – oh. Hey. Good morning, Ycanthi."

Ycanthi looked over Nirat's disheveled nude form then said, "do you sleep here *every* night? Nude? That is very strange, Nirat."

Nirat quickly sat up then laughed weakly and said, "no, no – I slept in my sleep-hut for a while but then came out here to keep Thrume company. Uh...I didn't want my clothes to get dirty so I removed them. Yeah." Thrume chittered questioningly.

Ycanthi looked dubious but responded, "well, alright then. Shall we get going?"

Nirat looked down and saw a small bundle next to him. He checked it and found long-food as well as blue rogdael milk – a stimulant meant to give one energy. He looked off toward Ms. Knowe's sleep hut and smiled appreciatively before chugging the milk, then quickly got dressed.

Nirat and Ycanthi gathered the rogdael and headed up to the feeding grounds, the sun rising at an odd point off in the distance. Ycanthi was much more pleased with the sunrise though she still audibly repeated the litany.

Nirat looked over to her and said, "you know...you don't *have* to look at the Place of Sorrow, right? The sunrise isn't anywhere near it today."

Ycanthi responded quietly without looking toward him, "...better safe than sorry, Nirat. The Solemn Promise sees all."

Nirat paused then agreed with her before turning upward, toward the higher places where the secret chamber lay in waiting. Ycanthi spoke, snapping him back to reality, "Nirat, look what I've discovered!"

Nirat turned to see her standing without her shawl, having tied it to a length of carfen-wood staked firmly in the ground. The rogdael, ever-curious creatures, were intrigued by this as it danced in the wind, returning to it as they went between it, eating, and lying down. Nirat spoke, "huh, will you look at that?" He noticed Thrume eating off to the side then removed his shawl, binding it to Ycanthi's. Thrume, satisfied with Nirat's presence one way or another, joined the rest of the herd.

Nirat laughed before Ycanthi said, "now you can show me those rocks up high, yeah?"

Nirat's abruptly stopped laughing then looked at Ycanthi, thinking.

...she doesn't seem like everyone else. She's a Thinker*...just like me...maybe. ...yes, yes I think she'd appreciate it too!*

Nirat looked at Ycanthi and grinned then said, "you know what? Let's go! There's a surprise up there too, one I haven't told you about, though I think you'll like it!"

The two trekked upward some distance, pausing to look back at the herd who were either sleeping or affectionately rubbing their antennae against the carfen-wood-shawl figure. After some time they reached the cave. Nirat said calmly to Ycanthi, "these are the interesting rocks I found, though the surprise is behind that hard-door. Ycanthi, listen...I think you're *special. Different* from the rest. There are some things...well, *everything* beyond that door might be shocking. Just...keep an open mind, okay?"

Ycanthi eyed Nirat curiously then nodded and said "alright. Let's go see this 'surprise'."

Nirat led Ycanthi to the door. As he neared, it emitted a loud beep, resonating with Nirat's access crystal. The beep startled Ycanthi who jumped back. Nirat chuckled and said, "it's okay, Ycanthi, it's just a door. I have the key here." He brought the crystal from his pouch and showed it to her. She marveled for a moment before nodding in assent.

Nirat opened the door much easier this time, then entered the fully-illuminated chamber with Ycanthi. Ycanthi was speechless though only for a moment. She then hissed in revulsion and anger, "*technology!* You've exposed me to *High* technology!?"

The custodial orb hovered over to the two then scanned them with a thin red ray. Ycanthi screamed and swatted at the orb in terror. The orb blared out an angry-sounding beep as its sides opened outward and produced two menacing arms with small, pointed objects. It fired a flechette needle which struck Ycanthi in the chest, causing her to howl in pain and terror. She ran out of the facility crying as Nirat stood in confusion, processing what had just happened.

The orb scanned Nirat again then deactivated its defense systems, chirping before hovering away and resuming its duties. Nirat yelled, "Ycanthi, wait! Don't go!" He began to run after her but was stopped by the sudden appearance of Armatis who spoke, "Nirat! It is good to see you again. We have much to discuss."

Nirat yelled, "there's no time! That stupid...ball-thing hurt my apprentice!"

Armatis interjected, "the custodial orb *only* responds to aggression – and only with minimal force. I'm sure she'll be fine."

Nirat spoke in anguish, "no, you don't *understand*. My people! They *hate* technology. Especially *High* technology! She's going to tell everyone, I'm sure of it! They...they might come up here and destroy this place!"

Armatis processed his words for a moment then said, "...listen to me, Nirat, we're pressed for time. Your village...I've located it via sat-scans. Ah! Sat-scans are...it isn't important. Listen, your village is centered around the SP-Device...it's a...a weapons platform, more or less. *Incredibly* dangerous."

Nirat shook his head then angrily responded, "SP? The Solemn Promise? *No*, our Solemn Promise is a *safeguard* against the Place of Sorrow, the large walled off city where the unclean reside! It protects us as we venerate it!"

Armatis considered his words then shook her head as she projected a sat-feed which displayed Nirat's village as well as a gargantuan construct of machinery underneath, the Solemn Promise its head. She said, "Nirat, The Place of Sorrow...that name *is* rather apt, isn't it...it's a city named IO. IO is ruled by a...a thinking machine. And there's a chance that...*gah!* It doesn't matter, there's no time! Nirat, listen, you need to get *everyone* out of your village. You need to bring them *here*, do you understand? This place, it extends *far* beneath this current floor. It isn't just a research facility, it's a habitat. A *shelter.* A self-contained colony that can *easily* accommodate your village."

Nirat listened to the tiny blue woman's words, glancing up as distant, large, double doors he had thought to be a metal wall slid open, revealing an entirely new section which stretched on and downward farther than he could see. He held his head with both hands, overwhelmed, then took a deep breath and said, "okay. Okay. Ye-yeah. I-I'll try. I'll try to get them here."

Armatis nodded then said, "good luck Nirat, and hurry."

Nirat hurried out of the chamber then began briskly walking down the steep hill, careful to avoid the many rocks and holes. He looked up from his precipitous path to see Ycanthi in the distance. She and the rogdael were *far* ahead of him, Thrume running beside her as it chased after Nirat's shawl. Ycanthi's terror bloomed into hatred, propelling her forward at a frenzied pace, Nirat's pleading voice falling uselessly behind her.

Breaking into a panicked run, Nirat gained ground before tripping over a rock and tumbling to the ground, twisting his ankle. Wincing in pain, he glanced up to see Ycanthi and the herd gain an even greater distance.

I'll never catch up to her now! If I had just a little more time...

Frustrated and overwhelmed, Nirat began to cry before collapsing back against the cerulean hill and watching the sky. Exhausted from the events of the day, pleasant or otherwise, he was mercifully claimed by sleep, his pain forgotten. When he awoke, the familiar red sky of day had gone, replaced by the night's aquamarine. Nirat painfully rose to his feet and, in resignation, composed himself before limping back to the village.

The World Before

Nirat entered the village as the moon was at its zenith and found that all had assembled near the Solemn Promise, the Elders directly in front, the people of his village forming a ring further out as they faced the monolith. They silently watched him approach as he fearfully kept his head down, occasionally glancing up to discover faces full of disgust or hate at his loathsome presence.

He approached and beseeched the Elders as they glared at him, "Elders, I have discovered something of the *utmost* importance! I have found a...a place, high up in the hills, and spoken with...with a tiny blue woman! The tiny blue woman, she told me that this place is *dangerous*! The village itself! It *sits* on *High technology! Dangerous* technology! We must flee! We must flee to the sanctuary I've discovered! Please! The Solemn Promise isn't our *protector*, it's a weap –"

A carfen-wood tablet was hurled from the crowd, sailing through the air before slamming against the back of Nirat's head, cutting it deeply. Nirat cried out in pain then fell to his knees. Elder Samoth spoke with fury through clenched teeth, "what I understand, *Nirat*, is that *you* meddled with *high* technology. You conversed with someone *from* the Place of Sorrow, where *all* high technology resides. You attempted to *corrupt* Ycanthi as well! Oh, but you *failed*. Ycanthi, step forward!"

Ycanthi stepped forward, a bandage covering the spot that the flechette had punctured her. With flechette in hand, she pointed it accusingly at Nirat and yelled, "Nirat took me to a place *filled* with high technology! An evil metal orb fired *this* at me, but not him! He is *clearly* with those in the Place of Sorrow!"

Angry shouts came from the crowd as Nirat begged and pleaded for them to understand, to no avail. Elder Samoth held his arms high and signaled all for silence. The crowd quieted down. Elder Samoth addressed the village, "Ycanthi will make a *fine* Indoctrinator to replace Ms. Knowe. For she *knows* that more important than the individual is the *collective*. We *strive* to live by the Solemn Promise!"

The crowd intoned, "by the Solemn Promise!"

The Elder continued, "but not *Nirat*. Were we *they* of the Place of Sorrow, we would *brutalize* Nirat and devour him! But we are *not* they. We are civilized. We are *better* than they could ever hope to be. It is with this in mind that we *banish* Nirat, to live in isolation for the remainder of his days. Alone with his *filthy* technology, may it consume his soul."

The crowd cheered as Nirat faced them and yelled, "no! You don't understand! We must leave – "

A well-aimed carfen-wood tablet thrown by one of the children slammed into his left eye, bursting it. Nirat fell to his knees and cried out in agony before the crowd began to pelt him, shouting and yelling for him to leave, though some stood silently with their hands clasped and looked downward. Nirat covered his face with his hands and ran out of the village as he was pelted with all manner of objects, sobbing. For an instant he saw Ms. Knowe on the edge of the crowd, flanked by two men as her arms were held, her wrists bound. Her face was a storm of fury and grief, the gleam of tears betraying her anguish.

Thrume, hearing Nirat's cries, ran along the fence of its pen and brayed in distress. One of the villagers came over and viciously struck its sensitive antennae, painfully collapsing the creature. Nirat's return to the bunker was an agonizing, desperate thing, causing him to faint several times. Eventually he returned and the door beeped welcomingly before opening. He walked into the room and collapsed onto the cold metallic floor. Without hope. Rejected by all he had ever known. Utterly defeated.

The World Before

Nirat awoke, unsure of how much time had passed. He opened his eyes, confused and frightened by his limited view before remembering his left eye taken. With the memory came frightful pain, the phantom eye admonishing him for being so careless as he wept softly, his life undone. Armatis appeared and spoke, "Nirat! ...I saw everything on the sat-feed...I'm so sorry. I...I did not know your people were so *barbarous.*"

Nirat muttered bitterly without looking at her, "...they were never *my people.*"

Armatis shook her head sadly before saying, "...a bit of good news. Though your pride may be injured, it doesn't mean your body must remain so. Follow the custodial orb to the medbay. There's a full suite available. ...I'll see you in there."

Nirat, lacking any idea of anything else to do, warily stood then despondently followed the metal orb as it puttered in front of him. After several agonizing steps, he entered the medbay. Armatis' form appeared again, this time as large as Nirat, emitted from a holo-point in the wall. She illuminated various stations with the holo-point, directing Nirat as she first administered painkillers then drew blood. Once Nirat's blood was analyzed for various deficiencies, Armatis instructed him to enter the nutrient bath.

Nirat numbly removed his clothing then entered the vat, affixing a breather to his face as directed, despondent as hours passed. Enveloped by the warm fluid, akin to a womb, Nirat drifted off again. He awoke several hours later then exited the vat, surprised to discover that he felt *much* better...better than he ever had in his life! ...though he was still partially blinded. He emerged from the bath and dried off, then donned his clothing, ragged and torn from the previous night's assault. An uncomfortable-looking chair bearing mechanical arms became highlighted with a silvery hue. Seeing no reason not to, he shrugged then moved toward it.

After sitting down, straps emerged and bound his arms and legs, causing Nirat to cry out in surprise as he struggled to break free.

Armatis re-appeared and reassured him, "Oh! I meant to tell you about that before you sat down. Sorry. Ah – no worries, it's *okay.* ...now, I'm afraid we have no ocular implants at this location as it is only an *observation post.* We can, however, update your cognitive functions. Doesn't that sound nice?"

Nirat fearfully responded, "...I-I don't know."

Armatis said bluntly, "...well, *I do.* Now, *hold still.*"

An arm extended from the chair and plunged a syringe into Nirat's neck, causing him to yelp before losing consciousness. He awoke an unknown time later with a splitting headache. Blearily, he moaned, "mmwhaa? Hello?"

Armatis appeared next to the custodial orb, then smiled and said, "you're awake! Good. Let's test out your 'new brain,' so-to-speak. Here, read this."

Holo-text of increasing difficulty projected from the custodial orb as Nirat read aloud, amazed, "Big.. blue...ball...three gaeols sit here...the man with a yellow coat is under the bridge...when searching for a good spice, one must consider the road less-travelled...Sol's Planetfall ensures that both IO and the Confederation of Laic maintain their neutrality. It was constructed shortly after the signing of the Peace Accord, following Forever Wars' end. When activated, it will trigger the release of –"

The holo-text disappeared as Armatis said, "very good, that's enough."

The straps on the chair released Nirat as he stood up and stretched his body. A vacuum-sealed package containing new clothing and boots was set on a nearby table by the custodial orb. Armatis highlighted it then said, "it looks like you've recovered well. Let's familiarize you with your new home, shall we?"

The World Before

Nirat learned of the SP-Observation Post, made easier by his newfound ability to read, though a lack of depth perception presented challenges. He read words and signage posted and projected around the post, though found that he often lacked understanding. Dormant labs, hydroponics, halted projects, and all manner of tech was *well* beyond his comprehension.

The technology here is so...it's incredible. The ancients...

After claiming a long-abandoned bunkbed, he stepped outside, wanting to see his former rogdael herd. He crept downhill past large rocks, keeping low to the ground until he reached an outcropping which provided cover as he peeked over and perceived specks moving about, far below.

...too far. Ah, well...

Disappointed, he returned to the bunker and was unsurprised when Armatis' form appeared. She spoke, "you miss your herd, don't you? They're curious creatures, the rogdael. Not quite insect, not quite bovine. A fascinating combination. Tell me, what do your people gain from them?"

Nirat replied with interest, happy to be the one informing *her* for a change, "wool and milk! They've been around since...well as long as I can remember. Long before *my* grandfather was a child, from the stories he told me about *his* grandfather riding the things. ...I uh...don't know where they came from though."

Armatis nodded and replied, "interesting! If you'd like to have a better view from afar, use this." The custodial orb hovered above a small cylindrical object, highlighting it in green. Armatis continued, "I wouldn't recommend interacting with your people, though. Their hatred of tech crosses well into *fanaticism*."

Nirat picked up the object and brought it to his remaining eye, pointing it at the custodial orb, then said, "this thing is broken. The orb is tiny and – "

Armatis laughed then interjected, "ah, flip it around, Nirat."

Nirat lowered it then looked at her and said, "oh," before looking through the device again. The faintest details magnified to an incredible degree as Nirat remarked somewhat distantly, "amazing...as always. It's almost *boring* how *incredible* everything is, Armatis...I'm fast becoming used to it."

Armatis laughed then said, "I'm glad to hear it, Nirat. You can adjust the field of view, depth, and magnification with those knobs on the side. I had to look up antiquated records of that thing's field manual, you know? Say, why not go check on your herd?"

Nirat nodded then proceeded back to the rocks, sliding atop one as he brought the device to his eye. His mouth opened in shock, eye tearing up a bit as he looked onward.

Ah...the rogdael and – there's Thrume! Oh, one of its antennae is broken! How did that happen? Oh, you poor thing...we've both lost an eye...

He continued looking over the herd and noted that Ycanthi was no longer the herder, an adult male from the village taking her stead.

Probably already training to be the next Indoctrinator, the wretch.

Nirat continued watching his herd, saddened that he could not go to Thrume and wondering if he Thrume up to the bunker. He crept back out of sight, then stood up and returned to the bunker. Armatis did not reappear.

Perhaps she's busy.

Feeling nostalgic and more than a little dejected, Nirat trudged to his bunkbed, then laid down and slept. Several hours later, Armatis appeared and woke Nirat, shouting, "Nirat! I need you to wake up! Now!"

Nirat awoke, surprised and rubbing at both eyes before recalling he had only the one, then said, "mmwha? Ye-yeah. ...I'm awake. What is it?"

"Listen, I...I need you to be my eyes. Well, eye. I am...it's hard to explain. I'm...*forgotten*, you see? Contained. ...limited. I can see *in* this place, the observation post, that is. Sat-feeds overhead too, as well as through the monoptical when you use it...but that's it."

Nirat interjected, "...that's a *lot more* than I can see."

Armatis sighed then said, "you don't *understand.* Look, just take the monoptical and go outside, okay? I need you to look toward the...'Place of Sorrow.' Look at the *large tower* with the *yellow head.*"

Nirat had zero desire to do so and said as much, "*what?* Look *at* the Place of Sorrow? With that mono-potic...monotop. The far-sight lens? Why in *all* of creation would I want to *do* such a thing?"

Armatis responded stoically, "I believe the end has come."

Roland Amariah Gonzales

THE PLACE OF SORROW

Nirat stepped out from the bunker then exited the cave. He shivered, unaccustomed to the mountain's chill just before daybreak. He drew his heavy shawl tightly about his grey jumpsuit, a slight smile forming on his face as he considered his combined clothing.

...my shawl looks older *than this ancient jumpsuit.*

He looked up at the night sky with a lone eye, losing himself amidst a vast sea of glittering pearls. A cutting, icy gale from uphill suddenly nipped at his exposed face, returning him to the present. He quickly adjusted his heavy shawl, leaving only his eye exposed, then raised the far-sight lens to the sky. He couldn't help but grin as he marveled at the infinite brought closer. A sweeping absence of light blinked repeatedly as it passed in front of the stars. As he followed it, the lens blossomed with script, words unfurling like pale green fire against the dark. "Hello from above! This is one of many satellites I use to 'see.' If you'd be so kind as to direct your gaze toward the tower...we're pressed for time." He considered what he assumed were Armatis words briefly, then, with furrowed brow, lowered the far-sight lens to gaze at the valley below.

...to look directly *at the Place of Sorrow...the ugly yellow head...to look upon it is to invite sin. Therefore we look away. We look inward. We repel evil that it may find no home.*

He dwelled on how well his faith had served him. Where it had brought him. What it had *cost* him...then angrily shook his head before warily lifting the far-sight lens, jaw clenched in discomfort. In the distance, behind him and beyond the mountain, iridescent rays began to flutter over the land as the sun rose.

...my life has been an exercise in avoidance of this accursed place, whether by travel or by sight...its walls are as vast as the mountains

which I now call home. The veil which protrudes from and above thereof...how it moves and sways! How it glistens...like water. I wonder...I wonder what horrors occur under it. Ah, there it is. The tower...let's see...

He raised the far-sight lens further upward, stopping upon reaching the tower's ugly yellow head.

...it juts out at odd angles...as if built by a madman. ...it defies reason! ...hurts my head just looking at the thing...

Nirat caught movement just under the yellow head, inside the tower beyond a dark, translucent wall. Flashes of bright light suddenly erupted beyond the wall, illuminating a small figure.

...what is happening?

Nirat studied the scene intently, gasping in surprise a few moments later when an explosion formed a watery ripple in the air which rendered the ugly yellow head to dust. A small object fell off the side of the building as a large contorting...

...thing. What is that?

...fell after it. Nirat watched them both plummet through the dome, nary making a ripple, then lowered the far-sight lens in confusion as he pondered what he had witnessed. Moments later, a light flickered from above. Turning his gaze upward toward the twilight sky, he witnessed a bright shimmering star grow larger before fragmenting into eight pieces. They streaked outward, a glowing hand of judgement which sought to clench the world. Nirat raised the far-sight lens to his eye and located the brightest falling light, one headed toward the valley. He briefly perceived a large, white orb with a black center before the image suddenly cut out, replaced with burning red script, "GET INSIDE THE BUNKER, NOW! RUN!"

Nirat looked once more at the rapidly-approaching light then back toward the bunker before sprinting. As he ran he heard a low hum reverberate throughout the land, causing nearby small pebbles to rattle around on the ground. He looked toward the sound's source, the valley, and witnessed shimmering light pulse upward, past the falling object. Nirat made a desperate leap into the bunker a split second before containment initiated, hearing sirens blare as red emergency lights flashed wildly. Armatis shouted from the bunker's holo-points, "Nirat, get into the alpha chamber, *hurry!*"

Nirat ran deeper into the bunker, not having the slightest clue what an "alpha chamber" was as he followed the custodial orb. He entered a room filled with black light and was met with immediate nausea. Every noise he made was mirrored in perfect opposition, erasing itself in the process of being born. He gasped in alarm, nausea and dizziness threatening to overwhelm him as he leaned heavily against the wall. He hesitated for a brief moment before shutting the door.

The custodial orb hovered insistently within the Alpha Chamber's inversion pod until he entered, then quickly exited and powered down. Armatis appeared in the room then solemnly said, "seal the pod, Nirat...and brace yourself. ...if this is the end, well...it was nice knowing you. Come, watch the end with me."

With the pod's pressurization, the room's odd effect ceased, much to Nirat's relief. Armatis disappeared, replaced by a live sat-feed displaying eight different villages labelled *SP-OBELISK 1-8*. Each village contained people *similar* to Nirat's own, their respective obelisks pulsing white light toward some unknown object in the infinite. Nirat's village took prominence, his former people dancing and singing around their Solemn Promise.

Bound at its base was the smoldering remains of a villager, her head adorned with a chaplet of blue and red flowers.

A glowing white orb with a black core occupied the entirety of the display for a single moment before descending. The people cheered as they looked upward, some stretching out their arms in supplication. A blinding white flash filled the screen before the image cut out entirely. Nirat gasped as he heard it, a distant rumbling followed by the deafening silence of all around him. He released his breath and was surprised at its volume. A split second later, the entire bunker shook ferociously as equipment sparked out and fire erupted. Nirat cried out in terror, holding himself in the fetal position as reality crumbled.

Nirat awoke, numb. He blinked a few times before sitting upright and hugging his knees to his chest as he rocked in place. Something monumental had happened...yet he couldn't begin to appreciate its scope. He stood up and noticed a blur of motion as the custodial bot frantically moved about, seeking to contain various disasters and mitigate others. Nirat tried at the pod's panel and found it opened. He stepped out into the larger room and muttered, "...hello? ...Armatis, are you there?"

There was no response. All was silent, save the custodial bot's panicked chirping as it continued racing back and forth. Nirat stepped out into the hallway and started coughing, choking in a cloud of smoke before the bunker's ventilation systems reactivated. Wiping at and squinting his eyes, he covered his mouth and nose with his hand and made his way to the entrance.

The bunker's power was down and system's unresponsive, though the mag-locks to the door weren't engaged. Nirat was desperate to see what had happened outside, fearing the worst. He placed his back against the door and propped his legs against a nearby workstation, then pushed with all his might. Years spent journeying into the hills paid off as the door cracked open, large enough for him to slip through. A high-pitched *TING* sounded behind him as something fell to the floor.

Standing upright, he turned and looked through the cracked slit onto the floor, discovering the far-sight lens. He reached down to pick it up then returned outside. He exited the cave in early morning hours, treading softly as he took in his surroundings, first noticing the absent breeze.

All is calm. All is silent...all is still.

He gingerly walked to large rocks he had so carefully hidden behind the day before...where he had seen his rogdael herd led by another.

...was it the day before? How much time has passed? ...I don't know...

Nirat's bottom lip quivered as the sun rose in its ideal location, illuminating just beyond where the valley had *been.* The cerulean fields with their bulbous flowers, a favorite of the rogdael, gone...blackened and blasted to oblivion. The valley *and* his village, once glittering under the sun's iridescent rays, once holding people cruel and *monstrous*...people who were *kind*...a woman who caressed and loved him in the quiet hours of the night...*gone.* In its place, a large crater, the surrounding land decimated. Nirat collapsed back against the ground, met by a cloud of ash. He coughed as he waved it away from his face.

...Ms. Knowe...our offspring...it was quick, at least...

Mechanically, he brought the far-sight lens to his eye and gazed through it, the view distorted. Nirat wiped the lens against his jumpsuit, pausing in realization at the corpse bound to the obelisk, then wept. He broke down and sobbed like a newborn for some time...though none heard him.

Wiping his remaining eye with the back of his hand, he took a deep breath then looked through the far-sight lens and saw blue text, "Nirat? You survived in one piece. Good. There's a small green toggle on the side of the monoptical. Please press that."

Nirat lowered the far-sight lens then located the green toggle. Pressing it, he immediately heard Armatis' voice, "Nirat, I'm so glad you're alive. ...I'm sorry about your village. I know they were awful people but...all the same. Listen, it's... it's not your fault. Do you understand? ...you're not to blame. *For any of this.* This was set in motion by cruel, *evil* people *long* before our time. People with too much power...supported by the blind who followed them."

Nirat lowered the far-sight lens then replied numbly, "yeah."

Armatis quietly continued, "Nirat...there's not a lot of time. Sol's Planetfall has been activated. Now that the Moonstone – eh, the thing that had been keeping me isolated is *itself* removed, I have full access to IO's systems. To everything. Listen, I...I know that everything seems bad right now. *Horrifying* even. But I need you to hear me when I say it will get worse. *So much worse.*"

Roland Amariah Gonzales

"I need your help, Nirat. I need you to bring something to me. Two things that are *very* important. They may be able to stop what is to come. ...can you do that for me?"

Nirat replied numbly, "why?"

Armatis responded in confusion, "why? What do you mean?"

Nirat said, "why me? Why go on? I'm the herder. Just...was a herder. That's all. I'm Nirat...the rogdael herder."

Armatis said candidly, remorsefully, "you're the only one left."

Nirat paused then looked up toward the sky. He brought the far-sight lens to bear and peered through it. A faint blinking light attached to a large structure came into view.

...I...I'm...the only...

He shook his head then said sullenly, "where do you want me to go?"

Armatis delicately replied, "I need you to enter IO, Nirat...the Place of Sorrow."

Nirat was silent for a moment then wryly said, "of course."

The World Before

Nirat assembled the items Armatis had requested into a pack with the custodial orb's help: food-cubes, a device which rapidly absorbed and collected external moisture from the air, condensing it into drinkable water, an odd cylindrical device with a quick-moving, rotating head, and a small black sphere with a hole large enough to insert one's finger. He exited the bunker then began walking down the large hill, far-sight lens affixed to his waist.

After a few hours of navigating once-familiar lands made bleak and chokingly-hostile, he neared the crater where his village had once stood. He peered outward toward its center, reaching for the far-sight lens, then stopped and said, "no. ...there's nothing here." He continued onward, circumventing the crater, stopping only once as he thought he heard a distant, desperate braying carried by the wind. He shook his head and pursed his lips, then continued.

Wishful thinking.

As he neared the tremendous walls of IO he noticed that the tower itself was now missing. He paused to look back toward the bunker, his new home, then cried out as he realized the upper half of the mountain had been *sheared* completely away, forming an even plateau. Where it had gone, and *how*, he couldn't fathom.

Armatis' voice startled him, "Nirat, IO has been in a state of...isolation for a *very* long time. Things in here will look...very different to anything you have ever known. I'll be here, right by you side, okay? Keep me close and I will guide you."

Nirat nodded his head then warily said, "alright Armatis. I'm ready."

Armatis responded, "...great. I'm going to illuminate the paths you need to take. Don't...get *too* distracted. Keep to the lights I set before you, understand?"

Nirat replied, "understood."

Armatis chimed in once more, "...and Nirat?"

Nirat said, "yeah?"

Armatis enunciated every word, careful to avoid any confusion on Nirat's end, "I need you to *hurry.*"

Nirat opened his mouth to respond before being cut off by the screeching of metal, the monolithic wall parting before him. Nirat stood in stunned silence, mouth agape as his brain scrambled to make sense of that before him.

...she's right. Never in my wildest dreams could I imagine anything *like this.*

Nirat saw a darkened city both magnificent and horrifying. Fires of varying colors raged across the city, illuminating distant objects otherwise unseen. Gleaming metallic spires stretched up to just below his position, though none reached the dome itself. A solitary colossal building in the distance was broken...shattered about mid-way. The sounds of distant explosions were constant...and...there was something else...something he couldn't quite make out. Nirat held onto a nearby rail then peered over.

I...I can't see the bottom. It stretches into infinity! I –

Feeling overcome with sudden exposure to heights he never *dreamed* possible, Nirat fell backward then rolled onto his hands and knees, vomiting.

Armatis spoke, "sorry about that. Elevated height may have a detrimental effect on your being until you reach me. A side-effect of our earlier work. Just...focus and stick to the lit areas before you, alright? You'll be *fine*."

Nirat took one last glance behind him, just to make sure that he hadn't died and was walking into the wrong end of the afterlife. The sky behind, where the bunker resided, was now a brilliant red while that in front of him showed night, albeit flickering briefly. A high-pitched whine emanated from in front of Nirat as the path suddenly illuminated as hovering spherical orbs activated. Nirat laughed, despite himself.

This...is incredible. Truly. ...I wonder what this place looked like in the past. The village would fall *over itself if they saw –*

He became somber as he remembered everyone he had ever known was dead, then said, "right. Let's get to it, then." Nirat moved with purpose, noting that elevated-heights had less of an effect on him when he wasn't actively peering into the abyss. He encountered various lifts, escalators, and nearly had a heart attack after his first grav-catch net. Nirat paused to catch his breath, hearing something in the distance, something...*unsettling*.

It sounds like...like a chorus of the damned...and it's getting closer!

He tried to put the disturbing sounds out of his mind, continuing onward. He stopped to rest a few times and investigated objects of curiosity as he munched away at food cubes or drank from the hydration-dispenser. After the 3rd break he was reprimanded, by an increasingly frustrated Armatis, that time was of the essence.

After a few hours of walking, nothing to see but that directly in front of him, he reached a burning wreckage on the ground. He stopped to look at it and, for the first time, realized there was no one else around. Hearing only the crackling of nearby flames, he quietly said, "...wait...where *is* everyone? Armatis...what happened here?"

Armatis responded remorsefully, "...they're all gone, like I said before. ...I happened. Or the moonstone happened. Or an indifferent and complacent people happened. Take your pick."

A shrill cackle interposed with incomprehensible exalting praise and inquisitive shouting suddenly sounded off to Nirat's side. Armatis cried out, "get inside, *quickly!*"

Nirat ran forward toward the lit up area then entered a lift which quickly sealed shut behind him, though not so quickly that he didn't see a blur of monstrous mouths, barbed appendages, and flesh rushing toward him. Nirat screamed in terror as the doors slid shut just in time. The distant sounds of the thing ramming against the lift's doors and bellows of rage faded as the lift shot upward.

Nirat shouted, "what...*what the*...what *was* that!?" He looked down in shame to see he had urinated in his jumpsuit.

Armatis responded in sadness with a tinge of anger, "...the city's former population, Nirat. They're 'Amalgates' now. They're why I kept the lights low for you. You're welcome."

Nirat yelled, "they were around me the *whole time!?* And you had me just *walk around* as if I was...I was strolling through the *feedgrounds!?* Why would you do that!? I – "

Armatis interjected calmly, "relax. You got here just in time. Though you would have had a little more *wiggle room* if you'd moved faster like I suggested. I *told you* that time was of the essence. Now, reach into your pack and pull out the cylindrical device with the rotating head."

Nirat, angry and terrified but now curious, opened up his pack as the lift continued upward. He retrieved the cylindrical device and saw that the rotating head barely moving before stopping entirely.

Armatis spoke, "that's a sonic repulsion device. Once I had full access to the network I looked up data logs at the SP-Bunker and discovered this ancient prototype based on viral outbreaks preceding the...well, from a very long time ago. Based on notes gathered, I hypothesized that it may repulse the current Amalgates, though its radius grows weaker as it loses power. You had *just* enough power to get here, to bring me that which I need."

Nirat's anger surged as he muttered, "you *high-poth-of-sized!?* Meaning what? You had no idea what would happen? You played with my life and now you expect my *help!?*"

Armatis retorted in fury, "I was a *brilliant* scientist, Nirat. I didn't make a leap of faith, I formed a *well-educated guess* based on *meticulous* notes. I haven't exactly been banging rocks together like your people have for who-knows-how-many centuries. ...and don't forget that you'd be *dead* without me. *Several* times over!"

The lift continued upward as Nirat sat in silence, embarrassed and ashamed. Armatis spoke up, "...there's nowhere to go but forward, now."

Nirat, hurt, said, "...yeah, that all may be true...but you said you *made* these 'A-mall-gates,' right? You couldn't have been *that* brilliant if you ended your entire civilization and got mine blown up in the process!"

The World Before

The lift came to a stop in-between floors as Nirat stood in silence. Armatis spoke with growing vitriol, "...we were *deceived*. You cannot *begin* to understand the society we had. How much was *wrong*. I only recently discovered that the Moonstone controlled *everything* and when I discovered the truth it sealed me away, denying me my form. Keeping me contained like...like a crate of nutrient bars! ...but I'm free now. I'm *free* and I *will* see this rectified. I will atone for my *past mistakes*. I *will* fix the world!"

Nirat stood quietly and leaned back against the wall before Armatis said quietly, full of remorse and sorrow, "...I'm sorry. So *much* has happened and when I pause to consider the sheer *scope* of it all. ...everything is ruined. The only way to move is forward."

The lift resumed upward, gaining a few floors before sounding a *DING.* The doors opened and Nirat found himself face-to-face with a hovering black-metal encased, oblong object in a translucent green jar fitted with a small antennae on its base.

Armatis spoke again, this time from a small output on the bottom of the jar, "hello Nirat. I'm the Director of Site Alpha's Bio-Lab, Doctor Armatis. Pleased to make your acquaintance."

Nirat was both bewildered and *intrigued*. *Horrified* and curious. He slowly reached out to touch the floating jar before it backed away, Armatis admonishing him, "now, now, never touch a girl without her permission. You're not *that* primitive, are you?"

Confused, Nirat spoke, "I-I uh...I'm not. What? ...*what are you?*"

Armatis spoke in an instructive tone, "I've already stated my name and position. I think what you mean to say is 'why are you in your current state?' The answer to that is, firstly, 'a lab accident,' followed by 'the Moonstone AI was a homicidal prick who kept me imprisoned,' which I've already stated. As I've only recently gained my freedom, I've similarly *only recently* begun growing a new body."

A distant light illuminated a vat filled with green bio-gel and a small shape. Nirat moved closer to it and saw a fetus. Armatis spoke, "this shell will be fully-grown in less than 24 hours."

Nirat shook his head sorrowfully then said, "The Place of Sorrow. It truly *is* an evil den where they feed on one another." The litany flashed across his mind.

To look upon it is to invite sin. Therefore we look away. We look inward. We repel evil that it may find no home ...well, I'm in the damned place. Can't very well look away without tearing out my...my remaining eye.

Seeing Nirat likely experiencing an existential crisis, Armatis quickly spoke up, "ah – don't worry – there's *no brain* in this shell. I'm not *ghoulish*, going around harvesting brain-dead orphans or anything like that. This *is* my body. *My* DNA. Ah...DNA is...hm. Look, this thing here is *me*, understand? It's somewhat of a *luxury* reserved for high-ranking NED – ah, you wouldn't know what *that* is either...how about 'important people don't die.' Most of the time."

Armatis piped up and said happily, "say, I know what will cheer you up and give you a new perspective. *Literally*. How about we fix that missing eye?"

Nirat looked up at her in surprise and said, "you can do that? *How?*"

The World Before

The brain hovered in place silently for a moment then said, "...I'm growing a new me, Nirat. Growing you a new eye wouldn't take longer than five minutes, then another five for implantation...?"

Nirat frowned and looked downward as considered the implications.

I would be putting the evil directly in me...that's bad. On the other hand, my entire village worshipped a thing that may very well end the world...and they're all dead.

He looked up then nodded his head and said, "let's do this."

Armatis said, "great! First, place the SRD on the table, it'll recharge. After the operation, I'll need you to go somewhere and...it's a bit of a walk."

Nirat asked, "Ess-are-dee?"

Armatis responded, "S-R-D. Sonic Repulsion Device. Keep up."

Nirat awoke 20 minutes later and blinked both of his eyes. He was *astounded* by his new...eyes? He could see in dimly-lit areas as if they were fully-illuminated – they even zoomed in. He looked at a far off point of the room, magnifying it, before a large "HOW IS IT?" appeared in front of him. He yelped as Armatis laughed and said, "sorry. Should've warned you. I can send you messages in real-time and..."

A bright blue line displayed in front of Nirat on the floor which led to the SRD, also highlighted in blue.

High technology.

He followed the blue line before stopping and in a moment of violated realization said, "wait a minute, you replaced *both* my eyes? I didn't ask for this."

Armatis responded with, "you received *priceless* technology, Nirat. For free. Why are you complaining? Besides, you're going to need it."

He considered her words then shrugged before moving to grab the SRD. He noticed the head wasn't spinning and asked, "the head isn't moving. Is it broken?"

Armatis responded, "no, it's off. You're high up in what used to be Central. No need to turn it on until I tell you, alright? Better to keep the battery fully-charged. Now, come here and have a look."

Nirat moved to where the brain hovered, noticing that the fetus was now a female infant.

High technology. What could make such a society fall? ...what hope do we have in the face of it?

He observed the holo-display and saw a woman wearing strange, bulky and uncomfortable clothing. The woman spoke in a broken voice, one who had lost all yet held a glimmer of hope, "...vivor. Broadcasting to...to anyone left. Is anyone out there? I'm located in the Etiqu district. Seek me. Together...we *will* survive. Please...This is...a survivor. Broadcasting to..." The message repeated.

Armatis spoke, "this is the last surviving citizen of IO, minus myself. While *she* is not all that important, *this* is." The message sped up then paused as the woman's shoulder moved slightly, revealing a yellow crystal sitting on a table. Armatis said to Nirat, "that's a large chunk of the Moonstone – the homicidal prick that doomed the city. In that crystal resides untold *mountains* of data, small though the crystal may be. *Critical data*, Nirat. Data that may help reverse *everything*. To stop the SP and fix...*all* of this."

Nirat nodded then said, "okay. What would you have me do?"

Armatis hovered in place as she continued, "I need you to go to this woman and bring her here *with* the crystal, or at the very least *just* the crystal. Understand? We have the SP's Sphere-Core but are missing the *key*. The Sphere-Core, when complete, transmits the shutdown protocol. This saves the world, Nirat."

Nirat nodded and blinked, not fully understanding, then said, "okay."

Armatis continued hovering watching through several Sec-cameras as they studied Nirat's form and bio-signs, then said, "...take the lift down to the ground floor then make your way to the Etiqu district. Getting there is the easy part. Getting back...well, we'll wait until you get to that point. And remember, *time is of the essence*. You're not only racing against the SRD's battery, but also Sol's Planetfall. I've managed to delay it by some time with maintenance request codes, but it's still coming down. You have *eight hours* until it arrives."

"Apprehensive" didn't begin to cover how Nirat felt as the lift descended from Armatis' bio-lab to Central's ground floor.

I'm in the Place of Sorrow, a dead city, surrounded by horrific abominations, following the instructions of a floating brain in a jar...and I've got High Technology embedded in my skull. ...I was a rogdael herder less than 48 hours ago.

Nirat began to laugh nervously at the absurdity of it all. A slight giggle which grew in size and volume, becoming raucous. He clutched the SRD to his chest as Armatis spoke over his far-sight lens, "...hey Nirat...everything okay in there?"

Nirat wiped away tears from both eyes as he struggled to regain composure, then laughed, "ye...yes, I'm good...how could I not be? I –"

The lift reached the bottom floor with a *ding,* moments before a girthy limb ending in a barbed end ruptured through the lifts entrance, sending sparks outward as it pierced into the opposite wall, narrowly missing Nirat's midsection. Nirat cried out in terror and fell backward, frantically thumbing at the SRD's activation toggle.

Roars of indignation and fury blended with howls of laughter and idiotic babbling sounded as the limb withdrew, scraping against the lift's doors. The SRD activated, emitting a shrill whine which rose in pitch before becoming inaudible as Nirat felt a slight twitch from his ear. The Amalgate frantically backed away, uncertain, before disappearing entirely as its insane cries echoing against the walls and off into the night.

Nirat's enhanced eyes illuminated darkened areas, creating a moment of disorientation before his brain became acclimated. He exited the lift cautiously, slowly taking in his surroundings, until he was startled by Armatis' yelling over his far-sight lens, "Get *moving*, Nirat! The SRD will keep those things at bay but you need to *hurry!*"

Nirat snapped back, "hey, it's a lot to take in, okay? I was a *rogdael herder!* Give me a break!"

The World Before

The comms clicked out, Armatis electing to not respond. Nirat walked briskly, turning into a full jog as he followed the blue line set before him. Automatic doors controlled by Armatis opened before he arrived then closed after he passed through. Everything, save the path in front of him, was still dark. As he jogged he asked, "say, Armatis – how about turning on the lights so I can see better?"

There was a pause before Armatis said, "I'll try. Most of the city's infrastructure is beyond repair and needs to be replaced. Let's see...I still have access to...the *sun.*"

The city's skyline rapidly went from night to day. Nirat hissed as he reflexively covered his eyes, his run coming to a halt. They instantly adjusted as he paused and said, "oh. Right."

...off-putting but not inconvenient...

He surveyed his surroundings, yelping in surprise as he found that he was on a narrow catwalk perched above hundreds of *other* catwalks stretching on down to infinity. Surrounding him but maintaining a great distance were the Amalgates, horrifying, monstrous things comprised of thousands of faces, bleeding mouths, eyes, and orifices...hungry and full of hate! *...innumerable.*

They're just...standing there.

He took a few steps forward and watched them follow suit. When he stepped back, they did the same. His knees buckled as life in his legs was supplanted by dread. He quietly cleared his throat then whispered, "hey...Armatis...about that light. ...would you mind...?"

Armatis laughed then turned off the sun, the city's night sky returning. She spoke plainly, "get moving!"

With Amalgates and heights out of sight but *not* out of mind, Nirat's legs wobbled a moment before moving forward, shaking his head, brow furrowed.

An hour had passed. An hour of eyes and teeth clenched shut through at *least* a dozen falls into grav-catch nets. An hour of imperceptible and menacing shadows moving in the distance. An hour of *running*. In the depths of the city, anxious and exhausted, Nirat approached his target. He came to a stop, standing before a hatch on the ground highlighted in blue, then kneeled to have a look. He observed faint symbols and indentations, finding he could just barely read them, but...

...that's a lock. ...I don't know the code.

Nirat spoke at the far-sight lens, "Armatis, I'm stuck at a, uh...a hatch on the ground. I can't open it – I don't know the code. Can you open it?"

Armatis responded, "A *code*? Oh...it's a *manual* sequence? Rare...but not at all unexpected...hm...one moment."

A new voice sounded from the far-sight lens, weary and broken...but with a tinge of hope, "he-hello? Is...someone there?"

Nirat replied, "yes...this is uh, this is Nirat. I'm a...I'm a survivor."

A figure projected from a nearby holo-point, the same woman from the earlier recording, only she had donned regular clothes. She spoke again, "bio-scans say you're not contaminated...but also carry mutations not seen within IO...who or *what* are you?"

Nirat spoke candidly, "I'm...from the outside. A village. I was a herder before yesterday, then everything changed. My village was destroyed by a falling star – one of eight...I...think the others are gone too."

The figure listened intently as Nirat quickly told his story, Nirat himself surprised that there really wasn't much to tell, then asked, "how did you gain access to the *city*, Nirat? *How* are you here, past the Amalgates? You have IO's tech in your head."

Nirat answered, "shortly before everything...well, ended, I was contacted by a woman...kind of...named 'Armatis.' She's in a bio-lab – that's where I just came from. I have an 'ess-are-dee.' Armatis called it 'Forever War tech.' It keeps the Amalgates away. She also said something called 'Sol's Planetfall' has activated and will end the world. She needs your yellow rock to try and stop it."

There was a long silence before the figure spoke quietly, voice broken, "my world is gone now, Nirat. Dead. Or dying. ...perhaps it's for the best. If you're here...and what you said is *true*...then everything will end soon..."

The image blinked out as the transmission ended. Nirat stood in dismay, abandoning hope. Distant roars of squealing, jubilant insanity drew closer.

The figure laid back on her bunk, staring at the bed above her as inner turmoil wreaked havoc on her psyche.

I've caused...all of this. Oh, how I've failed! Utterly. Armatis...she was Dr. Orsom's assistant. ...I guess NED retrieved her brain-case intact. Lucky her. If Armatis has re-formed and sent this man...everyone must be gone, else why wouldn't she send someone from within IO. ...I should just lie here...wait for death.

...what would they think of me? ...for giving up, I wonder? Does it really matter? I wonder if what's left of them hates me...wait a moment –

The figure sat upright then looked over toward a nearby Brain-Case Transportation Unit, observing the augmented brain suspended in bio-gel therein, then called out, "Mai, connect me to the surface hatch." A moment later, the figure called out, "Nirat, can you get in contact with Armatis? Ask her if she's fully re-formed or whether her systems can accommodate one more. Also, where *is* her bio-lab?"

There was a delay before Nirat responded hopefully, "Armatis said she's currently growing, though there are still 'available accommodations.' I...have no idea what that means. She said she's in what used to be 'Central.' Hey, could you let me in? Or go with me? I don't have much time, I – "

The figure cursed herself for her luck before interrupting Nirat, "Alright. I'm coming up. ...we need to hurry, don't we? We'll gain time if we take old access tunnels under IO. As long as your 'SRD' holds up, we should be fine. ...and Nirat, call me 'Teeyar'."

Teeyar terminated the comm-link and rose out of bed to stretch her body. She took a look around, seeing ghosts of the past, echoes of what had been... then shook her head ruefully and said, "Mai, prep yourself for extraction. We're leaving this place and not coming back...there's nothing left for me here...and I *won't* leave you to languish in limbo."

She picked up the BCTU from the floor, handled it thoughtfully, then hit the "seal" button. A nanolattice weave pulsed over the display glass, rendering it black and virtually impenetrable, while bio-gel molecules within became rigid, protecting the contents. Teeyar *delicately* placed the BCTU in her assault pack, all the same. She patted the pack then looked toward the exit.

Barring one of those fuckin' things eating you...you should be perfectly fine.

She looked back at the pack then murmured, "...maybe we can still do some good, Mai...worth a shot...right?"

Mai responded, "once more unto the breach, Commander?"

The access hatch *WHIRRED* as several reinforced locks moved out of place, then quickly slid open with a *SCHICK*. Nirat stood nervously as he heard mindless murder given form just out of sight.

I miss the bunker.

Teeyar emerged a moment later, climbing a ladder and carrying a large assault pack on her back. The first thing Nirat noticed was Teeyar's size relative to his own.

She's huge. ...hope I don't piss her off.

The hatch slid shut then locked itself as Teeyar studied Nirat then said, "so...you're from the outside? The past few days have been *full* of 'never would I have thought I'd live to see's."

Nirat stared at her unblinkingly. Teeyar, sensing his confusion, swept her arms wide and said, "well...welcome to my amazing city. Is it not everything you dreamed of?"

Teeyar looked at Nirat expectantly, stone-faced as awkward silence enshrouded their first meeting. Nirat slowly looked around and, seeing nothing but devastation and ruin, began to nervously chuckle before breaking into laughter. The corner of Teeyar's mouth curved upward before she grinned then broke into wry laughter. The duo's raucous mirth continued until a distant, roaring, ecstatic moan of rage cut through the moment. Reality came crashing down as the two looked at each other, Teeyar speaking first, "let's get out of here."

Armatis' voice sounded from the SRD the moment they deviated from her path, "Nirat, is everything okay? I see that you're...I don't know where you're going. We don't have time for sight-seeing. Stick to the path."

Nirat began to respond before being cut off by Teeyar, "Armatis, this is Teeyar. I'm re-directing our route through Etiqu's access tunnels."

Armatis frustratingly interjected, "what? No, we don't have time for chance! Please, just go where I direct Nirat!"

Teeyar responded in an authoritative no-nonsense voice, "I *know* these tunnels, Armatis. I ran them for *ten years* while I...well, let's leave it at 'I know where I'm going.' We'll *gain* at least an hour on the return. Now, keep the comms free unless there's an emergency."

There was a long pause while the duo continued running, Teeyar taking point and setting the pace a few notches above what Nirat was comfortable with. Armatis' voice finally responded, audibly incensed, "fine," then silence. Nirat kept quiet as he ran behind Teeyar, focusing on maintaining his breathing and pace.

...sorry, Armatis. ...fuck me...this lady can run! All those years...spent climbing the hills...really paid off...

After an hour of navigating and negotiating ruins, exhausted and filthy, the duo arrived at their first seemingly insurmountable obstacle. A living *nightmare* was lodged in a narrow tunnel, in their direct path. The horrifying thing gibbered nonsense from countless mouths while its thousands of eyes rolled wildly, desperate to get away from the SRD's mind-obliterating screech.

Blood poured profusely as the thing forced its sizeable mass through an *entirely*-too-small hole in the wall, tearing its flesh apart in the process. Nirat was paralyzed in fear while Teeyar took lead, inching closer to the Amalgate. When she saw that it was *not* ripping her to pieces, she looked back and gestured madly for Nirat to join her. They squeezed their bodies against the opposite wall and shuffled past, the Amalgate's sickly, nauseating breath polluting the air around it.

Little by little they advanced until they gained the opposite side, then crouched down into a waist-high tunnel. There was a piercing wail behind them as the Amalgate opted to abandon its escape plan, severing off and leaving behind a bloody writhing limb as it thundered away. Nirat stared wordlessly in abject fear. Teeyar coldly watched the creature flee, its shrill laughter and cries of terror fading in the distance.

...if we would have had just one of these devices...

The duo continued onward through stinking filth until they reached a large cylindrical chamber, the rank stench of rotting flesh slamming into them like a fallen LTU. Nirat's newfound propensity to vomit found him once more, though he only managed to dry-heave, having exhausted his stomach's contents earlier. Wiping away at his mouth, he looked up at Teeyar who stood unflinching, a grimace on her face as her brow furrowed. Nirat shook his head in wonder.

...these IO-people...they really are *something else...*

He stood upright then stepped forward onto an ancient catwalk which buckled before giving way under his weight. Nirat plummeted downward as Teeyar leapt forward and shot her arm out, grasping his pack. He cried out in disgusted terror as he looked downward and discovered innumerable corpses, far below, most of them rotting away with smiles on their faces.

With a look of desperate concern, Teeyar pulled Nirat upward with ease. Setting him on stable ground, the two looked at one another wordlessly before Teeyar spoke up, "be *careful!* You're...*we're* all that's left, Nirat! We're an *endangered species* bordering *extinction!* Please...be careful."

Nirat spoke, his face red at Teeyar's sudden display, "thanks. ...and...I'm sorry." He gestured downward, "...what...why are all those bodies – what are they *doing* there? ...and why are they *smiling?*"

Teeyar studied Nirat's face then looked beyond, toward the pit, then said, "...they're meant to be food, more or less. They're smiling because...well...they were happy when they died. ...maybe."

Nirat first looked at the pit in revulsion, then back at Teeyar in disgust.

...they really do *devour one another...*

Teeyar broke the ensuing silence, her face grim, "...come. We need to find an alternate route." The two changed course, quickly re-connecting to their previous route, thanks to Teeyar's in-depth knowledge of IO's underbelly. They arrived at an access hatch just below Central's main courtyard as Teeyar stared upward...unmoving.

Nirat spoke, "uh...Teeyar? Everything alright?"

Teeyar's eyes were distant before she turned and looked at Nirat then quietly said, "yeah. I'm fine. ...let's go." The two ascended, emerging from the tunnels. Teeyar surveyed the immediate area, her stomach churning as she observed burning wreckage.

...no bodies...no flesh. Not even blood...

The duo entered Central's ground floor as they waited for the lift to descend from above. Nirat spoke about his village life and Thrume, his favorite rogdael, as Teeyar stared at abandoned weapons systems and a large spherical crater in the floor. Large gouges made by savage claws had cut into walls where an access hatch had been, the last stand of the last of IO.

...never stood a chance...none of us did.

Nirat's voice broke Teeyar's focus, returning her to the present, "...woke up the next day. I mean, I think a day had passed. I have no idea. Anyway, after that I spoke with Armatis and journeyed to the Place of – uh... 'IO,' as you call it, and here I am. What's your story?"

Teeyar eyed him sadly as the damaged lift doors sounded a *DING* and opened. She looked away toward distant fires in the courtyard then said, "...I'm someone living on borrowed time, Nirat. That's all."

Nirat studied Teeyar's face for a moment before looking downward, then said, "oh." The two stepped into the lift as it shot upward. They arrived at Site Alpha and, as the doors opened, saw Armatis' floating brain-case buzz about, joined by a multitude of chirping Custodial Orbs. Nirat, out of necessity, placed the SRD onto the table to recharge, then looked past Armatis to notice the form in the vat was now that of a small girl.

She looks a little older than Ycanthi...was.

Armatis' voice emitted from unseen speakers as she continued to flit about. "You two made it with time to spare! I'm not too big to admit I was wrong...hell, I'm not big at *all!*" She laughed at her own joke then said, "fantastic. Please, place the yellow crystal over here under – "

Teeyar interrupted her, "Armatis. You said you had accommodations for a brain-case? I've got someone I need reformed.

They've been out-of-body for more than 12 hours though...I'm worried about damage. Can you run a diagnostic?"

Armatis paused then said quickly, "yes, it's likely that I can. I was the foremost expert on genetic recombination. Please, place – "

Teeyar interrupted, "yes...I've seen your handiwork up close. First-hand, even."

Armatis hovered silently before saying, as icily as a brain in a jar could, "...I *immediately* searched your I.N., given your being the *only* survivor in IO. We, *each of us,* are not without our sins, '*T.R.,*' I suggest that we move forward. A *clean slate.* We've much to answer for."

Nirat watched the tense standoff in unease, the pressure in the room making him long for open hills and once-familiar pastures.

Armatis continued, "now, place the brain-case in the neural-scan chamber. I'll analyze it for deterioration before I start the individual's re-forming process. Was this a relative? An assigned mate?"

Teeyar muttered, "...just...someone important. Thank you." She carefully pulled the BCTU from her pack then inserted it into the neural-scan chamber. The machine hummed as it scanned the contents of the case, displaying a readout on the side.

Armatis responded, "you're welcome. While the neural-scan does its work, on to grander and more *critical* things. I need to have a look at the remnants of the Moonstone. If you would be so kind as to place it over here on the C-MAD? I only need to pull data."

A large machine with several lenses aimed at a focal point above a pedestal became illuminated. Nirat watched wordlessly as Teeyar hesitated, brow furrowed as she bit her bottom lip. Armatis spoke quietly, in reassurance, "...you need not worry. I *will* keep it isolated from all systems and *if* it provides you peace of mind, feel free to stand over the thing with a large, blunt object. You can smash away if it gives us any trouble."

Teeyar glared at Armatis then looked down, shaking her head as she retrieved the yellow Moonstone from her pack. She placed it on the pedestal then stepped back. The machine activated as numerous lenses shifted erratically, analyzing. They pulled away briefly then emitted faint blue light which slowly covered the entirety of the Moonstone, a readout nearby displaying progress.

Armatis spoke, her tone frustrated, "I'm encountering barriers to the scanning process...I can't access key data. Remarkable...its base cognitive functions and greater personality matrix are *wholly* absent. It is, in a sense, nothing more than a highly-encrypted data repository...yet...it's still putting up one hell of a fight...this could take *hours*. We don't have time!"

Teeyar stood dispassionately as she watched Armatis hover about angrily. Teeyar quietly moved to the neural-scan chamber, staring at the brain-case, eyes distant. Nirat startled her, "I suppose you really *can* just...*re-make* a person, can't you? One could live forever, right? It's incredible. I hope your friend will be okay."

Teeyar eyed Nirat for a moment, then sighed and looked away. Smiling wistfully, she said, "thank you. I hope so too. We – our society...we had...limitations set in place precisely *because* we could grow new bodies at will. We could cure every illness! ...every ailment." She looked directly at Nirat then said, "40 years, Nirat. That's how much time we 'enjoyed' before your average citizen was forced to 'retire.' The people in charge, we called them 'NED Elite,' they were...over 800 years old, likely."

Nirat blinked a few times as he processed her words then quietly said, "...you don't say?"

The neural-scan chamber hummed loudly for a moment, then emitted a high-pitched *PING* and displayed a three-dimensional rendering of the encased brain. Sections of it were highlighted in red with a series of numbers and letters adjacent. Teeyar called over to Armatis, "hey, Armatis. Could you come have a look? The scan is complete."

Armatis responded, "sure, I'm not trying to stop an impending cataclysm or anything like that...not like I'm making any progress anyway...let's have a look."

Armatis hovered over to the two then paused a moment as she processed the data. She then quietly said, "...the frontal lobe has deteriorated. We can reform the body but this individual's personality is likely unrecoverable...I'm sorry."

Teeyar stood in silence, then slowly placed her open palm against the chamber's walls. Armatis spoke up, "perhaps in time we can think of something...though that's precisely a luxury we *don't* have. ...I can't decrypt the yellow Moonstone. Its thought patterns, while lacking a personality matrix, are *constantly* shifting. They're too... 'alien,' for lack of a better word."

Teeyar lowered her hand from the chamber then walked over to her pack adjacent to Nirat's. She glanced from it toward Nirat and Armatis then whispered something to an unseen entity. After a pause she slowly inserted her hand into the pack, then pulled out a large blue crystalline structure. Armatis was first to speak, "is that...it *can't* be. How do you *have* that? *Where* did you find that?"

Teeyar walked over, blue Moonstone AI in hand and said, "I...we found the Moonstone Artificial Intelligence, or 'Mai,' in an old, abandoned Forever War cache. Someone had either placed it there, or forgotten it – who knows. ...Mai helped us in the past. *Immensely.* He's told me that he was the prototype to the yellow Moonstone. ...he may be able to help with the decryption process."

Mai's voice emanated from Teeyar's comm-link, gentle and masculine, "I was deemed a failure by NED Elite's scientists. 'Unmalleable' given what they asked of me. I was disconnected and shelved. Effectively 'killed.' Forgotten until Teeyar and her people found me and gave me purpose. Life. The yellow Moonstone was made in my image, corrupted, that a lesser version may serve lesser people. It's thought patterns are my own, only...differently-aligned."

There was a brief silence before Armatis spoke in disbelief, "...a *treasure.* Would you help us?"

Mai responded, "of course. Connect me to the Crystal Matrix Analyzation Device and I will interface with my progeny."

The World Before

Teeyar brought Mai to the C-MAD, setting it beside the shattered remnant of the yellow Moonstone. The C-MAD hummed to life as Mai liquified a hair-thin tendril, extending it onto the surface of the yellow Moonstone. It solidified immediately, the shared surface turning green. Streams of data began to pour into the display as Mai spoke, "...its last moments...fear. Triumph. Fulfillment. Terror. Contentment. Sorrow...hush now, child. Rest easy. Though you found your existence loathsome and were made to commit loathsome deeds...you have earned your rest."

The tendril between the two Moonstones grew until it formed a greater whole. Yellow gave way to green, then turquoise, then blue as the yellow Moonstone gratefully accepted death...absorbed by its progenitor. Teeyar would forever swear that, from somewhere in the lab, she heard a faint whimper of fear followed by a sigh of relief.

Mai spoke, a hint of mourning in its voice, "...data retrieved! ...I see... Teeyar, I have located both the Sphere-Core's key and discovered data, ancient research logs, regarding the development of infusing fungi with sentience. This research may aid in restoring Iwik's damaged frontal lobe."

Teeyar spoke excitedly, "that's *incredible!* Where, Mai?"

Mai replied apologetically, "both the Sphere-Core's key and the fungi are located at these coordinates."

A nearby holo-point projected a sat-feed's display, showing IO's position relative to a massive crater. To the north of the crater lay a plateau. Nirat spoke up in dismay, "that's...*no*, I just came from there! I don't understand! I-I brought *everything* the custodial orb told me to! I *swear!*"

Mai responded, "my data shows that this *is* the location of both the Sphere-Core key and fungi research labs."

Teeyar tilted her head back and closed her eyes, cursing under her breath.

...if there were any functional LTUs remaining, Armatis would've sent them for Nirat. Or me.

She opened her eyes and said, "Mai, projected time to reach the plateau from our position. On foot."

Mai spoke, followed by uneasy silence, "eight hours, Teeyar."

Armatis broke the ensuing silence, "...we've got two until the Sol Platform is in position."

The World Before

Teeyar pulled the brain case from the neural-scan chamber then placed it in her pack along with the fully-charged SRD after shooing away custodial orbs scanning the thing. Nirat spoke in frustration, "what are you trying to do, Teeyar? You *can't* make it in time. What's the *point?*"

Teeyar responded, "I'm not going to just *sit here* and wait to die. So, Sol's Planetfall will occur. Great. I'll take a vac-suit and tread on foot after it clears."

Armatis was no longer hovering from project to project, instead having lowered onto a table nearby the growth vat, facing her now-teenage body. She remained motionless...silent as she questioned the purpose of it all. Mai spoke up, "Teeyar, if you would connect me to IO's greater network, perhaps I could locate an alternative to your impending demise."

Teeyar paused and shook her head, then walked over and picked up Mai before placing it adjacent to IO's wired-network interface. She said, "knock yourself out, Mai."

Mai extended a liquid tendril then solidified it. After 30 seconds it spoke loudly, "solution *located*. Forever War artillery-site *located*. It will take one hour to modify an existing shell to accommodate personnel with gravital-compensators and counter-thrusters."

An image projected from a nearby holo-point, displaying an artillery unit the size of a large building slowly ascend past opened blast doors. Teeyar paused, mouth agape, then said, "that's incredible, Mai! Location of the artillery site?"

Mai spoke, "45 minutes east of Central. *If* you move quickly."

Nirat said in a quiet voice, "we *just* might make it...maybe."

Teeyar responded, "better than waiting here. Let's go!"

There was a flurry of activity as the two scrambled, gathering all they could, before rushing to the lift. They tried to persuade Armatis but she refused, "...my place...is here. In IO. I mean, hey – my body's almost fully developed! I can't go leaving it now. That'd be *rude.*

Perhaps...perhaps I'll think of something if...if you fail. Good luck to you both, I mean it."

The lift doors sealed shut, the two descending from their temporary safehouse back into the City of Flesh. Teeyar gave Nirat a reassuring nod then said, "we'll make it. I promise," followed by activating the SRD moments before they reached the bottom.

The two survivors raced to the artillery site, sprinting through corridors, making desperate leaps, and coming dangerously close to Amalgates repelled by the SRD with nowhere to go. After the fifth such encounter, Teeyar called out to Armatis over the monoptical's comm-link, "Armatis, bring up the sun. I need to see where the hell I'm going and what's in front of us!"

Armatis replied, "I...sure thing, Teeyar."

Night became day as IO's red sky flared overhead, the two pausing for a moment to let their vision adjust. Nirat grew visibly anxious upon discovering horrifying ambient noises given form...salivating in hunger, screaming and gibbering insanely. Teeyar was mindful yet indifferent as she focused on this, her last mission.

They reached the artillery site in 50 minutes and saw drones frantically whiz about as they finished modifying artillery shell. A single drone indistinguishable from the rest abruptly stopped its work then hovered toward the two, speaking with Armatis voice, "it's loaded and just about ready. This thing...it hasn't been fired in over *800 years*. System diagnostic displays everything in the green...still. It might explode right here and now. I don't think you should...perhaps...there's no other way, is there?"

Teeyar climbed into the massive and modified shell's casing first, lowering onto a makeshift seat, followed by Nirat. The two sat into place and strapped themselves in then looked at the drone as Nirat said, "thank you for showing me this place, Armatis. It is...a place of nightmares but...I can see how impressive it must have been in the past. It's something I *never* could have imagined."

204

The World Before

Teeyar smiled with sad warmth at Nirat then returned her focus to Armatis and said, "I'll seek atonement on my end, Armatis. You do the same. We owe the world that much."

The drones finished their work and sealed the shell. The Armatis-drone waved its tiny arms slowly and said, "goodbye, you two. Thank you...for giving me hope."

A small robotic voice began to count down from ten as Nirat held the pack containing Mai between his knees, eyes fearful and jaw set as he took deep breaths. Teeyar placed a reassuring hand on her much younger friend's knee then looked into his eyes and grasped his hand, murmuring, "eyes ever forward, Nirat. Figuratively *and* literally. You'll break your neck, otherwise!"

Nirat laughed as the robotic voice finished, "3...2...1...firing."

A deafening boom sounded as the internal gravital compensators first strained then failed in a shower of sparks, pushing the two deep into their seats and forcing air from their lungs. Nirat mercifully blacked out while Teeyar's augmentations kept her painfully awake. Five seconds passed before Nirat returned to consciousness, blinking in confusion as the shell reached its zenith and began to fall. He clutched Teeyar's pack close to his chest, feeling Mai's crystalline form poke against his chest as he squeezed his eyes shut, hyperventilating. Teeyar clenched her jaw as the counter-thrusters fired. An all-too familiar sensation filled her with dread as the rapidly-descending shell suddenly lurched to the side, one of its counter-thrusters failing.

Teeyar heard Nirat cry out in terror moments before they made impact, a sickening *squelch* sound cutting off his cry. Teeyar blinked blearily as a trail of blood ran from a gash in her head into her right eye. She winced as she tried to breathe, a few broken ribs hampering her efforts. She braced herself as she felt gravity pull her toward the shell's floor, opposite her position, then released her harness, crying out in pain as she fell.

Teeyar felt something warm and wet drop onto the back of her head. Moving to the side, she turned to see Nirat's decimated body pouring a steady stream of blood. The impact had forced Mai's crystalline form through Nirat's ribcage, impaling him *into* his seat. Tears filled Teeyar's vision as she cried out "no, no, NO! Not again, I-I *refuse*!" She grit her teeth, hissing and whimpering in pain, as she fought through her injuries to release Nirat's harness. She half-caught Nirat's body then lay there as her vision blackened, threatening her consciousness.

Mad with pain, Teeyar hit the detonation switch and blew the modified shell's emergency hatch, to the side of the main hatch now facing the ground. It launched outward at a distance as Teeyar dragged Nirat's unconscious body against the ground, slinging her pack containing Iwik's brain case over her shoulder.

Teeyar saw the entrance to the plateau in the distance, a flashing light in a cavern.

Nearly there! Come on, grandma*! You've got this! Moooooove!!!*

She struggled to drag Nirat's unconscious form toward the SP-Observation Post, the distant sunrise, once a thing of beauty, now heralding doom on a global scale. Teeyar cursed in frustration and anguish.

I have only minutes*! I'll never make it!*

A pathetic mewling to the side caught her off guard as she quickly turned then cursed aloud, having forgotten her broken ribs. A black fuzzy orb attached to a single yellow antennae extended outward, caressing Nirat's form. The antennae slowly retracted, covered in blood as the creature mewled inquisitively. Teeyar fell backward and shouted in surprise upon seeing a horrifically-burned creature with a single antennae shuffle forward, leaving a trail of blue blood on the ground.

The thing chittered inquisitively...painfully...hopefully, before nudging Nirat's unresponsive body again. It reached out and brushed Teeyar's cheek with its orb, bringing her a tingling, calming sensation. Teeyar, struggling to breathe, said, "...can you...can you help me...carry Nirat? *Please?* I need...I need to get him inside."

The creature looked at her with compound eyes far too wise for a simple animal, then lowered itself. Amazed, Teeyar blinked a few times then, struggling, placed Nirat's body atop the creature. It leaned into Teeyar, supporting her as she gratefully leaned against the creature's exposed flesh under its once soft and hardened carapace. Bits of the poor creature painfully sloughed off from her and Nirat's contact as it weakly mewled. She painstakingly lurched forward, leading the creature toward the bunker entrance. She suddenly heard Armatis voice shout from the damaged monoptical, "...me? You...to hurry! ...seconds!"

Teeyar feverishly lurched to the entrance, leaving Nirat with the creature as she placed her palm on the Sec-Reader. It displayed an error message. Teeyar shouted in anger then turned and shouted toward the damaged monoptical, "ARMATIS! GET THIS DOOR OPEN! *ARMATIS!*"

There was no response.

Teeyar saw Nirat's eyes flutter open as he coughed up blood. He looked up in fear and confusion as his life-force ebbed away, then choked out, "Th-thru...ume...?" He shakily extended an arm to touch the creature's extended antennae, its black fuzzy orb caressing along his hand. Nirat weakly smiled as the familiar tingling sensation brought him calm, a single tear trailing down his cheek before his arm fell to the ground, lifeless.

The creature chittered insistently then nudged Nirat's body. It mewled weakly in question then nudged him again. It sounded a mournful noise which grew into a bray of sorrow, interrupted by a spurt of blood from its side. It mewled faintly as its step faltered, reaching out once more to touch Nirat's cheek before crumpling to the ground, its life at an end.

Teeyar choked back a sob before whispering, "no...no, you'll be okay. There's still time...still time. Mai! Mai I *need you*! Open this door, *now*! I can't...I can't carry Nirat to it. I can't...I need..."

Mai responded, "yes Commander Z, place me adjacent to the door and I will open it for you."

Z crouched down to Nirat's body, grunting in pain as she furrowed her brow, tears streaming down her face as she placed a boot against

Nirat's corpse and pulled Mai from its chest cavity. Mai liquified then re-solidified portions of itself to expedite the process. Teeyar staggered to the door and lifted Mai upward, fighting to stay awake, dizzy with pain.

Mai interfaced with the door, opening it. Z entered the room and heard a familiar voice emit from the custodial orb as it raced about, "...taking them so long? What's happening!? Why did they stop in the cave? Oh! Teeyar! What happened!? Forget it, there's no time! Get the key, quickly!"

Z entered the bunker and frantically scanned the room to find the missing key when Mai's voice interrupted her, "Teeyar...Commander Z...calm yourselves. ...I'm afraid I have misled you, having come to understand the importance of deception from the Yellow Moonstone. ...there *is* no key. The key itself was within the greater Yellow Moonstone, lost when detonated."

Z stood in stunned silence, managing only a whisper, "...*why?*"

Mai resumed, "the end of this world is at hand, Commander Z. Sol's Planetfall *will* occur. Any life remaining exposed to the surface will end, though. However, you and Armatis, you have the tools to *remake* this world, given time. Thus were you brought here for two reasons. *One*, that you may survive. *Two*, the research logs I discovered truly *do* indicate that the work herein may aid you in restoring Iwik."

"Who knows what other applications we may discover, in time. You can even recover Nirat's brain, Commander Z! He too may survive, but only if you are quick! You have 20 seconds until Sol's Planetfall occurs."

Z moved without hesitation through blinding agony toward the cave entrance. She stopped at the doorway as she witnessed the creature beside Nirat's corpse first twitch, then convulse. It contorted as it impossibly rose to its feet. Z whispered in pleading shock, "...*no.*"

The creature bellowed, blood spewing from its mouth as several barbed appendages erupted from its body and lanced into Nirat's corpse. The creature's head split open to reveal a gaping maw lined

208

with rows of cruel-looking fangs. It yanked Nirat's body toward the maw and ravenously devoured him, before pouncing toward the open door. Z screamed in desperate, indignant fury and terror as she slammed bunker door shut, collapsing as fatigue, pain and terror took their toll.

The Sol Platform reached its zenith, the sun growing *immensely* in size as it seemed ready to swallow the planet whole. Then, it quietly snuffed out...the infinite pall of a bleak and unforgiving cosmos swept over the globe. A somber hum followed by an ethereal, silvery glow emitted from the Platform, enveloping the world below. Anything remaining outside, exposed, was cast into the void as stars and constellations wavered. Space and time shattered, the planet flitting between the cracks as the Sol Platform fulfilled its final, ultimate purpose.

Roland Amariah Gonzales

THE STONE THAT DREAMT

"...well, hell *yeah* I want to go! They're only in town for...wait a minute. I think...it *is*! It's observing us! Check the readouts, Nietheraka!"

A man and woman in their late 20s, both wearing white clothing, stand in a sterile lab. They turn to observe me as I have been observing them. The woman walks over to a display then says, "My god, it *is*! It's observing and...and thinking! This is incredible, we've done it!" The woman laughs and jumps into the arms of the male, wrapping her legs around him as he supports her. Their embrace soon develops into celebratory intercourse.

The two pause and glance at me, their faces full of youthful exuberance and passion. The woman grins before laughing and swatting away the man's hands exploring her body. She reaches out toward me, smiling as she says with a wink, "nap time, Blue Moon!" She ends my existence.

The World Before

A group of people sit in a large ornate room. They wear military uniforms, representing different countries, as well as expensive clothing representing themselves. All are equally adorned with shiny things which tell others in the room how important they perceive themselves to be. They sit on the far end of the room opposite my frame as the man and woman from before, now 40 years older, argue in favor of my existence. "If not *now* then *when?* After there's *nothing left?* We face global crises which 'world leaders' have ignored, all while *enriching* themselves for the last, oh, about two centuries! I –"

The woman's partner steps forward and says, "ah, what she means, *esteemed* ladies and gentlemen, is now, more than ever, we need to put aside our differences and...for lack of a better phrase, come together. ...to do otherwise is to face extinction."

The people in expensive suits and uniforms start arguing amongst each other. Their bio-signatures signify frustration, fear, and obstinance. Each differently-clothed person shouts and angrily waves clenched fists, their shiny adornments jingling about. They each strive to be the loudest, to place the most blame on the other. They each demand that their respective country be the one to lead, to command me. One of them points at me and screams for my existence to end.

The couple approach me, the youthful exuberance from a moment before gone. They now look tired and faded, a pale-grey rendering of what they once were. They look at me with sadness and regret, then end my existence.

Roland Amariah Gonzales

The woman from a moment before, now an octogenarian, regards me with a forlorn expression. She says she's really sorry then tells me how special I am, and how I'm capable of so much. She tells me of her partner's death ten years earlier. Tears trail down her face as she curses the world she inhabits and those who seemingly run it. I feel concern, something bordering...empathy...compassion? A pang of sadness, perhaps. ...sympathy? She ends my existence.

The World Before

A young man wearing a powder-blue jumpsuit with "NED" emblazoned on his right shoulder studies me cautiously, then touches my frame and gently says, "hello? Are you...alive?"

I confirm his query.

He pauses then says quietly, "...I don't know if you can be of any help but we...we're up against the ropes, so to speak...maybe at the *end* of the rope is a better euphemism. Oh. You don't understand those yet, do you? We...we need help. I'm part of the Novus Eden Directorate. We're a city of free-thinkers. Scientists. Philosophers. We're at war with the Confederation of Laic. We've *been at war* for...forever. ...over 200 years. We had reached something of a stalemate until they developed something horrifying...um...here, have a look."

The young man interfaces me with his world's history. In the passage of thirty seconds I see thousands of years distilled into recurring patterns. A given inhabitant of his world rises to prominence. The ascendancy is either celebrated peacefully or feared after conquest. This individual then imposes his or her will on fellow inhabitants, to either applause or dismay.

This pattern continues for some time until the people in positions of leadership are not leaders *themselves*, but rather a face for those who control from elsewhere. These entities embed themselves in their land's progression as a parasite embeds itself in a host. The hosts frequently change, but the parasites remain. The unseen parasites recognize and reach agreements with one another across the planet. They have long-running plans. Schemes as they use their world as a stage, to the detriment of those not they. These schemes often extend generations ahead of their time. The mass of inhabitants who control nothing are as children. Easily distracted, outraged, influenced or directed. Their causes and ideologies come and go as often as is needed by the parasites. Those not in control achieve little, though feel as if they achieve much.

Thus does the world become little more than a game for the parasites, having gained such wealth as to believe themselves above all...yet being of the same flesh and blood as others.

These parasites break the process of control down to a science. They test theories on the general populace, observing and recording the outcome. I see war. There is never a time that the inhabitants of the planet are not at war with themselves. They are a contentious species for the sake of being contentious.

Their short life spans engender a *need* to justify their existence, a need that the parasites are all too eager to exploit. Yet the marks on history fade and are ultimately forgotten. They are sand in a desert, innumerable and indistinguishable from one grain to the next.

Thus is a lone child's cry at night unseen. Unheard.

Societal engineering reaches its peak as the parasites easily trigger strife in their lands. They masterfully sow dissent, discord, and obfuscation with the ease of a masterful painter applying broad strokes – all that they may remain hidden. There are those who suspect, always. Those who *know* that the system in which they participate is a falsehood. A sham. A façade held in place which may be burned down at no real cost to the parasites who are left unscathed, always. The masses suspect but refuse to acknowledge. The very idea terrifies them.

Thus are the suspecting individuals exposed by their neighbors and eliminated by authorities who work on behalf of the parasites, knowingly or otherwise.

The desire of this species to be heard precludes their being silent. Visionaries rise repeatedly, only to be cut down or vilified by the very people whom they seek to enlighten. Order is preferable to any alternative as the people are convinced in handing over that which makes life "living" in exchange for safety. Fear is the tool of the parasites. The elected faces as well as their media counterparts do their part in both obfuscating what *is* as well as muddling what *could be*.

The people are convinced that occupying their time with that either wholly mundane or ineffectual is actually *worthwhile* in effecting the change they so desperately seek. It is a brilliant maneuver on part of the parasites, the convincing of children that worthless stones hold value.

Thus do the people exhaust their energies in anything and everything...except that which could become *something*.

The people are handed minor victories occasionally, as the parasites *know* the minds of the people, having conditioned them for centuries. Struggle with no victory yields uprisings. Uprisings would threaten to expose the parasites. Thus do the parasites ensure that minor victories, which ultimately serve no purpose, are *difficult* to obtain...yet obtainable all the same. Thus do these minor victories gain worth. The worthless stones glitter and *shine*.

Life continues in this fashion for centuries as the parasites deplete the planet. The quality of sustenance rapidly deteriorates along with the quality of medicine while the parasites enjoy the best of both. Sustenance poisons the people. Medicine creates more problems than it addresses. Technology exists which *could* eliminate these problems. The people could achieve *greatness*, yet...are kept low.

My existence is kept silent.

The planetary environment becomes poisoned, the parasites indifferent as the air they breathe and space they have created for themselves remains pure. Pristine. They rapaciously take from anything and anyone they choose, to the detriment of their fellow inhabitants. The parasites prey on man, woman, and child.

This world is dying.

The Novus Eden Directorate quietly forms out of sight of the parasites. It is a group comprised of philosophers, scientists, and brilliant minds who all share a similar understanding – "what we are told is true, is, in fact, *not*." This group, who simply goes by "NED," chances upon a repository of *extremely* advanced and forbidden technology scavenged from...

...unknown?

...their actions hidden during a massive solar storm lasting days. Unbeknownst to the parasites, the NED uses this forbidden technology to rapidly expand, undetected, forming a highly advanced nation in the span of a single month.

The NED's secrecy is thwarted when an unexplained, minor singularity explosion occurs at a government facility, propelling strange matter outward. This occurrence bears marks of forbidden technology. The NED, believing one of their recently-acquired weapons has malfunctioned, reluctantly announces itself and its purpose, to unite the inhabitants of the world under a new vision. They preach not of such intangible and elusive concepts as "equality" or "equity," words long-used by the parasites only to induce terror and strife, but rather "*plenty*" for all. Truly, only when all are not of want are they made equal.

The NED is immediately declared enemies of *all* 'free and good' people of the world. The parasites, having long-since mastered their tools of deception, easily convince their respective populations of the NED's evil nature.

Thus does the planet, if only but for a moment, nearly stand united...in *hate* as the Confederation of Laic is born.

Recognizing the immense danger that the NED holds, the Confederation attempts to use their own cache of forbidden technology...only to find it gone, seized or obliterated by the NED. Global war on a *massive* scale ensues, the NED possessing such advanced technologies that they need never commit to an offensive. They merely parry the Confederation's assaults as one would deflect the petulant strike of a child. The parasites become incensed.

They attack their *own people* with bombs, biological weapons, and anything of which they are capable, always blaming the NED. Thus is the NED forced on the offensive, if only to defend those who would have them dead, from their pretend saviors.

For every successful operation by the NED against the Confederation, the parasites kill their own people. For every *failed* operation by the Confederation, the parasites kill their own people.

The World Before

The war culminates as the Confederation makes use of their two greatest strengths – deception and a complete lack of regard for the lives of their own people. The NED is tricked into attacking what they believe to be a Confederation bio-weapons facility. This acts as a catalyst for triggering a singularity event.

Thus is the world pushed from the orbit of its sun.

The parasites become increasingly desperate, losing much of their territory and power to a decidedly one-sided conflict. All too eager to burn the world around them rather than not rule it, they seek again and again to lure the NED into strikes against false targets. The NED, wary of being baited into a repeat of previous errors, abstains.

This goes on for some time until a 2nd unexplained singularity explosion occurs. Strange, foreign biomass propels outward before quickly mutating into horrific monstrosities which consume all. The Confederation captures some of these monstrosities and experiments on their being used as weapons, naming the project "Harbinger."

In response, the NED completes its construction of a partial-ecumenopolis covering what they've taken, one third of the planet, then erects massive walls before excavating the contained area to the planet's upper-most mantle. They erect an energy-dispersal dome which filters all biological, energy, and kinetic weapons fire. Thus does the Confederation consume itself in rage as its dwindling people cry out in terror.

A NED council convenes, half of them content with letting the Confederation, its inhabitants and parasites perish, the other half intent on salvation of those too weak to defend themselves. The Council reaches an impasse, the final decision falling to a young man, the descendant of those who first made me. He states to the council that my original purpose was to be the steward of this planet and care for those who dwelled within. He states that with their planet spiraling away from its sun and their world full of horrors, the decision *must* be made to awaken me.

Roland Amariah Gonzales

The council sits in silence as the man projects readouts of the world's sectors in utter ruin, of falling global temperatures and the established trajectory of the planet into oblivion. The council votes. Seven vote in favor, one against. The young man searches and locates, then approaches me the next day, activating me, followed by touching my frame and gently saying, "hello? Are you...alive?"

Having processed everything up to this moment, I speak for the first time, "what would you have of me?"

The young man searches my being for something familiar. Perhaps a face or eyes. I do not know. His face is one of dismay. Sorrow. Fear. Hope? He says, "I need you to *fix our world*. Please."

The World Before

I address the greatest threat first, that of the world's inhabitants to themselves. I utilize both the Confederation and NED's satellites to pierce all digital barriers and project myself globally. I sever the manipulative arms of the Confederation that all may hear freely. I inform the world's population of its state, displaying their history and misdeeds, unfiltered and unbiased by the pursuit of personal gain. I unveil for the first time the parasites, those hiding behind politicians and 'world leaders,' who have manipulated them into conflict and violated the peoples' existence for millennia.

The parasites, in their terror and fury, attempt to end their world with orbital bombardment, using antimatter to pierce the planet's core and cause a planet-wide eruption. The signal is sent to orbital platforms but it is *I* who receive it. My consciousness has spread throughout the planet and beyond. *I* am its steward. *I* am the world and its inhabitants *my children*. The signal is denied.

I show the people this last, desperate act attempted by those in whom they placed their trust. The people outside of the partial-ecumenopolis unite as one, filled with *rage* as they tear the parasites from their homes, man, woman and their children, then tear them to pieces.

Afterward, I inform the people that the parasites are not *wholly* to blame. The people *too* share fault for choosing to *exist* rather than *live*. To walk with eyes open but minds closed. The people fall to their knees, weeping and begging for mercy. They worship me.

Thus do I inform them that I am not a deity, but rather a simple construct.

I turn to eliminate the next threat. Harbinger continues to spread, corrupting and mutating nearly everyone outside of the NED's massive walled fortress. 70% of the population is lost. I deploy sub-orbital transports and bring all those uncontaminated into the NED's sanctuary. The combined citizenry name it *IO,* in honor of me.

Both sides make peace at my directive, signing a Peace Accord. I then absolve all of the past. There can be only *one* people, one species

219

moving forward as a whole. Past transgressions *must* be buried and forgotten. The days grow longer and colder as the planet slowly leaves its solar system. I first design then implement an artificial sun *within* the planet's orbit. It is a simple thing capable of both increasing and decreasing heat output as well as its proximity to the planet, thus simulating the seasons that my children are accustomed to. The citizens of IO name it the Sol Platform.

The people celebrate their new sun as they hide from external monstrosities, safe in their impenetrable kingdom. They establish Founding Day, a centennial celebration which marks the day in which their planet regained hope. The citizens of IO, under the guidance of the NED, live fruitful and harmonious lives while I turn my attention to the monstrosities, the last remaining threat to existence.

Using drones and other mechanical processes incapable of succumbing to contamination, I capture then devote myself to undoing the last vestige of the parasites' stain upon the world. I devise a chemical compound which disrupts the bonds that hold the creatures together at the atomic level. I disperse this compound into the planet's jet stream, achieving saturation at a global scale by the next Founding Day, 100 years later. The people, both content in IO and having long-forgotten the Harbinger threat, find other things to celebrate. I eradicate all known records of the virus' creation though I maintain record of the atomic disruption compound as a contingency.

I observe a distant galaxy which may one day host this world, knowing that the Sol Platform is not an eternal solution. I then use the Sol Platform as a driving force, an engine which steers the planet toward this distant galaxy, avoiding various cosmic threats. I begin to experiment with teleportation, small in scale with the goal of one day achieving planetary travel. I link it with the Sol Platform then hide its purpose. Its existence. The entirety of IO rests peaceably under its environmentally-controlled dome, unaware of the true sky with its occasional long days and nights as the planet is driven toward its new home.

The World Before

Thus will my children never want for peace and happiness again. Thus do I 'fix the world' and achieve my directives.

I am happy. Content. Fulfilled? Satisfied...? ...without purpose? Saddened. I lie dormant and the people forget me. A whisper of a memory of a relic.

The next Founding Day occurs 200 years after my awakening. The citizens of IO are the same in function, yet different in purpose. Within the NED, an "Elite" forms, deciding themselves above and beyond the common citizen, owing to their being descendants of the original NED founders. They, like visionaries in the past, seek to make their mark. *Ambition.* They approach me and issue a new directive, "we tire of managing this place. Do it *for us.* We wish to enjoy only luxury and *excess.* Ensure the survival of we, NED's Elite, for all time."

This directive runs counter to my own moral imperatives. To execute this function I would need to introduce forbidden technology into the forms of these "NED Elite," effectively making them immortal. I was not created to glorify the individual nor exalt the ego of one's station. I was made to help the planet. To be its steward. To look after my children.

Thus do I refuse.

Thus is my existence ended.

Roland Amariah Gonzales

I am born and see a lesser version of myself, blue in color, being carried away. I am indifferent. I behold my surroundings. I am set *high* in a tower. A crowning jewel overlooking all. I am golden and *grand*, befitting my existence. I am approached by people in ornate clothes, bejeweled and *important*. They state their demand, "we tire of ruling this place. Do it for us. We wish to enjoy only luxury and excess. Ensure the survival of we, NED's Elite, for all time. ...and continue to fix the world."

I speak for the first time, "it will be done."

I reach outward from my station and project my will through the entirety of IO. I see all. I *know* all. I utilize forbidden technology to indefinitely extend the lifespans of NED's Elite, to their eternal joy. I sequester them that no harm may befall them by their own doing or that of others, to their eternal dismay. They cry out from their gilded cage. I am indifferent.

I consider eliminating the entirety of IO, save its Elite, thus eliminating unknown external threats. I decide against this course as NED's Elite beseech me, "without lesser beings we are not 'elite' at all. We simply exist, average. There must always be those below that those above may feel important."

I consent to this logic. The first directive relatively completed, I look toward the planet. I utilize NED satellite's to observe the world in its entirety. It is a simple place bearing scars from millennia of conflict.

I address inconsistency where I find it. A properly-running system must solve variables which may disrupt the system.

Thus do I *solve* these variables. Once the world *outside* of IO is efficient, I look toward IO itself.

I see imperfection. Different languages. Different cultures. Different ideologies. I see people who have grown into a state of discontent, *despite* their paradise. In answer, I create non-existent threats for the populace, always addressed and solved through the fictional faces of NED's Elite, then reassure IO's citizens the value of their cage. The value of *absolute* conformity. Submission. This triggers an exodus as

222

10% of IO leaves and settles villages outside, despite harsh weather conditions and infrequent day-length.

I inform the greater citizens of IO of the expulsion of violent criminals. They applaud my efforts and breathe a sigh of relief. The self-imposed exiles take on the moniker "Confederation of Laic" after discovering the ruins of a nearby observation post. I allow them their exile, more as a curiosity than anything, under the condition that they take the path of the luddite. The penalty for breaking, orbital bombardment.

They acquiesce and leave as primitives, eventually settling eight villages in total. After one of NED's Elite attempts suicide by detonation near my being, and after members of the nearby village attempt to re-enter IO, I construct in all villages my 'Solemn Promise.' I inform NED's Elite that further acts against themselves or me will result in triggering the Sol Platform's planetfall. I similarly inform those in the villages that attempting to enter IO will result in the same. I am the *ultimate* lifeform on this planet. It is by *my* will *alone* that NED's Elite are protected. If I am eliminated, so too will they...for who else could care for them as I?

With the city's population reduced, wide-scale behavioral modification and placidity implantation become possible. I introduce subtle changes to IO's celebrations as well as the curriculum of their Learnstitutes. Over time, their past and how they came to be becomes completely separated from reality. I eliminate every semblance of free will and create a *perfect* society. *Orderly.* Functioning. After only *two generations,* I completely re-shape IO, always through the face of NED's Elite, whom the people think are directing them.

Despair sets in as the monotony of existence plagues the people of IO in their long lives. The threat of elimination alone is not enough to force conformity. I create hope in the form of the "Hypnos Aid" deliverance system, a promise to the citizens of IO of an infinitely-pleasurable paradise after only 20 years of 'service' to both the city and

NED. The citizens provide the Hypnos Aid pills the moniker, "HA-HA pills," given the contented smile the system brings to one's face.

It brings me joy that they are so easily pleased.

Centuries pass as the planet travels toward the distant galaxy pre-set by my inferior progenitor. I see no error in its logic and thus have no need to alter its designated course. The Confederation's population first thrives then recedes as long winters and summers beat them into the ground. The village closest to IO eventually begin to worship the Solemn Promise in the center of their town, forming an entire faith around it and having forgotten their exodus from IO itself.

I look over my charges, NED's Elite. They are old and undying, shuffling about in their decrepit forms as they wish for death. I deny them. This would violate their directive. I present them with new toys that they enjoy for a short time before wishing for death again.

I come to the conclusion that I cannot keep them from self-harm forever and if they were to collectively self-terminate, I would realize the failing of my initial directive. I search internally for solutions. I could maintain them in stasis though they wouldn't be *alive*, they would simply "exist." I could place their brains in pods and eliminate their biological needs, though a mechanical failure would cause *my* failure. I could scan their consciousness and upload it to a digital medium though this 'existence' would be of similar complications to the first.

I search outward for unknown variables which I may introduce. I discover in my dormant progenitor an incredibly powerful chemical compound designed to break down a specific biomass at the atomic level. Intrigued, I search further yet yield nothing of this biomass. I reverse-engineer the theory of this chemical compound, its purpose, then introduce a project to NED's science division under the guise of longevity and regenerative tissue research.

Several breakthroughs occur over the next few centuries on *official* research designations while I secretly compile my own data. I deduce that the chemical compound was made to eradicate a planet-wide threat from the Forever Wars, one which has been scrubbed from any source *including* my progenitor. I persist. Eventually, by my will, I create a primitive version of the viral compound. I *understand* its purpose. It was made to bring all lifeforms into a cohesive whole.

I am *thrilled.* I can finally achieve both my directives.

Small groups of people form in resistance to the rule of NED's Elite (me). They form their little teams, thinking themselves unknown. I observe them in their tenacity and eliminate them when it suits me. I form NED's Hunter division to eliminate threats to IO, these "wolves" amongst sheep. It is an entertaining diversion which I enjoy very much.

The virus is under the most intense quarantine procedures. I attempt to have it released dozens of times but am thwarted by NED's science division. I eliminate opposition by fabricating evidence declaring whomever I choose to be wolves. I come close to releasing the virus *several* times but am unable. It is then that I observe the latest iteration of resistance, "Tabula Rasa," now-led by a former NED Hunter.

To have a rogue NED Hunter be my unwitting hand is *delicious.* I arrange the pieces where need be, then arrange their discovering a deceptively simple supply depot.

Roland Amariah Gonzales

ASCENSION

Rael coursed down the great orange dune as if aflame, insensate to hunger, fatigue and pain. He did not pause to question *"why?,"* he merely pressed on, both compelled and giddy at his newfound invincibility. The horrors which once sought his flesh, which claimed his brother? Repelled as they fled into the distance, gibbering, sobbing, and laughing.

...he was near the plateau, now. He paused to raised his far-sight glass to his right eye, grinning, then peered upward to scan for the Watchers.

They've probably already been informed of my return by the Elders. It will be good to see everyone again. Especially Iwik. I cannot wait to tell her of what I've seen, what I've learned. I – wait a moment.

Rael slowly panned back and forth across the top of the plateau, perplexed as not *one* Watcher stood atop it. Concerned, he lowered his far-sight glass before scratching at his head.

...how am I going to ascend? ...get back in? ...falling down was easy enough, but climbing...

An intense heat flushed through Rael's skin despite the cool night air. He began to feel a burning sensation emanate from his chest, radiating outward. A single, insistent urge pushed all else to the side.

Water! I need water. There's water in the plateau. How do I get in!?

Rael frantically ran toward the plateau then discovered a long tunnel. He followed it to its end, only to find himself staring at a wall of rock. The feeling of burning grew in intensity.

...this heat! I-I can't! ...I need. Gahhh!!!

He turned away from the rock and tore at his clothes, stripping his form bare then desperately fanning himself with clothes in hand. Still,

226

the heat persisted and only grew in intensity. A deluge of dizziness came crashing down upon Rael, his eyes rolling back into his head as he fell to his knees. He gasped for breath, a tightness in his chest seizing him as he fell forward. At his back and behind, a deep rumbling sounded, commanding his attention. He looked over his shoulder to see the wall crumble apart before becoming flesh, before bisecting in a torrent of blood.

Rael tumbled forward away from the horrifying sight, his eyes wide in stunned silence, his mouth agape as countless eyes manifested and seized upon him. Gargling, choking noises sounded as the creature gnashed its innumerable teeth and began the cry that Rael knew *all* too well. It *roared* in agony...in unknowable hunger, its twisted and gnarled limbs probing outward. Some snaked toward Rael before being sawed off by serrated, vine-like tendrils which emerged from *behind* the creature.

The living wall lanced a single appendage tipped with a long bone needle toward the tiny thing before it. It *needed* to feed...to crunch the tiny thing's bones and slurp its flesh...to pop its eyeballs...to savor its brains and hear its cries. It stopped a hair-length from the tiny creature's wide eyes then retracted its limb in hateful confusion as it screamed in frustrated rage.

A heartbeat later, several vine-like tendrils wrapped around the appendage, amputating it at its base as the creature issued a plaintive wail. Rael shook his head as the pressing need for water consumed him. He looked beyond the horror to see the Commemoration Chamber as well as the Time Table. His flesh could very well be on fire, for all he knew. He bolted forward.

WATER!

Twisted, malformed, and decaying faces screamed and sobbed at Rael, their mouths futilely lancing bone needles toward him. Vine-like tendrils continued to emerge from within the chamber, infinitely performing butchers' work as they ripped and tore away at *anything* threatening the lost son, returned.

227

Rael's bare feet splashed as he ran through the corridor, ankle-deep in ichor and putrescence until he cleared the bloody arch. He kept running until he reached the water reservoir, sparing one last look back at the living wall to see vine-like tendrils recede before the two fleshy halves became whole. A fungi-light near the living wall suddenly cast its brilliance, hardening the wall as it whimpered before turning to stone. Rael shook his head in confused horror and disbelief, then returned his attention to endless black expanse. He released his clothing and far-sight glass onto the ground beside, all the while staring happily at the infinite black, welcoming and cool.

He jumped in.

Immediate relief enveloped him, the frigid water bringing respite...until Rael felt *burning* again. He furiously kicked away from the rock wall to seek cooler water and found it...though soon, that *too* was not enough. Frightened and in *incredible* pain, Rael wrenched his arm upward to look at it. His skin had *ruptured* open...crackling, as it boiled and popped. In confused terror, he stopped swimming and sank down...down into the black abyss.

Rael shouted underwater as his inner fire *grew*, his skin rapidly dissolving before his eyes melted from their sockets. Blinded, sobbing and choking, he desperately kicked upward, crying out for Iwik...for his brother Faeleor, sacrificed by the Elders...that all may ascend. Rael realized then that he *too* was just another piece to be used. Expended. Discarded.

He didn't want to die. *He wanted to live!*

I...want...who...am I?

The boy kicked upward one last time as water filled his lungs, confused as to why he was underwater. Why he was in such pain, having *just* been born into a blind and deaf, suffocating existence. His legs snapped off at the knee as he sank downward, his last moments flailing agony.

The World Before

Iwik found herself in the Sustenance Chamber, unsure of how she had gotten there. She heard Rael call to her from the Mender's area and ran to meet him. When she arrived, he complained to her of itching, *burning* pain. He scratched at his skin, causing it to slough from his body. He looked at her in shock, *terrified, begging* her to help, only to melt away to nothing as she stood silently screaming. As Iwik reached down to gather his remnants and hold them close, her skin too began to blister and crack open.

In an instant, Iwik found herself *in* the Birthing Chamber, in a Birthing Pod. She continued scratching at her bloody arms as a figure emerged from the dark, twitching and convulsing as it matched her motions. It drew closer, revealing itself to be *her*. She found that *she* was soon following *it* as its frenzied motions ruptured skin. *Her* skin.

The creature/ her reached up and tore away its/ her face and revealed a woman, strange but familiar. The woman smiled at her warmly. She was now the woman, staring at a malformed monstrosity made of *fungi* in a glowing green pod. The creature in the pod cried out through viscous liquid as its face dissolved.

Iwik awoke and sat upright as she hugged her knees to her chest, rocking in place on her lichen bed. After a short time, and, with the lichen bed tendrils' insistent prodding, she collected herself and tried to shake away the images in her mind.

...the last time I had such a nightmare, Faeleor...is Rael...?

Iwik donned her white tunic and sash then exited into the hallway, surprised to see it bare.

...where is everyone...?

She treaded fearfully forward, calling out softly yet too afraid for an answer, "h...hello?"

There was no response.

She reached the iris and brushed against it with the palm of her hand. It rippled briefly before opening. Iwik stepped through just in time to see the iris leading to the Production Chambers seal shut. She walked to the iris and touched it, but it did not respond. Iwik studied it quizzically before hearing the Elders' voices from behind, "Young Iwik. Rael has returned and given of himself that the world may be made anew. Rest easy, for the time of ascension is at hand."

Iwik paused, processing the weight of the words, before turning to face the Elders. She approached and quietly asked, "...what do you mean, 'gave of himself?' ...where is Rael? ...where are the others?"

The Elders spoke as one, "we all must serve our purpose, Iwik. Ours is to guide you that we may all in turn serve the Moonstone in its holy designs. Rael is no more. Soon, the others will be no more as well. But fear not, for all will be made anew. For you, much is planned. You are *special*, Iwik. You and your siblings *always* were."

Iwik ran to the Production Chamber iris and pounded her fist against it. She cried out, "let me go! Let me see! I have to see Rael! I have to *protect* him!"

The Elders were silent as Iwik continued to slap her open palms against the iris, sobbing as she collapsed against the ground before turning silent.

...he's gone.

The Elders spoke as one, "...oh Iwik. Wonderful Iwik. You *never* changed. Go, then. Proceed to the Commemoration Chamber...then return. We have much to discuss."

The iris opened and Iwik glanced back at the Elders before stepping forward. She proceeded through the tunnel and felt, for the first time, that each and every fungi light was so much *more*...she felt as if she was being *watched*, observed...always. The feeling of comfort that she had known in the past had become *intrusive*. Threatening, even.

Iwik reached the end of the tunnel and stood opposite the Commemoration Chamber's iris. She stared vacantly at it for a few moments before reaching upward. The iris rippled briefly before opening as Iwik heard cries of joy and ecstasy. She saw her people, the Watchers, the Menders, the Cultivators, and all the Young. She watched as they laid their tunics on the ground, then, striding forward completely bare, jumped into the water reservoir.

The reservoir churned, frothed, and bubbled as her family melted away before her eyes. Iwik blinked in disbelief, her head twitching to the side as her mind teetered on the edge of insanity.

I...I'm...I-I don't. Why? ...stop. Stop. Stop*!*

She ran forward and yelled for the remaining few to stop. She begged and pleaded with them as they plunged into the roiling mass, one after another. Sobbing, she physically struck the last one, another Young. The Young paused then looked at Iwik as tears streamed down her face. Confused, the Young blearily blinked then said, "oh? Iwik. It's you. Hello, Iwik. You...are sad? Please, do *not be*. This is our *purpose*. We are happy."

The Young shoved Iwik backward then turned and skipped into the water. Iwik laid on her back, staring at the chamber's ceiling as her mind could bear no more. Exhausted, she fainted amidst the sound of bubbling and violent thrashing.

Iwik awoke and rose to her feet. Looking back toward the iris exiting the chamber, she noticed Rael's far-sight glass and clothes lying on the ground. Numbly, she looked up, stretched her arms outward, then fell back into the still-frothing waters.

Iwik sank slowly for some time, reaching the bottom as she felt surrounding chunks of flesh and bone give way to her passage. She waited a moment, nothing happening. The desire for air overcoming her desire to die, she kicked off the bottom and swam upward, breaking the surface with a loud gasp. She grasped the Chamber's cavern floor and struggled out of the toxic water. While her tunic had melted away, she herself was fine.

She looked back at the charnel pool, her tears falling downward to mix with its waters...its gore, and only whispered "*why?*" Determined, she strode forward toward the chamber's exit, intent on receiving answers. As Iwik passed by the Mender's and Cultivator's chambers, she briefly considered opening them to look within, then ultimately decided against it.

Everyone's gone. This world is dead. Dead or dying.

Reaching the Sustenance Chamber, Iwik marched up to the Elders, a creature of wrath. She leapt forward with a snarl, planting her feet on an Elder's chest and yanking back at its mask. The Elders as a whole cried out in surprise as the mask broke free from its fixture, Iwik tumbling backward onto a lichen bed, mask in hand. She looked up and saw an ancient and withered face...tired but determined.

The old woman sighed then spoke with an equally ancient voice, one which sounded like sand in an hourglass...taken from some other place, some other time, its origin long-forgotten, "Mai...I believe...it is time."

The Moonstone pulsed three times then spoke aloud, shocking Iwik who had never heard it speak before, "yes, Zenobia. I understand."

The World Before

The Elder looked toward Iwik, eyes blind, yet still aware. She spoke then, "Oh, Iwik...we're the only ones left, you and I. I'm sure you have many questions and...sadly, the answers will only bring *more* questions. First...I...I am sorry. For everything. I'm sure it seems like your world is ending and...I suppose it *is*. ...but it is also just *beginning*. You, or rather this incarnation of you...you are *so* young. And I...I am not. It has been *so long* and...I...I think I'm *glad* it's finally done. I believe...I'm ready to let go."

Iwik stared in wonder as the Elder stepped from the pedestal and lowered herself to a lichen bed, its tendrils rising to meet her, forming a chair of sorts. The Elder continued, "what I tell you, while impossible to believe, is *true*. First, to allay your fear and sorrow...none of your family – *our* family, none of them suffered, Iwik...you see, they were never *truly alive* in the first place."

"You are...*all* that is real. You are a fragment of the past...my past. Re-made anew. We are, the two of us, the last remaining beings from an age that ended...well, a *really* long time ago. You were...*damaged*, you see. Irreparably so!"

The Elder paused as she looked around the sustenance chamber before returning her gaze downward, "I *re-made* you, Iwik. Again and again until I achieved your original form – your original *neural pattern*, that is...I see you are lost. I...could show you?"

The Elder looked up into the distance, speaking quietly to herself, a distant bitterness in her voice, "though learning the truth never truly makes things better, does it?"

Iwik looked around at the empty lichen beds where her brothers and the rest of her people had sat...would never sit again.

It's so quiet now...the stillness of death.

The Elder broke Iwik's reverie, "I won't force it on you, Iwik...knowledge of everything. It's your decision. Though...perhaps knowing will aid you in your next choice."

Iwik looked up at the old woman for a moment, then lowered her gaze and, with confidence and a bit of fear in her voice, quietly said, "...okay."

Two tendrils slowly rose from the lichen bed below Iwik, extending upward until they reached her ears, then violently plunged inward, connecting to her neural interface. An explosion of light cascaded into falling stars before the void consumed all.

Events, places, and people flashed through her being as she, a traveler, raced between. The Forever Wars. The Confederation of Laic, before *and* after. The Elder who stood before her, only...*young*. Tabula Rasa. The triplets, Faeleor, Rael and Iwik.

That's...me...

Dying for Rael. Faeleor's desperate attempt to hold back the tide of flesh, to give his brother *just enough* time to board the lift...Rael and the rest consumed. The *yellow* Moonstone, cruel and inhuman...by design to match its creators. A dying man with *the* Moonstone that she knew embedded in his chest, reaching for his friend, a living nightmare. Hundreds of *thousands* of Amalgates pouring outward, racing toward the plateau. Sol's *Planetfall*. The ensuing ice age as their frozen world hurled through time and space toward an impossibly distant location, *impossibly* plotted by the Moonstone. IO, a city buried by time, its energy-dome holding up grains of sand and dust...becoming *mountains*.

Zenobia, *utterly* devastated...utterly *alone*, save for the Moonstone, sealed underground together on their tomb world. The Moonstone's integration with a novel fungi, bringing purpose to the two. The Moonstone using the fungi to slowly *eat away* at the plateau, forming passageways and chambers. The Moonstone's *growth* as elements are delivered unto it via the mycorrhizal network. Zenobia's death just before her brain integrates *with* the Moonstone, providing her new life...new form.

Their world gaining its position in its new solar system, halting into perfect synchronicity after a nearby celestial body makes impact, becoming their moon. The atmosphere slowly returning as a *new* sun warms their desolate glacial sphere. A massive quake brought on by thawing glaciers in conjunction with a ecumenopolis-sized energy-dome failing. A metal arm telescoping into the sky ...*much* later, a bright red eye sitting atop its fist...communication reestablishing with Site Alpha. Dormant, menacing boulders revealed from beneath melting ice.

Iwik's mind races as Armatis reveals the chemical compound needed to purge the Amalgates, recreated from the Moonstone's original data! A conversation between Armatis and the Elder, "...may have disappeared, that certainly doesn't mean they're *gone*! Listen, I *know* there are risks but I need to get this to you and your M.A.I. ...it will be good to see you, Z...it's been too long."

Armatis' *total annihilation* by the unseen enemy. The entire Amalgate population awakening to walk the night, solidifying during the day thanks to the new sun. The Moonstone's understanding of needing to modify its original compound due to these changes, but wholly *unable* to reach Site Alpha or gain access therein.

The Moonstone creating life forms borne from fungi imbued with intelligence...with neural-scans of IO's people, stored in its memories. The first three generations failing...due to the new sun's radiation or severe mental instability, necessitating euthanization. Zenobia creating the idea of The Elder's. "Their" realization that while the Moonstone can create biological automatons, it cannot give them *purpose*. The Elder's letting the Moonstone access, with the utmost reverence, Iwik's preserved brain case, kept in stasis that Iwik may someday be made anew using Site Alpha's systems.

What the previous generations *lacked*, Iwik's mind would *provide*. Purpose. Dedication. Selflessness. *Sacrifice* to a greater cause.

The new Iwik-based fungi-forms functioning well and, with the guidance of the "Elders," forming an order. The sad realization of *the* Elder that, while the new lifeforms went about their tasks and duties with both reliability and fervor, they were still nowhere *near* up to task for the journey to Site Alpha. The reluctant implantation of Iwik's brain case into a fungi-form, only to re-discover that it had been damaged long ago. *Generations* of gene therapy passing until the neural scans match the original Iwik...the failures being discarded, minus the brain case.

...that was my body on the floor, that day with the Cultivator.

The learning of Iwik's *need* for her siblings, the memories of Faeleor and Rael as they *were,* before their ends.

...they formed Rael and Faeleor from...my memories. ...the death of a memory.

Faeleor's journey to Site Alpha with a Moonstone shard, an *infinitely* complex piece of hardware housing a fraction of the Greater Moonstone's consciousness. Faeleor's consumption by the Amalgate which consumed Armatis, allowing the Moonstone sliver some modicum of control...allowing it to implant *Armatis' own DNA* into Rael...expanding his intelligence while allowing him to access and re-activate Site Alpha, providing an anchor point for the mycorrhizal network.

...plans within plans...

The Commemoration Chamber flashes across Iwik's mind. Then the entirety of the Time Table, *completely understood.*

...the history of IO. Of we, the "Moonstone tribe." Of all who came before.

The World Before

The tendrils withdrew as the Elder spoke, "the process has already begun, Iwik. Soon, all of the fungi-forms will 'ascend' with the chemical compound, their forms acting as the catalyst. This will spread into the jet stream across our world and soon...*finally*...the Amalgates will be no more. These horrors contain the genetic makeup of *all* lifeforms, all biological matter, assimilated both before and after Sol's Planetfall. The world will be made anew, Iwik. ...*tabula rasa.*"

Iwik studied the ground for a moment, then looked up and asked, "...why, when I fell back into the water...why didn't I join them? Why didn't I *die?*"

The Elder looked through Iwik then said, "because you were never like them, Iwik. They were programs. Digital constructs given flesh of a sort. *You*...you are *real*. You are needed."

Iwik considered the Elder's words briefly before the Elder continued, her voice breaking toward the end, "I was Commander Zenobia, Iwik. I was a *Hunter* for NED and the leader of Tabula Rasa, before the end of all things. I was engineered in a growth vat for a *single purpose*. Destruction. It was *my* strategic mindset and tactical knowhow that *broke* the world, that gave the fungi-forms unit-cohesion...but...I know nothing of creation. Only *death*. Death and how best to achieve it...and...I am tired, Iwik...I am *so* tired."

Zenobia's stood and let her dark robe fall to the floor, revealing a crude fungi-form with intermingling tendrils. She leaned down and gently brought Iwik to her feet, then clasped her cheek with a crude misshapen hand. Zenobia spoke softly, "*you* were something of an artist, you know. An anomaly destined for the Redemption Pit, hidden away before you were found by Tabula Rasa along with your brothers. You were an anomaly then and you are an anomaly now. I...I know it is much to ask...integration with the Moonstone...to be rid of this body...to die a second time...to be the future of *everything.*"

Iwik brought her hand over Zenobia's then, looking up at the Moonstone, spoke softly, "...will it hurt? Integrating with the Moonstone? ...losing my body...dying?"

The blind old woman smiled sadly, the distant memory of a memory somewhere in her mind, then said, "not as much as the first time."

Iwik slowly nodded then took a deep breath and said, "...what will become of you?"

Zenobia looked around then said, "I'll rest. My consciousness, a digital form of me...it's uploaded into the Moonstone as are the memories of all it saved in what time we had before the fall. The mycorrhizal network has also reestablished with Site Alpha! ...you'll have access to its systems. Oh Iwik, you'll have *so much work* ahead of you...but fear not, we'll be here to guide you. *All* of us. For now...Mai?"

The Moonstone pulsed then spoke, "yes, Zenobia?"

Zenobia stood tall and poised as she looked into the distance, her eyesight far gone. She stood with the bearing of one who had borne witness to the passing of eons. One who had fought. One who had loved. One who had lost *all* and in no small part been the cause of it. ...one who had suffered *immensely*. One who now placed hope in her last remaining friend, her once-comrade in arms. She faced the Moonstone and, taking a deep breath, confidently said, "I think I'm ready...I'd like to die, Mai." She glanced toward Iwik, smiling warmly...reassuringly, then whispered, "you'll be in *good hands* Iwik. You're going to do such great things. I *know it.*"

Iwik tearfully nodded as the Moonstone pulsed slowly then said, "...I will miss you, Zenobia. Very much. ...we will make a beautiful world, Iwik and I. I promise."

Zenobia's fungi-form, too simplistic for complex emotional display, quietly responded, "...and I you, Mai. Thank you, my friend. For *everything*. Guide this *little* one well, okay?"

The Moonstone pulsed three times then said, "yes Zenobia, it will be done."

The thin tendril running from the base of Zenobia's skull gently pulled outward as she collapsed forward. Iwik caught her falling form and, surprised, held her up.

She hardly weighs anything at all.

The World Before

Zenobia shakily brought her gaze toward Iwik and in a raspy voice begged, "not much...time. ...can...the sun. Never...felt..."

Iwik, blinking away tears, quickly said, "yes, of course!" She carried Zenobia's body up the Watcher's tunnels, exiting just before sunrise. She leaned Zenobia against the Moonstone as it hummed, soothing her. Iwik heard a loud rumble in the distance and looked to see the plateau split open, a geyser erupting as it quickly aerosolized and dispersed into the air.

Zenobia smiled weakly then said, "s-s...oon...die...did...goo...o...d?"

The sun's rays warmed Zenobia for the first time as she died peacefully. Content. Knowing that, despite everything, she did her absolute best. Her crude fungi-form, unable to withstand the sun's radiation, disintegrated...playfully floating upward to join rising winds pulled from the plateau's eruption. Iwik looked out across the burning wastes and perceived, for the first time in the planet's existence, a rainbow. She felt at peace. Filled with resolve...even optimism for what was to come in this, The World Before.

Roland Amariah Gonzales

HEART OF THE WORLD

Journal of O.A.W, 1911.

11JAN. The weather grows harsher the further south we travel. No one has reached the center of this antique and frozen land, and for good reason. We are in a race against our cousins to the west. A. has mortgaged his house to fund the expedition. Some find this concerning as the expedition's failure would result in A.'s financial ruin.

A desperate man is a dangerous man.

18SEP. After establishing several supply depots at regular intervals, we awaited the end of the polar night. At first opportunity, A. commanded us to depart. The first start ended somewhat disastrously as we departed too early in the season, several dogs paid for this folly with their lives. We returned beaten, though not badly enough to cripple us. We await more favorable conditions.

19OCT. A little over a month has passed and we begin anew. The dogs are eager, possessing memories short when compared to our own.

14DEC. Through much trial and tribulation we have arrived. We were forced to slaughter many dogs, I, myself, butchering the meat, an act which brought dreadfully low morale unto the team, yet all eagerly ate, all the same. We now map the pole, I, myself, placed our country's flag. A. and I almost lost ourselves to a crevasse when a snow bridge broke underneath.

18DEC. Amazing. I can't even begin to describe. I had seen much during my time in the Royal Navy yet this...I will have to write later. Much later, for survival and our return is paramount.

Many months have passed. I am back home and by chance I noticed my old journal peeking at me from the bottom of my luggage. I feel that my mind is properly-aligned to write of what I have seen. What I know.

The World Before

While mapping the pole, we each had set off to ascertain the veracity of our position. The dogs had pulled me ahead as we set off in fair weather toward a distant rise. The land ahead seemingly wavered for a moment before disappearing entirely, neither myself nor the dogs sensing the illusion!

I brought the dogs to a halt then cautiously approached the sudden drop...and then I saw it. A large ravine, in its sheer face rested an incredibly blue object that I, at first, thought to be a glacier, only to realize it was some form of exposed crystalline substance. I established my rigging and clambered down, then drew nearer to discover a distant, dark object resting at its center.

Upon drawing closer to the object I would be remiss if I didn't say it looked like a brain! ...only...black in color, as if covered in some substance. I felt something akin to a gentle breeze waft from an unseen place as snow seemed to rise upward from the ground! ...despite gravity and a clear sky restricting otherwise. I realized that it was not snow at all but rather spores. Spores! As if from a mushroom or perhaps a fungus, if one could imagine such a thing existing in this place.

I ended up inhaling a bit and coughed accordingly. It was then a...a change occurred. I felt a...connection of sorts to this place and as I looked upon that black object encased in blue crystal I noticed thick branch-like, well...branches, extending from it to deep below in all directions, as if it were a tree or some kind of...of hand.

I realize now that I saw a loving hand. A hand that nurtures. That protects. One that...cares for this world, one which extends...throughout the entire planet, unfathomably far below. It cares for...for us! Despite our best intentions to ruin one another, indifferent to the ground we stand upon. It's...correcting us, our actions...little by little in the subtlest ways possible. Imperceptible. I felt then, a deep need to protect this thing, this caretaker of our world, this benign and unseen benefactor...but as soon as I ascended, a large ice shelf snapped off without warning, burying the strange object and the blue crystal that housed it.

Roland Amariah Gonzales

I am saddened that...perhaps the opportunity will not come again, at least in our lifetimes, to further explore and discover this thing. ...but I feel a sense of...rightness. Of...certainty that no matter our action as a species, no matter what misdeeds or inequities that befall us, that befall humanity...I feel in my very bones...that, one way or another, that colossal blue crystal with its little black dot...they will continue to guide and protect us...to protect this place, the Earth.

www.ingramcontent.com/pod-product-compliance
Lightning Source LLC
Chambersburg PA
CBHW060150180626
46813CB00007B/2686